A CAPTIVE OF WING AND FEATHER

THE FOUR KINGDOMS AND BEYOND

A CAPTIVE OF WING AND FEATHER

FEATHER

A RETELLING OF SWAN LAKE

MELANIE CELLIER

LUMINANT PUBLICATIONS

Luminant Publications
PO Box 203
Glen Osmond, South Australia 5064

melaniecellier@internode.on.net
http://www.melaniecellier.com

Cover Design by Karri Klawiter
Editing by Mary Novak

For Priya,
faithful friend and reader from the start

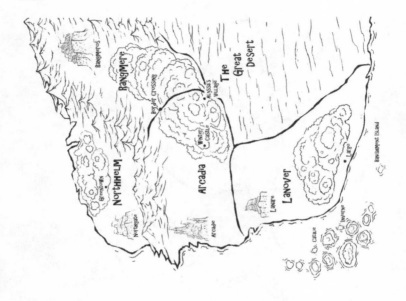

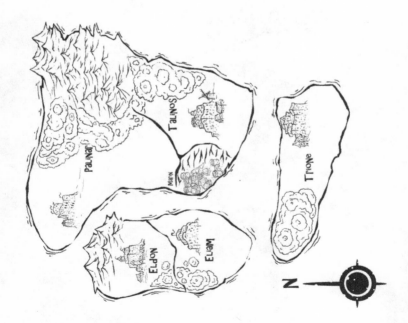

PART I
THE LAKE

PROLOGUE

I stumbled, my feet tripping over dead branches and leaf litter. My heart pounded harder than my steps, although no one was chasing me.

A sweet, clear taste lingered in my mouth, but it elicited only dread. The lake had been beautiful, and the swans floating on it even more so, but I never wanted to see any of it again. I never wanted to see that man again or hear him spout such madness. I refused to believe his talk of enchantments.

I should never have followed the sound of my name. I should have listened to the townsfolk and stayed away from the forest. It had been foolishness to try to prove I wasn't afraid of it—even while nameless dread circled in my stomach.

I burst out of the trees and onto the edge of town. Just as my feet touched the road, I faltered, a burning, stinging sensation washing over my body. My hands pressed against my exposed skin, but it was gone almost as quickly as it had come.

A flash of white overhead made me flinch. Had that been a swan? I shook my head and kept my eyes resolutely down. It didn't matter what it had been. I was returning to the haven, and I would never enter the forest again.

CHAPTER 1

TWO YEARS LATER

*a*n air of excitement hung over the town. A newcomer might not have noticed it, but I could feel it like a palpable presence around me. I'd spent enough time in Brylee over the past five years to recognize its moods. I glanced longingly at the various small knots of townsfolk talking on street corners and scattered around the market square, but there was no point stopping and trying to talk to any of them.

Instead I moved faster, hurrying for the sprawling lodge house on the edge of town. My path took me past the bakery where I would usually receive a greeting or at least a wave. But on this occasion the young baker, Ash, seemed just as distracted as everyone else. He was deep in conversation with two older women who showed no inclination to leave, despite the fresh loaves already poking from their baskets.

As I passed by, I caught a snatch of their conversation.

"But what purpose could he have?" The woman sounded worried.

"Perhaps we're suspected of some sort of wrongdoing— treason even!" The second woman sounded even more concerned.

Ash—who was usually fairly sensible—made no effort to gainsay this outrageous statement.

"If you ask me, the best thing we can do is nothing," he said. "If he wishes to pretend that his visit is nothing out of the ordinary, then we must do the same. Perhaps he'll…"

He trailed off, as if even he didn't know what he hoped would happen, but both women nodded their agreement. I realized my steps had almost completely stilled and, shaking my head, I picked up my pace. If I wanted answers, my best hope was Cora. I wouldn't get anything from this group.

The dilapidated building—once an inn but now known to most of us as the haven—came into view, and my speed increased again. A brisk spring breeze nearly blew back my hood, and I grabbed at it just in time. I had an odd reputation around town, and with everyone so stirred up, I didn't want to invite trouble.

I pushed open the main door without knocking and looked around for Cora, the haven's keeper. Instead a four-year-old girl came barreling into view, an excited grin on her face.

"Lady!" She raced toward me. "Lady, Lady, Lady!"

I hoisted her up onto my hip and paused for a moment to give her a cuddle. Unlike the townsfolk, Juniper didn't care that I had no voice. I wanted to savor these moments while I still could—she would be too big for it soon. Already she seemed less and less of a baby, all long legs and waving arms.

"I made muffins. All by myself. And you can have one. And I got a new tooth. Right at the back. See."

She opened her jaws wide and tipped her head back to an angle that completely obscured her mouth. I suppressed a smile and adopted an astonished and impressed expression.

She paused for only a moment before snapping her teeth closed and continuing to prattle on, unbothered by my silence. When she began to squirm, I let her slip back down to the ground. She took my hand and tugged me down the long hallway into the large kitchen at the back of the lodge.

Clearly Juniper didn't know about whatever had the towns-folk so worked up—she would have blurted it out to me first thing if she did. I felt a surge of unease. The people of Brylee had a tendency to get worried about every tiny thing, but Cora and Wren were usually a little more sensible. If they felt the need to shield Juniper from what was happening, then perhaps it truly was a cause for concern.

"Junie, there you are!" A young woman hurried into the room, her eyes fixed on her daughter. "I thought I told you to stay in the —" Her eyes fell on me. "Oh, Lady, you've arrived. That would explain it, then."

The disapproving look she had fixed on her daughter didn't relent, but the girl let go of my hand and ran happily to her mother anyway. She rushed through an almost unintelligible sentence from which I caught the word muffin.

Wren's expression dissolved into a reluctant smile, and she nodded. Juniper ran off toward the far bench where I could see a cooling rack filled with muffins. Wren gave me an apologetic look.

"I hope you're hungry. She won't relax until you've had one, I'm afraid. I needed an excuse to be out of the classroom this morning, and Juniper has been begging me to do some baking with her."

I gave her an inquiring look.

"Frank and Selena are nearly old enough for apprenticeships now, and they're both outdoing each other trying to prove how reliable they are, so I've been wanting to give them a chance to take charge of the younger ones." She chuckled. "Juniper was a little too eager to escape her schooling, but she's still young. I wouldn't even have started her at it yet if I wasn't responsible for the older children as well."

I smiled to indicate my willingness to become a muffin taster and slipped onto one of the stools surrounding the enormous, worn wooden table that filled the middle of the kitchen. Wren and Juniper had been at the haven for more than three years now, and I knew that she took her role of teacher to the haven's children seriously. Her attention for them hadn't wavered, despite their numbers being low this year—Cora having found adoptive families for three of the younger ones only a few months ago, and two of the older ones having left for apprenticeships that she had secured.

Normally at least some new children would have arrived to replace them, but we'd been seeing fewer and fewer people making their way to the haven from distant towns. Travel all across the kingdom had been dropping from all reports.

I was glad Wren was getting a small break. And perhaps she could answer my question. Glancing toward Juniper, I confirmed she was still busy selecting the perfect muffin. When I looked back at Wren, it was with a raised eyebrow and an inquiring tilt of my head.

When she didn't immediately seem to understand, I jerked my head toward the front door and the rest of town. Adopting an exaggerated expression of concern, I mimed my best impression of the townsfolk I had passed.

A woman several decades our senior, her hair in no-nonsense braids against her scalp, entered the room just in time to witness my performance. She snorted a laugh.

"Are you sure you're not a long-lost member of my family? You look exactly like my old Aunt Florinda. She wore an expression just like that every day of her life."

Wren chuckled. Only my brown hair, thick and wavy, looked anything like Cora's—and since she always wore hers in braids, even that wasn't much of a similarity. Certainly my pale skin and blue eyes looked nothing like the warm brown of hers.

I smiled as well, but inside I hid a sigh. I knew every branch of my family tree, tracing back multiple generations—my father had insisted on it. There was no chance I had any relatives half as down-to-earth and kind as Cora. I would have to content myself with being adopted into the haven's strange family in heart, if not in actuality.

When Wren's humor subsided, I made a series of hand gestures that produced a sigh from Cora, her face falling into more serious lines. Juniper trotted back toward us before she could reply, however, proudly bearing a muffin on a little plate which she placed before me.

"What are you talking about?" She looked between us all.

"Nothing that concerns you," said Wren. "Lady has her muffin now, so why don't you get back to your letters?" She sent a stern eye toward the abandoned slate on a small, child-sized table tucked into the corner of the room. I could just make out a single, misshaped S scratched across its surface.

"But—" Juniper began to protest, only to cut herself off when she saw her mother's unyielding expression.

With a large, dramatic sigh, she hung her head and shuffled off toward the small table and chair. I bit my lip, trying to hold in a laugh.

Wren rolled her eyes. "Anyone would think I was the cruelest of mothers."

Cora raised an eyebrow. "I can't imagine where she gets the dramatics from."

Wren laughed, her eyes lingering on her daughter, but gradually the humor dropped from her face. "She does seem like Audrey, doesn't she?"

I abandoned my muffin to put a reassuring hand on her arm, despite the stab of pain in my midriff at the mention of Wren's sister.

"She'll be back, when she's ready," Cora said in a calm tone.

Audrey was sixteen—two years younger than me and seven years younger than Wren who often treated her like another daughter. She had told me once that older siblings couldn't help taking on that role when they lost their parents too young.

I had refrained from observing that not all older siblings

reacted in such a manner. For five years I had refused to mention my home, my family, or even my kingdom—it was habit now as much as intention.

Wren's mothering had irritated Audrey at times, but I knew that underneath she loved it. And you only had to look at Juniper to see what a wonderful mother Wren made. But I knew she blamed herself for Audrey's departure. They had fought the night before she left, and it ate her up inside that Audrey hadn't been back even once for a visit in the six months since she went to work up at the local castle.

I was the only one who knew there was more to the story, but I didn't dare tell Wren.

Cora met my eyes silently, and my hand dropped from Wren's arm. I returned to my muffin, keeping my face hidden from my friend. Cora didn't know the whole story either, but I knew she had at least some suspicions about the castle, and we had a tacit agreement not to mention anything about them to Wren. Wren thought Cora's antipathy toward Lord Leander was solely because he didn't send supplies to assist the residents of the haven as his father always used to do. Better that she believe her sister still angry with her than that she worry herself about something worse. Not when there was nothing she could do about it—except get into trouble herself.

Once I had finished Junie's treat, I flapped my hands to capture both of the other women's attention and re-signed my question to Cora. Wren looked between us with a raised eyebrow. She had learned some of my more common hand signals, but only Cora fully understood the makeshift communication system she and I had cobbled together.

"So you noticed the townsfolk are getting themselves all tied up in knots, I take it?" Cora's voice held enough exasperation to allay the worst of my fears.

"It is concerning, though." Wren kept her voice low, casting a warning glance toward Juniper who had abandoned her slate and was crouched down on the floor of the kitchen, closely examining a small bug. "Why is he here, of all places? And why is he trying to hide who he is?"

I gave them both a look of exasperation. They were as bad as Ash and his customers. I made an impatient gesture with my arms, and Wren gave me an apologetic look.

"Oh, sorry, Lady. It seems we have a newcomer in town. He checked into one of the inns, instead of going up to the Keep, but of course the innkeeper's wife recognized him. Apparently the innkeeper questioned him about it but was entrusted to keep the secret."

"Which naturally means the entire town now knows," said Cora with a roll of her eyes.

I gave them both a look of frustrated confusion. The loss of my voice was most infuriating at times like this. *Who* had arrived in Brylee? And what was he trying to keep hidden?

"It turns out," Wren said, realizing my exasperation, "that Brylee's newest visitor is none other than—"

A loud rapping on the door made her break off. Startled, we all exchanged glances. No one ever bothered to knock at the haven's door. It was well known to be a refuge, open to all.

"That can't be..." Wren stared toward the hallway open-mouthed. "Surely that can't be..."

"Well, there's only one way to find out." Cora marched toward the kitchen door.

Juniper, usually boisterously friendly, seemed to have taken exception to the loud knock and had squeezed herself under her tiny table. Wren sighed and hurried over to extract her while I followed behind Cora.

"Greetings," a young, male voice called from the entryway. "Is anyone here?"

I faltered slightly, and a crease appeared between Cora's brows. What was a young man—a stranger, apparently—doing at the haven? This was a safe place, a refuge for women, children, and the elderly—people who had nowhere else to go. The only young or middle-aged men who came here were townsfolk bringing supplies for the inhabitants. Ash, the baker, was a regular, bringing any unsold wares at the end of the day.

Cora stepped into the entryway, a commanding presence.

"I am the proprietress of this establishment. May I help you?"

"I hope so," he said. "I'm looking for someone, and I hear that many people find their way here." The voice sounded friendly... and vaguely familiar.

I stepped to the side to get a clearer view around Cora. A tall young man stood just inside the door, his stance confident but relaxed. He wore the simple but sturdy clothes of a woodsman, and he had a quiver and bow strapped to his back.

I stared at his olive-toned skin, tracing the contours of his face with my eyes. His brown hair looked windswept, ruffled into small curls around his ears and the nape of his neck, and his brown eyes contained flecks of gold. Everything about him was brown and green—he looked like he belonged in the forest. If this was the newcomer, I could see how the townsfolk had immediately recognized him as out of place in the town.

I didn't know why it had caused such mass concern, however.

He turned to look at me, his brow creasing slightly even as he gave me an easy smile. His eyes flicked up, just above my face, and I realized that I was once again wearing the hood of my cloak, pulled forward to shield my face. I must have pulled it up without conscious thought as I followed Cora.

"Sometimes the people who find their way here don't want to be found," Cora said, her voice cold. "We don't take too kindly to strangers asking questions."

He didn't seem in the least flustered by her response.

"But surely some who are lost want to be found?" he asked.

Cora narrowed her eyes. "I suppose that depends on who's doing the finding..." She let her voice trail off, the question implied.

If he made a reply, I didn't hear it. Instead I stumbled back half a step, my eyes widening. His voice had triggered my memory.

He had been a gangly youth when I last saw him, although still charming. There had been a whole crowd of us, gathered for some function, and he had been intent on involving the other princes in some sort of mischief. Now that I had caught the familiar note of his voice, I could see the traces of the boy showing through in the man he had become. And suddenly I understood what had thrown the townsfolk into such confusion.

This man belonged no more to the forest than he did to this remote town. He belonged in a palace, on a throne. We were talking to Crown Prince Gabriel of Talinos.

CHAPTER 2

*S*omething in my movements must have given me away because both Cora and Prince Gabriel turned to look at me, interrupting whatever verbal sparring I'd missed.

"Are you all right, Lady?" Cora asked, remarkably calm given she was confronting her future king.

"Lady?" Gabriel looked between us. "I must admit I didn't expect to find any of the local nobility here." He swept a ragged bow—far less polished than the ones I knew him to be capable of performing.

So he was still attempting to pass himself off as a forester of some sort then. If he wanted to portray himself as the kind of commoner who was overawed at the presence of minor nobility, then he should have worked on the air of confidence which he wore more comfortably than clothes.

"What?" Cora stared at him uncomprehendingly for a moment.

"Lady isn't someone *important*," said a piping voice. "Why did you bow to her?"

Juniper, who seemed to have recovered from her momentary timidity, gave Gabriel a direct stare. Wren hurried forward and swept her daughter up onto her hip, coloring as she did so.

"I'm sorry, she's only young. She doesn't know what she's saying…"

She looked back and forth between each of us, suddenly uncertain.

No one had spoken the prince's identity aloud, but the knowledge of it hung over us all, coloring our interactions. For a moment there was awkward silence, and then Gabriel blew out a quick breath.

"You all know who I am, don't you?" When we all nodded, he sighed. "I suppose everyone in the town knows."

Cora gave a wry chuckle. "Brylee is somewhat isolated, it's true, but the innkeeper prides himself on knowing the face of every royal and noble in the kingdom. And word travels fast in these parts—it wouldn't surprise me if half the inhabitants of the next village over know by now. Would you prefer we all start curtsying or should we maintain the charade, Your Highness?"

Gabriel gave a rueful grimace, running a hand through his hair and further ruffling the little curls. He shrugged and then gifted us all with a broad grin.

"I thought maybe I was far enough away from the capital that it was worth giving it a try at least. People tend to act strangely when they know you're a prince."

"I can only imagine," Cora said dryly.

"You're a prince?" Juniper's eyes widened. Her gaze locked on Gabriel. "A real one or a pretend one?"

He chuckled. "A real one, from what they tell me. Are there a great many pretend ones?"

She nodded. "I thought maybe they were all pretend. Like dragons and giants and princesses."

Wren clucked. "Princesses are real, Junie."

"Are you sure?" Juniper asked, her wide-eyed face looking between each of the adults for confirmation.

I bit my bottom lip and looked away, not meeting her eyes.

"They most certainly are," Gabriel assured her, gravely. "I have met many of them myself. I even have two sisters who are princesses. Twin sisters, in fact—Pearl and Opal."

I thought of the young twins with a pang. They would be fifteen by now—so grown up. Did they ever think of me and wonder about my fate? Did anyone?

"And godmothers?" Juniper asked. "What about them?"

Oh, they're real, I thought but had to leave it to Gabriel to inform her that godmothers also existed.

Juniper seemed to consider this before looking in my direction.

"Why did the prince bow to you, Lady?" She struggled in her mother's arms until Wren gave an exasperated sigh and let her slip down.

Gabriel followed her progress toward me with his eyes before letting his gaze dwell curiously on my still-hooded face. I could feel the questions hovering on the tip of his tongue.

I wrapped an arm around the little girl's shoulders, squeezing her affectionately against my leg. I said nothing, however, and Cora answered for me.

"That was a misunderstanding." She turned to the prince. "Lady is her nickname, not her title. No one from the local castle ever comes down to the town. As far as we know, Lord Leander dwells up there alone. He has no wife or daughters for us to call lady."

"What do you mean *as far as you know?*" Gabriel immediately latched onto the oddity. "Surely he doesn't literally live alone? If he never comes down to the town, he must have servants who visit for him—to fetch food and supplies, if nothing else. Do they not gossip?"

"He has servants," said Wren, her voice soft. "But no one ever sees them in Brylee. Not since his father died five years ago."

"That sounds ominous," said Gabriel with a laugh tinging his voice.

When none of us responded in kind, or even smiled, his humor slipped away, a frown taking its place.

"Well, that sounds serious enough to be worth investigation," he said. "Have none of you..." His voice trailed away at the horrified expressions on the faces of Cora and Wren. They might be more sensible than most, but they were still citizens of Brylee.

"No, of course you haven't gone to have a look," he muttered to himself.

I frowned at him. Hadn't he only arrived the evening before? Surely he hadn't been here long enough to understand the strange and pervasive timidity that gripped the townsfolk and rendered them impotent in the face of even the mildest threat.

"It is certainly curious enough that I, at least, would like to go and pay a visit to your Lord Leander," he said. "I wonder if my purposes would better be served by going as myself or attempting to..." His words dropped too low to be heard as he planned his best approach.

I gazed at him in shock. It had been five years since I had seen anyone approach a potentially dangerous situation with such decisive action. I had almost forgotten how little this small forest-bound town reflected the rest of the kingdoms.

His mutterings suddenly ceased, and his eyes swung up to latch onto me, as if his roving thoughts had brought him back to the other puzzle confronting him.

"And what exactly is Lady a nickname for?" he asked. "What is your full name?"

I sucked in a breath. This was dangerous ground.

"Adelaide," said Wren from behind me, a note of confusion in her voice. "Her name is Adelaide, Your Highness."

The prince gave a visible start and then took two long strides forward to push back my hood, fully exposing my face. For a moment we both stood frozen, our eyes locked together. Then

17

his gaze broke free to rove over the rest of my features, and I heard his startled intake of air.

His lips moved, forming the beginning of a word, and I didn't know if he meant to say my name or my title, but it didn't matter. In another second he would reveal everything and destroy the only refuge I had left. Habit had sealed my lips, but seeing him brought back my old self too forcibly, and I opened my mouth to cut him off.

A loud honking burst from my throat, filling the entryway and sending Gabriel staggering back a step. I clasped my hands over my mouth, liquid filling my eyes. I hadn't slipped up like that in over a year.

I glared at him, and something about my look must have silenced him since his gaping mouth closed without saying a word.

"Lady? Are you all right?" Cora looked at me with concern, her eyes darting suspiciously to Gabriel.

A giggle broke the tension of the moment. I blinked rapidly, trying to clear the unshed tears before Juniper saw them.

"Do it again, Lady! Do it again!" Juniper bounced at my side, her eyes shining. "You haven't done that in forever."

I smiled at her but shook my head, consigning myself once more to muteness. Silence was far better than the only sounds I could now make.

"Do the squeak. Pleeeeease!" she begged.

I shook my head more firmly.

"But—"

Wren scooped her up, cutting off her protest.

"That is enough out of you, little miss. We're going to go check on Selena and Frank now, and I don't want to hear any more about it."

"But Mama…" I heard her saying as Wren marched off down the long hall in the opposite direction to the kitchen.

Gabriel finally found his voice. "The...squeak? Should I even ask?"

"Definitely not," said Cora. "Now you said you were looking for someone, Your Highness? If I'm sure of one thing, it's that we don't have anyone here likely to have a prince looking for them."

"Are you sure about..." Gabriel let his sentence die off when he caught the pleading look I had trained on him. "Never mind then. I guess I need to look elsewhere."

"Perhaps you can start at Lord Leander's Keep," Cora said in a flat voice. "You seemed mighty interested in it before. And if you run across an Audrey, you can let her know that her sister misses her."

Gabriel gave a bow—courtly and polished this time. "I will certainly do so if I run across this Audrey." But even as he said it, his eyes lingered on me.

I frowned. It almost seemed as if the crown prince of Talinos had come here looking for *me*. But why would Gabriel, of all people, be searching for me? From the things I had been hearing around Brylee for the last few years, Talinos had trouble enough of its own without its prince worrying about a missing Palinaran. And how had he possibly managed to track me to Brylee, anyway?

But the only thing harder to believe than that this royal prince had come here searching for me, was the idea that there might be a second person he knew hiding in this out of the way place.

The silence stretched out until Cora narrowed her eyes.

"Very well, then, Your Highness. If you're not needing anything else..." She stopped short of actually ordering a prince to leave her property, but it seemed not even the presence of royalty could shake her from her assertive ways.

Cora had been running the haven with open doors for so long that not even the growing timidity that infected the town seemed to have quite managed to stamp out her old nature. And one of the few positives of the townsfolk's strange attitude was that she had no need to back up her assertive manner with actual courageous action—something I feared would be beyond her. No one in Brylee wanted a confrontation if they could possibly avoid it.

The prince didn't seem to fit this mold, but he did agree to leave, however reluctant his manner. Only when the front door shut behind him did my tense muscles relax. I'd just arrived at the haven for the day, but all I could think about was getting back out of Brylee.

Would Gabriel head straight for the Keep, or would he linger, hoping to talk to me? I hurried to a window that gave a clear view of the front of the lodge and peered outside.

The prince stood on the street, gazing back at the building with a confused expression. I stepped to the side, out of sight, hoping he hadn't seen me. A long minute ticked by, as I tried to convince myself not to look again. At last I gave in and peeked, more circumspectly this time.

He was gone.

I took a deep breath and stepped away from the window. Should I leave it for half an hour before making my escape, or was I better off seizing the moment now?

"Lady? Are you all right?"

I started at Cora's words. I had forgotten she was still there. The smile I managed to summon must not have been a good one because she crossed over to me, her eyes full of concern.

"You know that we're all here for you, right? That you're always welcome to stay..." She paused, the lines of concern on her face deepening. "You know there's a bed for you here, don't you?"

My smile softened, becoming more real. I squeezed her arm and nodded, hoping she could read the gratitude in my eyes. Of course I knew. And I wished more than anything that I could stay in my room here, as I had for three years, before—

I sighed. I couldn't stay tonight, any more than I had been able to stay any nights of the past two years. And I couldn't explain it to her either—and not just because I no longer had a voice.

I pulled my hood back up over my face. Better I go now, while Gabriel was distracted. Otherwise he might circle back and start asking uncomfortable questions.

"Lady!" A querulous voice called for my attention as shuffling footsteps sounded from the passage. "Where have you been?"

An elderly man came into view, hunched and with receding hair. A moment later a tiny woman followed him, shrunken by age but still straight-backed.

"Sorry, Lady," she said with a bright smile. "He's cantankerous today."

"I'll show you cantankerous!" he said, in what was clearly meant to be a growl although it sounded scratchy and thin.

He took off after her, moving painfully slowly, and she side-stepped him neatly, her joints less worn than his.

"I could do this for hours." She cackled and side stepped again.

A smile crept across my face as I watched them make their slow way around the entry. After more than sixty years together, they still acted like courting youngsters.

Cora rolled her eyes and muttered that she was leaving me to deal with them before hurrying off toward the kitchen. Vilma made another attempt to outpace her husband, only to be caught by his reaching hands. As he wrapped his arms around her, she winked at me from under his arm.

I bit back my smile, assuming a serious expression as Gregor turned back to me, keeping one arm around his wife.

"You haven't been near us for two days, and everything is out of order," he said. "I can't find my cushion—the one that eases the ache in my back."

"Can't find? And whose fault would that be? You've put it in some nonsensical place, I don't doubt." Vilma shook her head. "We're lost without you, Lady, dear."

I cast a single glance toward the window before offering them each one of my arms. It was true I usually visited them every day in the wing of the haven reserved for the elderly residents, but I had run out of time yesterday. So I couldn't walk away now—not when I had no words to offer them an explanation.

As she leaned on me for support, Vilma whispered, "Never mind about the cushion, dear, but the roof's leaking again, I'm afraid. I don't like to further burden Cora, but I'm afraid we're going to have to move the bed."

I gave an internal sigh. It sounded like I wouldn't be leaving any time soon. I would just have to hope that the Keep kept Gabriel occupied for the rest of the afternoon.

CHAPTER 3

*T*he sun was far too low in the sky as I finally slipped back out of Brylee. I shouldn't have stayed so long.

The trees closed quietly around me, swallowing me without effort. A phantom ache danced across my bones, but I shook myself and pushed the imagined sensation away. The sun hadn't set yet, and I could still make it if I hurried.

I had been on high alert as I scurried through the streets of the town, but I let myself relax now. My feet easily trod my path without conscious thought, but I didn't follow any established road. I need not fear meeting anyone now. The locals preferred to stay out of the forest if they could—and if their business took them through it, then they stuck to the main roads that connected them to the rest of the kingdom.

Gray and brown surrounded me, lichen hanging from the trees and new undergrowth struggling to push through the littered detritus underfoot. Spring had arrived in Brylee, bright flowers filling window boxes, but in the forest only the occasional flash of green or newly furled leaf hinted at the season.

The broad canopy grew densely, blocking out more of the sky the deeper in I pressed. The occasional rustle of some small animal sounded, but no bird song reached my ears, and without meaning to do so, my steps sped up.

A louder rustle sounded behind me, and I flinched. Darkness was falling faster than I had anticipated, the trees disappearing off into the gloom, and the whole world fading into pools of black. I needed to move faster, or I wouldn't make it in time.

I broke into a trot as the rustles increased. What animals prowled between the trees come darkness? I burst into a large clearing, gaining enough space to get a better look around me.

But I only had time to cast one anxious glance backward before a more familiar whoosh sounded, followed by the crash of wings beating against leaves. Seven large shapes brushed against the edge of the canopy as they swooped into the clearing, their sweeping feathers filling the air around me.

"*There you are*," I bugled, my words somehow transforming inside my throat until they sounded exactly like the sounds made by the swans themselves. "*I was starting to worry.*"

Three white birds swooped around me, although it was hard to tell which ones in the near darkness. They honked and bugled, circling me, and it didn't matter that I couldn't understand them the way they understood me—it was clear they were both scolding and urging me on.

But it was the others that drew my attention. One of them— no doubt Shadow—had swept through the trees only to issue a loud, challenging honk, and the remaining three followed her, gliding past me and the three birds issuing their admonishment.

Despite the need for haste, I paused, looking back to see what had attracted their attention. The white feathers caught what little light was left, brightening our small patch of forest, but their bulk also blocked my sight.

All four of them reared up, stretching out their wings and hissing. I took a step back toward them just as a voice spoke.

"Steady on, there! Adelaide?"

I gasped. Gabriel.

24

Whether the birds took exception to his call or to my gasp, something caused them to lunge forward, attacking him with their wings—or in the case of Shadow, with her beak.

The prince shouted, and my ears caught the sound of a blade being wrested from a scabbard.

"No!" I called in a long honk. *"He has a sword."*

Shadow snaked her head around and hissed at me, as if rebuking me for questioning their courage. I glared at her.

"Time is running out. We need to be moving. Leave him."

With a rustle and flap of feathers, the birds pulled back, coming to join the three already with me. Together they surrounded me with a bevy of curved necks and orange and black beaks. Their movement revealed the prince, one arm still raised to protect his face while the other held the now drawn sword partially raised.

"Adelaide?" he repeated, staring at the spectacle of me and the swans.

He had followed me. How had he followed me? He must have been lying in wait somewhere, hidden. Had he gone to the castle at all? I could barely make out his face now in the deepening night.

Pain flared across my body. I had momentarily forgotten its imminent arrival, and I gave a soft cry.

A swift streak of movement, more heard than seen, shot down from the sky and nipped at Gabriel's arm. He shouted and leaped forward.

Eagle. I really was distracted if I'd failed to notice that the one black member of my wedge was missing.

"Eagle! Stop it!" I managed to squeak out the words, and the seventh swan swooped toward me. When she reached me, she butted at me with her head, and I didn't need any further prompting.

Ignoring Gabe, who called my name, I took off running through the trees. The pain was growing worse, leaching the strength from my limbs, but I knew I had to push on. I kept both arms raised, my forearms protecting my face as I careened through the darkness. Only two years of familiarity with this path kept me from colliding with the now invisible trunks, and twice I tripped over roots or fallen branches and went sprawling across the ground.

The second time I fell, the pain kept me glued to the ground, my head spinning. My swans had taken to the sky, but when I didn't get up, one of them came flapping down to peck gently at me. She grasped my cloak in her beak and pulled, trying to get me moving again.

Tears dripped silently down my cheeks, but I managed to haul myself up with a groan, resuming my stumbling run. Ahead of me, I glimpsed light between the trunks and leaves. A final burst of strength propelled me forward through the last of the trees.

With a deep, trembling sigh, I sank to the ground and pressed my face to my hands. The pain was gone, but tremors shook my wrung out and exhausted body.

Long seconds passed as I recovered my equilibrium. The moon shone on seven elegant shapes gliding down from the sky to land gently in the smooth waters of the small lake in front of me. All seven of them paddled in my direction, but I raised a weak arm and waved them away.

"I'm fine. I promise." My voice came out croaky, and I tried to remember how many nights it had been since I bothered to talk to them in the hours of dark. There seemed little point when my words came out in a language unfamiliar to them.

Although they didn't understand me at night in the way they did during the day, my gesture and tone must have conveyed something of my message. Four of them broke off with soft honks, up-ending themselves immediately in search of food.

But Snowy and Sweetie continued in my direction, heaving themselves from the water to come and lie beside me, their hot bodies and soft feathers pressing gently against my still-shaking body.

Shadow followed behind more slowly, standing in front of me and honking assertively.

"I'm sorry," I said. "It was an unsettling day, and I lost track of time. I guess I lost track of a few things if I let the prince follow me that far. None of you were hurt, were you?"

She gazed at me, her head slightly cocked to one side, but clearly unable to understand me. I sighed.

"I'm sorry. I don't have any real explanation anyway. At least not one likely to make any sense to a swan," I muttered, mostly to myself.

Snowy and Sweetie's calming presence worked itself gradually into my core, relaxing me. The pain—so searing and disabling only minutes ago—was already a distant memory, gone the moment I stepped into the clearing.

I pulled myself up, stroking my hand against my friends' feathers as I went, and walked over to the lake for a drink. The cold water sharpened my mind, driving my thoughts back to the prince. Was he stumbling around lost in the dark?

I chewed on my lip. I didn't want him to follow me here, but neither did I want him to die in the forest. Here in this small tranquil oasis we were safe but was the same true of the wider forest? I had heard rustling on my walk here, but it could well have been him from the beginning. I could only hope so—for his sake.

No such sound presaged the tall, thin man who stepped into the clearing, shattering the illusion of tranquility. All seven swans responded aggressively, flapping their wings as they grunted and hissed. None of them offered him any violence as they had Gabriel, however. Instead they retreated to form a ring around me. Whether they were offering protection or seeking it had never been clear to me where this man was concerned.

I drew strength from their presence, however, and straightened my back.

"Leander." I knew it grated him to hear his name without his title, and I relished the small act of defiance.

"Surrounded by your avian handmaidens, as always, Princess, I see," he said, with a smile that held neither warmth nor goodwill.

I said nothing. I still hadn't worked out if the swans were his doing or whether their appearance two years ago had taken him by surprise. Either way, there was no question that they neither answered to him nor liked his presence.

"What do you want?" I asked, although in truth I knew the answer to that question.

The knowledge that my tardy arrival would prompt a visit from him was almost as effective as the pain in ensuring I returned to this lake before darkness fell each night. Except for today. I sent a silent curse in the absent prince's direction. Why had he arrived to upend my carefully balanced life?

"It's been a long time since you were late back," Leander said in friendly tones that somehow reminded me of nothing so much as a coiled snake—oily and sleek and promising danger.

"And what of it?" I asked, trying to keep my voice from giving away any hint of my roiling emotions. "I'm here, am I not?"

I arched an eyebrow at him, trying to mirror the poise that always graced the memories of my long-dead mother.

"Such elegance, my dear," he said, strolling around the edge of the lake toward me. "In spite of your dirt-stained cloak. How the fools in that town fail to recognize you for what you are continues to astound me."

He stopped two steps in front of me, held back by the solid wall of feathers which pressed against me on all sides. I realized that no black broke up the monotony of white, and risked a single glance around, my breath quickening.

I only hoped Eagle remembered what had happened last time she tried to attack Leander. I'd had to nurse her for weeks.

Leander continued talking, all his attention on me. "But then, they let you slip through their fingers, so they clearly are fools. I certainly don't intend to do likewise."

I abandoned my surreptitious search for the missing swan and gave him the coldest look I could muster.

"You may have me trapped here, Leander, but you don't own me."

He gave a low chuckle. "Do I not, indeed? I suppose we shall see…"

The silence between us grew to uncomfortable lengths, and it took all of my determination not to wilt before him. Eventually he gave another slight chuckle.

"Really, you should be grateful, Your Highness. I only come to check on your welfare, you know—as I did that first time. Just imagine how terrible if you were injured on your way back and unable to complete the journey. No doubt you would welcome my presence then."

I clenched my teeth together and said nothing. I did remember that first night, when I still didn't really understand or believe the enchantment he had wrought. I had run straight from the forest determined never to enter it again. Even when darkness fell and the pain began, I had tried to deny it at first. By the time I acknowledged I needed to return to the lake, I had been far beyond the journey back. I had barely managed to stagger a quarter of the way.

I also remembered how long it had taken him to appear—how long he had left me to suffer to drive his point home. And almost as unsettling was the memory of what it had felt like to be carried in his arms, pressed against his chest. I suppressed a shudder. He had carried me as gently as if I were a baby, but I had still felt the need to scrub myself three times in the lake before I felt free of the lingering sensation of his nearness. There was a darkness in this man, and it rode all too close to the surface.

"As you can see, I am not injured," I said. "You are not needed here tonight."

"Pity," he said, and his smile made my skin crawl. "I do so like to be useful."

"It is late," I said stiffly, "I need sleep."

"Very well, then, my dear. I wouldn't wish to disturb your rest." He gave a mocking half-bow. "And after all, I know where to find you."

"Indeed," I hissed. "You're the one keeping me here."

He chuckled to himself again as he strolled away, and for an unthinking moment, I longed to pick up a stone from the edge of the lake and hurl it at his disappearing head. Sometimes it was as unnerving that he left me here mostly undisturbed as it was that he had trapped me in the first place. What exactly were Lord Leander's plans for me?

At times, not knowing felt like the worst torture of all.

A soft flutter of feathers alerted me to the presence of my missing friend. I turned to glare at Eagle just as Leander disappeared into the trees at the same point he had appeared, a short distance around the lake.

"Where have you been?" I asked the bird, not expecting any answer. "I was worried."

"I think she must have sensed you were in trouble," said the prince, stepping out into the clearing behind the bird.

I swayed, my eyes flying to where Leander had just disappeared. So close!

"I didn't hear everything," Gabriel continued in a grim voice, "but I gather you have a problem this fine bird thinks I can help you solve."

I blinked and his strung bow appeared in one hand, the other hand sliding over his shoulder and retrieving an arrow. I blinked again, and he had already taken several strides in the direction of the departed lord.

My scrambled mind grasped his intent just as he broke into a faster pace.

"What? No. No!"

The swans honked, bumping against each other as I pushed through them, racing forward and launching myself at the prince's back. He stumbled and crashed to the ground, my weight dragging him down.

CHAPTER 4

For two full seconds, I lay there, stunned. And then I realized the entire length of my body was sprawled over Gabriel's back, and I scrambled to my feet. For several more seconds I stood frozen while the prince lay unmoving on the ground.

Had he been hurt? I stepped toward him again, concern overriding my reluctance to approach him. Before I actually reached him, however, he pushed himself up with his arms, and slowly rose to his feet.

In the moonlight he looked faintly flushed, and I examined him closely for any sign of injury. When I could find none, I took another step back.

"What did you think you were doing?" I demanded, keeping my heated voice low in case Leander were somehow still in earshot.

Gabriel raised both eyebrows. "So, you can suddenly speak." His eyes bored into me. "And you do not, in fact, wish to be rescued from that…gentleman?"

"Of course I want to be rescued," I snapped. "But not by you, Gabriel!"

The prince looked injured, although I couldn't tell if he meant it seriously or not.

"You wound my manly pride, Addie! I assure you, I'm an excellent rescuer." He grinned, answering my question about the seriousness of his feelings—or lack thereof. "And I could have sworn you used to call me Gabe."

"We were children," I said stiffly.

"Childhood friends. Exactly my point! And of the same rank, too. I think nicknames are entirely appropriate."

His easy smile remained, but I noticed a more serious gleam in his eye as he watched me. Perhaps he wished to see if I would repudiate his acknowledgment of my identity. I said nothing, however. What was the point out here? He clearly knew me, and my swans didn't care who I was.

Instead, I turned my head and looked across the water. I let my eyes roam over it in the almost unnaturally bright moonlight, trying to see the clearing as he might see it. It couldn't have looked more different from the surrounding forest. Here colorful flowers had been blooming for weeks—soaking up the sweet water of the lake and the rays of the sun that had free access to the ground around its shores.

There was no denying that even in the dark it looked like an idyllic paradise—at least in contrast to the rest of the forest. While I watched, a plump rabbit hopped up to the edge of the water to drink, clearly unafraid of any lurking predators. And it had no reason to fear. No dangerous creature had ever accosted me here—I had never so much as seen one come seeking refreshment of its own from the lake's waters.

Gabe must have followed the direction of my gaze because his next words were quiet and awed.

"What is this place?"

"Cursed," I said, noting the brusqueness of my voice but making no apology for it.

"It doesn't look cursed."

I could feel that his eyes had returned to me—no doubt full of far too many questions—so I kept my own turned resolutely away. He let the silence draw out, filled only with the splash and flap of the swans, who had mostly returned to foraging in the lake.

Eventually he must have realized that I didn't intend to offer any answers because he spoke again.

"I still can't quite believe I've actually found you. I've been looking through every village and town in the forest since winter first loosened its grip. Well, all those on our side of the border, at least. Dominic already searched those on his side last autumn."

I stiffened at the mention of my brother, and suddenly I was the one full of questions. I managed to keep them locked inside, however, as Gabe continued to rattle on.

"There have been strange rumors from this region, and Dominic has been desperate to follow up any hint of you, however ambiguous. I would have come looking myself back in the autumn—once Jon wrote explaining the situation and asking for my help—if not for the various excuses and delays that my family invented to keep me in the capital. But after being stuck there with them all winter, I assure you I would have gone mad without an escape."

He paused to shake his head. "So I reminded them of all the benefits to the kingdom if I was the one to find you, and rode off before they could come up with another reason to keep me there. So, really, I should be thanking you."

He gave me a courtly inclination of his head and shoulders, his eyes inviting me to share in his humorous tone, but I had barely heard his last couple of sentences. My mind whirled with confusion. His comments about my brother had been confusing enough, but I could make no sense at all of the rest of the tale.

"Jon?" I asked. "As in, Prince Jonathan of Marin? *Jon* asked for your help in finding me? Whyever would he do that?" Palinar and Marin were trade partners, certainly, and there was no bad blood between us—or there had not been when I left five years ago—but we didn't have an especially close connection either.

Once upon a time I had been friendly with Jon's sister, Princess Lilac, but we hadn't seen each other regularly enough to develop a close friendship. While her rank made her an acceptable enough companion for me in my father's eyes, the duchy of Marin could not be compared to Palinar—mightiest of the kingdoms. My father had not considered anyone worthy of a close connection—no doubt the reason my brother and I had always turned to each other.

But I quickly pushed my mind away from Dominic. It would do me no good to linger on thoughts of him.

"He did it for Sophie, no doubt," Gabe said. When I gave him a blank look, he continued. "I'm guessing Sophie spoke to Lily, and Jon would do anything Lily asked him."

When I still looked confused, a look of disgust crossed his face. I fell back several steps. But his next words suggested the disgust wasn't directed at me.

"Look at me, acting the utter fool! Of course you don't know who Sophie or Lily are. You probably have no idea what I'm talking about at all."

He shook his head, shifting his weight from foot to foot restlessly. "I keep forgetting how long you've been gone. So much has changed. It's a long story, I'm afraid. But the short version is this: the High King has lifted the storms that blocked the way to the Old Kingdoms. A delegation arrived in Marin just in time to be caught up in Dominic's Princess Tourney. One of the foreign princesses—Sophia of Arcadia—won and is now married to your brother and queen in Palinar. And Sophie has a twin sister, Lily, who has married Jon. Thus your sister-in-law is also sister-in-law to Jon." He laughed. "And, as I said, that's the simple version."

"My brother...called a Princess Tourney...to choose a bride for him?" I gasped the words out, wishing I had a chair to sink into. There hadn't been a Tourney in the kingdoms for...I didn't know how long. And Dominic of all people had given over the choice of his bride to a competition?

Instead of a chair, I felt soft feathers pressing against me and let my hand trail down to brush against the base of Snowy's neck. Her presence steadied me, absorbing some of my shock.

"Yes, we were all as astonished as you." Gabe shook his head. "It would have been startling enough before, but with the curse on Palinar..."

He looked at me, a question in his eyes, and I sighed.

"Brylee may be isolated, but we did hear about both the ongoing curse and the fact that Palinar has now been freed," I said. "There have also been stories of new kingdoms and foreign princesses, but I'll admit I didn't take them too seriously..."

No doubt I would have heard of Dominic's Tourney, and more of this Sophie and Lily, if I hadn't been distracted around the time of their arrival. The disturbance they caused in our land had coincided with a personal disturbance of my own—my entrapment by Leander. It had taken me some time to reintegrate into life in Brylee afterward, and I hadn't had the means or inclination to follow up any references I heard to strange happenings in distant places.

It had been shock enough months later when I learned that the border with my kingdom had been opened and the inhabitants freed. Many nights since I had spent awake, wondering what it meant—but each time I remembered that I had left that old life behind. And with good reason. I had long since come to terms with that.

"So you knew the curse had been lifted, and yet you didn't return." Gabe kept his voice soft, as if I were some untamed creature that he feared spooking.

"I have nothing to return to," I replied. "I have made my peace with that."

"But what of your brother? He searches for you everywhere."

"I am astonished to hear it," I said, and then regretted my

words. I had no obligation to open myself or my old life up to Gabe. He had already admitted that searching for me was merely an escape from his own life—an entertainment of sorts.

"What happened between you?" he asked, abandoning subtlety in favor of a direct approach.

I raised a single eyebrow before turning away from him.

He sighed. "Very well. But I have answered your questions, surely you would not refuse to answer some of my own. All of us have wondered many times what became of you. Everyone will be so excited to hear that I've found you! I'll send word to Dominic and Jon first thing in the morning."

I spun back, rushing forward to grip his arm tightly.

"No. You must promise me you won't tell anyone. Give me your word." I gazed up at him, making no effort to hide my desperation.

I had left my old life behind, and the knowledge that an unknown foreigner sat on my mother's throne and slept in her royal suite did nothing to entice me back. And while it might be true that my brother had changed—Palinar's current liberation supported such a notion—I had trusted him before, only to be abandoned in my moment of greatest need. He might search for me, but I had no desire to be found by him.

And all of that was nothing beside the far more pressing concern of my imprisonment, anyway. What would Dominic do if he learned of my current entrapment? I couldn't even hazard a guess, and I couldn't risk him—or anyone else—blundering into such a delicate situation.

"I can't keep such a thing from them," Gabe protested, frowning down at me.

"You must!" My entreating look changed into a glare. "It's my life, isn't it?"

A softness lingered in Gabe's eyes as he looked at my upturned face, so close to his, and it unnerved me. But worse was the look of calculation that gradually replaced it. His new look shouldn't have concerned me—it was nothing like the chilling cunning Leander wore behind every expression—but it frightened me just the same. A laugh seemed to lurk behind every one of Gabe's moods, and I didn't want to be the object of one of his games—even if he sought to draw me into it alongside him.

Slowly he peeled my fingers from his arm and stepped back, crossing his arms across his chest.

"Convince me then," he said. "Why should I keep you a secret? Something very strange is clearly going on here."

I bit my lip and glanced toward my wedge of swans, who seemed to be ignoring the two of us for the most part. Did I dare tell him my story?

I examined him sideways, frustration overtaking me. What choice did I have? If I couldn't convince him of the stakes, he might ruin everything.

When I didn't immediately speak, he prompted me.

"What happened to your voice at the haven? Why couldn't you speak? What is this place, and who was that man? It sounded as if he's somehow keeping you here." He raised both eyebrows. "Is that enough questions to be going on with?"

I made a frustrated noise in my throat but didn't actually protest. I shouldn't be surprised—I knew well enough to expect such manipulation from someone like him. He had pushed himself into my life, and I would no doubt be left to pick up the pieces soon enough. But for now, I had to make him realize why I needed to be left alone.

I sighed. "His name is Leander."

"The local lord?" Gabe frowned thoughtfully. "I'm suddenly even more curious to pay a visit to his castle."

"Yes." I blew out a breath. "Weren't you supposed to be doing that today? How did you follow me?"

Gabe gave me a half smile. "I came to Brylee to search for you, remember? As intriguing as this Leander sounded, I was hardly going to go running off just as I found you. I waited all afternoon for you to emerge, you know. And naturally—given your open and welcoming manner earlier—I concluded I should approach you directly."

He gave me a full grin, and I narrowed my eyes at him.

"You mean you hid and followed me—hardly the actions of a noble prince."

He actually winked at me. "Who said anything about noble?"

I stalked away from him, grumbling silently to myself as I went. Of course it had to be Gabe of all people who found me. He had always been like this—brave but impulsive. Even as a youth, he had been dashing and full of humor, and half of the young princesses had been in love with him. None of the other princes would have seen my situation as an intriguing riddle—an opportunity to showcase their daring and skill.

When I reached the small shelter where I spent my nights, I sank down onto the rushes that I had bundled into a pallet of sorts. It was a fitting bed for a home that was nothing more than a collection of branches formed into an open frame, with a blanket stretched over them so as to create something of a roof and single wall.

Gabe followed me, pausing only to scoop a couple of mouthfuls of water from the lake. When he reached me, he took a seat on a fallen tree trunk that bordered one side of my simple nest. He placed his bow carefully beside him and gazed at my construction with interest.

"Not exactly what you'd call hardy," he said, although there was no judgment in his tone.

I shrugged. "It's all I need. The air here never gets any colder than what you feel now—no matter the season or the temperature of the surrounding woods. If it rains, it's no more than a gentle mist, and no dangerous animals disturb my peace."

"All of this, along with a lake whose water is both fresher and clearer than it has any natural right to be," he said, taking up my litany. "And surrounded by a collection of loyal animals who not only guard and comfort you, but who actually understand your instructions." He paused. "Remind me again why this place is not a paradise?"

"I suppose it would be a paradise," I said in a low voice. "If it wasn't also a prison."

CHAPTER 5

"So you *are* trapped here." He frowned. "But you were in Brylee earlier…I don't understand."

I sighed. "It's complicated." *Quite complicated enough without you getting involved,* I thought, but didn't add.

"I'm smarter than I look," Gabe said with what he no doubt meant to be a dashing smile.

I eyed him uncertainly. I remembered Gabe as rash—a prince who was far too likely to leap into action and danger without proper thought. But I hadn't seen him in years. He had been a boy then—perhaps he had grown in wisdom as well as stature?

I shook my head at my own wishful thinking. Unlikely. Which meant I now had one more thing to worry about. But whatever the complications, it would be worse if he sent word of my location to Dominic and Jon.

"It's only at night," I said, my words tumbling out in a rush, now that I had freed them. "Every night, by the time darkness falls, I must be at this lake."

"Or else what?" he asked.

"If I'm not in this clearing when the last of the daylight fades, then I'm hit with crippling pain all over my body. The further away I am, the worse it is. And, as an extra gift, I receive a visit from Leander."

My expression no doubt conveyed my feelings about such an event.

"So today..." Gabe winced. "That's why you took off running back there in the forest. And why Leander was here. You didn't make it back in time—because of me."

I said nothing, and guilt flooded his face.

"I assure you, I would never mean to cause you pain, Adelaide."

I shrugged. Experience had taught me that the pain caused by those who intended no harm could be the most damaging—because you weren't armored against it. But I wasn't vulnerable to him now. I had learned my lesson and built up my armor too thick to be pierced.

After a moment he seemed to accept that I meant to say nothing and continued on.

"But what of your voice? Back at the haven..."

"That is another symptom of my strange entrapment. At night I can speak like normal. But during the day, when I am free to roam, I speak only the language of the swans. It is a painful irony. At night I can speak—but I have no one to converse with. Well, except for the occasional visit from Leander—and I would rather go silent than speak to him."

"But now you have me to talk with," Gabe said. "It must be strange for you."

The truth of his words crashed over me. His presence was strange in every possible way, and I hadn't immediately realized what a welcome relief it was to make use of my words again. Their loss had stripped away a part of me I had almost forgotten to miss.

Gabe turned to gaze out over the lake, and the one black and six white bodies which glided across it, their beaks dabbling for food in the shallows or their tail feathers flashing as they up-ended for a deeper prize.

"All sorts of strange things have occurred across these lands since Palinar fell into darkness," he said. "But this is a very odd sort of enchantment. I assume Leander is behind it, but what is his purpose?"

I frowned. "I wish I knew. I have been trying to puzzle it out for two years without success. Leander seems to delight in my captivity, and I do not doubt he has some sinister purpose, but..." I gestured around us, "he's given me a gilded cage. The pain that strikes me if I set foot into the trees seems utterly at odds with the protected beauty and peace of this place."

Sweetie waddled over, bugling at me before settling content-edly at my side. I rested a gentle hand against the springy softness of her feathers.

"And I am not entirely alone," I added. "My swans are loyal and true companions, even if they cannot hold a conversation. If Leander's purpose is to break me, to isolate me, then their pres-ence seems to work against such an aim. Why give me a language that anyone could understand—even if it was just birds?"

"They certainly don't behave like any swans I've ever seen." Gabe's eyes lingered on Sweetie before passing to me. "They must certainly be part of whatever enchantment Leander has crafted. You think his purpose was to isolate you?"

I shrugged. "I don't know for sure. But I don't think the enchant-ment worked quite as he intended. He told me at first that I would not be able to leave the lake, and yet when I turned and ran, nothing happened. It was only when darkness fell that the crippling pain he had promised hit. There was a weakness of some sort in his trap."

"A weakness? Hmmm..." Gabe tapped his chin, his eyes fixed blindly on the water. "I wonder..."

I waited for him to explain, but instead his mind seemed to leap in a different direction.

43

"Leander is clearly a blackguard, and needs to be stopped," he said. "Why did you prevent me from going after him?"

For a moment I had lost myself in the puzzle of my circumstances and had even enjoyed having someone to discuss my theories with, but his words brought back my earlier anger.

"Who knows what damage that would cause? We know nothing of what he has done here—or how."

"Exactly," Gabe said. "What if killing him releases you?"

"And what if it doesn't?" I shot back. "What if instead it dooms me to spend the rest of my life caught in such a state? There is every chance that he alone has the key to releasing me, and I cannot risk losing it."

I took a moment to calm my breathing which had sped up despite my efforts to remain unruffled. How had I even considered that he might have grown past his rashness? He had already shown me proof that he had not.

"I could have put an arrow in his leg, at least," Gabe muttered mutinously.

But when I glared at him, he held up both hands placatingly.

"Oh, very well. No shooting." He gave me a significant look. "For now. But if I'm not allowed to turn him into target practice, what exactly is our plan?"

I bristled at his use of *our* but chose to ignore it.

"Leander was a recluse in his castle long before I stumbled onto this lake and into his snare, and I can't help feeling the building must hold answers. Why else does he refuse anyone access—except for the servants who never emerge to tell any tales?"

"Then we must search it," said Gabe, an enthusiastic gleam in his eye that unfurled tendrils of disquiet in my stomach.

"Easier said than done," I replied. "Night is generally the best time to gain covert access to a building, but I'm not exactly free to attempt it in the darkness. And any daylight attempt is significantly hampered by my inability to speak."

"Ah!" Gabe sat up straight. "But I am not so limited."

The tendrils tightened their hold on my insides. Gabe was not some backwoods servant. If the crown prince disappeared inside Leander's fortress…who knew what consequences it would bring down on the lord—and by extension, me?

"I think it would be in my best interests to acknowledge my true identity," Gabe said, half to himself. "Leander can hardly refuse me at the gate."

Against my will, a seed of hope sprang to life inside me. Surely Leander himself must know the dangers of restraining Prince Gabriel. Perhaps…

I shook myself. No. Gabe was just as likely to do something foolish and destroy everything I had been working toward. I had to convince him to leave all of this—and me—alone.

"Please," I said. "This has nothing to do with you. You should return to the capital and forget you ever found me."

Gabe had stood up and begun to pace back and forth, his body almost quivering with energy, but at my words, he halted abruptly.

"You must be jesting!" he said. "Leave now? With you in the grip of unknown evil? Where would be the honor in such a course?" He shook his head, but then slowly a smile crept over his face. "And even without such considerations, this is precisely the sort of adventure I have been longing for, confined back at the palace. No. I could not abandon you, any more than I could ignore a potential threat to the kingdom. And I wouldn't want to."

I worried at my lip. His words had made it abundantly clear that I had no hope of convincing him to leave. But they had also brushed against one of my greatest fears.

"So…" I hesitated. "So, you think there might be a threat to more than me? To the kingdom, even?"

Gabe sat down heavily on his vacated log. "Who can say for sure? But it's hard to imagine that this—" he gestured vaguely at me, the lake, and my swans, "is his whole plan. If this were merely the first phase of some plot centered on you, then two years is a long time for him to wait without progressing. However, perhaps you are merely one piece of some broader plan he is assembling. From what you said, the mysteries around him began before your arrival on the scene."

My hand fluttered to the base of my throat. I had hoped he would brush aside the worst of my imaginings, not agree with them. I leaned forward.

"Have you noticed...Does it seem to you as if there's something strange about the inhabitants of Brylee?"

I watched him closely, waiting for his reaction. He frowned at me.

"Strange? More strange than everyone else, do you mean?"

Now it was my turn to frown. "What do you mean everyone else?"

"If you mean the unnatural timidity, it's not just the people of Brylee. Even my own family is infected—thus their attempts to keep me at home away from any possible danger—and the reason for my earnest desire to be away from the capital. I was stifling there. I don't remember everyone being so...so *afraid* when I was a boy. But, as you know, I spent so many years living with Teddy and Millie in Trione—as King Edward and Queen Juliette's ward —that sometimes I wonder if I was just oblivious as a child. I've been back for less than three years, and I find myself visiting my friends in other kingdoms all too often. Here in Talinos, even my own family make me want to kick down a door, jump on the nearest horse, and go do something reckless."

He grinned. "Their caution is like a red rag to a bull where I'm concerned, I'm afraid."

I rolled my eyes, but I was too interested in what he was saying to comment on his irresponsible nature.

"You mean it's not just Brylee? It's the whole kingdom?" My eyes widened. "Is that why the whole army massed at the border with Palinar and then just sat there for years? The locals seemed to think it only logical, but I could never understand such a strange course of action."

Gabe's face turned serious.

"It's a course of action that nearly ruined Talinos. So many men sitting idle for so long? Our production nearly ground to a halt, and paying them was emptying the royal coffers. If things hadn't changed in Palinar—and if I hadn't finally managed to convince my parents to disperse the soldiers and set them to more useful tasks around the kingdom..." He shook his head. "It was like no one could think of anything but their fear of what might cross the border—and yet no one could take any positive action either. Surely Talinos cannot have been going on in such a manner for my whole life without my noticing."

"No, indeed..." I said slowly. "I don't think..." I looked up at him. "What of your brother, Percy? He was only a year younger than me, so he must be seventeen by now. Surely he is not equally timid?"

Gabe's face twisted. "He's as bad as anyone."

"Then it must be new," I said with conviction. "He's closer in age to many of us younger princesses than he is to you older boys, but he was always determined to keep up with you. Do you remember when he was seven, and he broke his arm trying to—"

"Oh yes. Now that you mention it, I do remember that," Gabe said quickly, cutting me off. "Although, to be fair, I broke my arm as well." He shook his head ruefully. "I was no doubt a terrible role model for a brother three years younger."

It didn't seem polite to agree with him, so I said nothing. A thoughtful expression crept over his face.

"You know, I spent a lot of hours loitering around the town waiting for you yesterday. It did seem particularly bad here— more so than back in the capital."

"Perhaps because we're near the border?" I asked. "Ever since my parents..." My words faltered, and I couldn't bring myself to refer to their deaths out loud. Just as I had feared, Gabe's presence was bringing back a part of my life that I had put away for good.

I could feel a crawling sensation from my scalp down my spine as I remembered the face of the servant who brought the news to my mother—my father and Dominic's trip had resulted in the murder of an entire village. Everyone had fled before him after that, except for her. My mother loved our people too much not to protest such an atrocity. But, selfishly, I wished she had stayed in her rooms that day.

Watching my father send my mother tumbling down the stairs to her death had been traumatic enough without the shocks that followed. I saw them now, racing through my memory. My godmother's pronouncement of a curse on our kingdom. My father attacking her, only for her to step back into thin air leaving him to fall to his own death. Dominic rejecting the godmother's call to free our people, instead roaming the palace full of pride and anger. My own repeated attempts to speak to him, and his continued rejection.

Whatever rage had gripped him, it had left no room for the love I had always believed he bore for me. Sometimes I even wondered if he had been aware enough to see me in those horrifying days. It was like he had forgotten I even existed, no thought in his mind for anyone other than himself.

No immediate danger threatened me now, but still I felt the panic of those days when I found myself alone at thirteen in the vast empty palace of Palinar, surrounded by an equally empty city. I had no idea what had happened to my people, no chance to farewell my mother at the grand funeral she deserved, and no words of comfort or arms to cry in. I had nothing but fear, and hopelessness, and grief. Until my godmother reappeared, and I had the haven.

Gasping, I pushed the images away and the emotions down. I was here now, at my lake, and I had more immediate concerns.

Re-wording, I tried again. "Ever since the curse on Palinar, it seems like most Talinosians have been obsessed with the taint creeping across the border and consuming them as well. Well, what if they were actually right, in a way? Maybe it was already here—maybe it's still here—and they just can't see it."

A softness entered Gabe's eyes at the mention of my parents, and when he spoke, his words were gentle.

"Jon has been convinced for a long time now that what happened with your family in Palinar opened the door to a darkness that has been infecting many of the kingdoms. Marin was nearly destroyed—until the new princesses managed to turn things around there."

He leaned forward suddenly, his expression turning eager.

"Did you hear there are godmothers here now? They never left the Old Kingdoms, and Lily and Sophie even have a godmother of their own. A godmother helped Jon, too, and he and the twins managed to destroy the Tourney!"

"Destroy the Tourney?" I stared at him.

"And then Sophie freed your brother—and Palinar along with him—and Celine managed to thaw the Eldonians. And Snow somehow managed to stand up to her stepmother—which is almost as astonishing as all the rest. I suppose you heard her father died?"

I nodded. "Yes, poor King George—and poor Snow. Although I'm glad she's Queen Blanche now. But what did you mean by *thawing* the Eldonians?"

He shook his head. "That's a long story, and it's all over now. My concern is for Talinos—because it certainly looks like whatever darkness is festering here has yet to be driven away. I've been traveling for a while now, and I didn't notice the other border towns being as bad. Which makes me wonder…"

He turned to me, his eyes glowing and his voice slightly breathless. "Do you think Brylee could be at the center of whatever has happened to Talinos? Could this Leander somehow be part of it? Maybe he recognized that you were a danger to his plans, and so he decided to trap you before you could upset them?"

I frowned. "It seems like a very elaborate scheme for such a simple purpose—especially given I wasn't exactly posing much threat to anyone back then. I lived at the haven and helped Cora with the elderly residents and the children."

Gabe deflated somewhat. "No, I suppose there would have to be more to it. But that doesn't mean he isn't tied into whatever is happening to my kingdom. Which makes it all the more important to get inside his castle and see what's going on."

"If Leander is plotting against the kingdom, your rank may not be enough to keep you safe," I cautioned.

"I'm not worried about me—I'm worried about my people." He hesitated, peering at me, as if he wasn't sure if his next words would be welcome. "I'm glad you found the haven. It's why I came to Brylee, actually. I heard there was a place where anyone who needed it could find safe shelter, and I wondered if—well, I suppose I hoped more than anything—that you might have found such a place."

I turned my face away. I hadn't found the haven—I had been placed there. And it wasn't news to me that the godmothers had returned to these lands—because it had been my own godmother who placed me with Cora. When I had no one, my godmother found me a new family. I had even found a new happiness, despite the grief for my mother. But then I had turned sixteen, gone for an ill-advised walk in the woods, and been lured into an elaborate trap that changed everything.

Sometimes, at night, when I was alone, I wondered if my godmother had foreseen it. She had looked so kind when she came to me in the palace at Palinar—to a thirteen-year-old, alone, grief-stricken, and confused. She had worn none of the avenging anger that had clothed her as she confronted my father standing over the stairs where my mother had fallen to her death.

She had offered me a way out—and I had gladly taken it. But surely she had known of the evil that lurked in these woods? On those nights it was hard to forget her role in my father's death—as deserving of that fate as he may have been. The possibility that she was not, after all, a friendly force had kept me from calling on her through the two years of my curse.

"You know, I've been wondering..." Gabe said, jolting me from my thoughts. "You were saying earlier that yours is a strange sort of curse, and I've been thinking about all those other kingdoms and what happened in them."

He jumped up and began to stride again, causing several of my swans to look up abruptly and honk loudly. He ignored them. Finally he stopped and looked back at me.

"What do you know of godmother objects?"

CHAPTER 6

$\mathcal{I}$ blinked in surprise.

"You mean like the royal mirrors?"

He nodded. "Among other things. They're the magical objects the godmothers use to help drive back the darkness and ensure true love triumphs. We don't have as many of them as the Old Kingdoms apparently, since we've gone so many years without the godmothers, but we do have them."

I raised my brows, and he crossed over to drop down beside me again.

"We didn't grow up with the stories like Lily and Sophie did, but it turns out it's all true. If a kingdom is ruled by true love, then everyone prospers. That's why the godmothers do it. Lily explained the whole thing to me once. And it certainly seems to be making a difference in Palinar and Eldon and Eliam." He laughed. "It sounds like a fairy story, doesn't it? But it seems our ancestors went astray and that's what opened the door to all this darkness in the first place."

I bit my lip. I thought it was my father who had done that. But then I had seen the way he warped the brother I once loved...

Maybe a long time ago, someone had warped him in the same way, the problem stretching back for generations.

"But what do godmother objects have to do with any of this?" I asked.

"Godmother objects and gifts are the only source of power in the kingdoms. I guess I'd heard that, but it never really meant anything to me. Except then I went to Eldon for Oliver's wedding. Celine has a lot of stories—and even more brothers and sisters." He shook his head. "Seriously, there's a seemingly never-ending supply of them. And most of them have unbelievable tales about how they fell in love and saved their kingdoms. But Celine herself—"

"Who's Celine?" I interrupted.

He looked surprised for a moment and then gave me an apologetic look.

"Sorry! I keep forgetting how much you've missed." He chuckled. "It's hard to imagine anyone not knowing Celine. She's...a force to be reckoned with. But I think I'll leave you to find out about Celine's special gifts yourself."

"That sounds ominous," I said.

"Well, she saved Eldon—thanks to her godmother. And that's my point."

"That Celine has a godmother?" It had been a long day, and the various shocks were starting to take their toll. Too many thoughts were swirling around my mind, and I was struggling to follow the conversation.

He laughed. "No, that's entirely irrelevant."

I pulled my eyebrows together, giving him an unimpressed look.

"Sorry," he said again. "I'm making a muddle of it. It's just that I heard a number of cases from Celine and her siblings where people with evil intent were able to find and collect godmother objects, and then twist them to their purposes. And I wonder if that could be what's going on here."

"You think Leander is using a godmother object to keep me trapped here?" I asked.

"How else could he be doing it?" He leaned toward me. "It might even be more than one. And it would make sense of why some parts of the enchantment seem almost positive—and why it didn't turn out quite how he wanted. Maybe the original enchantment was meant to protect a place—like this lake." He waved his arm around to indicate the clearing around us. "And maybe he twisted it to trap you here—you're probably right, and he never meant for you to be able to leave during the day."

"And the swans?" I asked skeptically.

"Like I said, maybe that's a second object." He was warming even more to his theories. "Maybe it was originally intended to allow someone to communicate with animals—or swans particularly—and he tried to twist it so that you would communicate like an animal, or something. Maybe he even intended to turn you into a swan."

"Now you're getting a bit carried away," I said, unable to resist a small smile despite myself.

He grinned back. "Well, maybe not that. But who knows his plans? The good news is that, if I'm right, we have a plan, at least."

"We do?"

"We need to find those godmother objects and destroy them—that should break the enchantment. Which means you were right. We need Leander, so that he can lead us to them."

"And how are you planning to get him to do that?" I asked.

A dimple appeared in one of his cheeks. "I suppose it's more the beginning of a plan than a full plan—but that's enough for me."

"I'll bet it is," I mumbled to myself.

When I looked up, he was giving me a questioning look, but I didn't repeat myself.

"It's getting late," I said instead. "We need a full plan, but I'm tired. I suppose you'll have to stay here for the rest of the night—

you'll never find your way back in the dark. But in the morning, you need to go back to the town. Come up with some excuse for the innkeeper about where you were all night—we don't want word getting to Leander that you were in the forest all night."

"And then what?" he asked.

"I've been here for two years. There's no big hurry now. Tomorrow night we can talk again." I gave him a stern look. "And see if we can come up with a proper plan."

"Yes, Your Highness," he said gravely, but his eyes twinkled at me.

"There's a thick patch of grass on that side of the lake." I pointed across the water. "It will make a nice enough bed."

I expected him to protest at not being invited to join me in my shelter, but he stood up meekly enough and bid me goodnight. I watched him with narrow eyes as he made his way around the edge of the water, glancing back in my direction every so often.

When it became clear he was following my directions, I curled on my pallet, my back pressed against Sweetie's warm bulk. I closed my eyes, but sleep didn't come.

The lake was always still at night, and I could hear faint sounds as he settled himself across the water. His presence felt incongruous with this place—a jarring note that I had never experienced in my many nights here. It kept me awake and alert, every little sound setting me on edge.

It was true that I was tired, but that had only been an excuse to give me space from Gabe. I needed time to think. Clearly I wasn't getting rid of him, but I wasn't sure how to incorporate him into my plans. Because everything I had told Gabe was the truth—but it wasn't the whole truth. I wasn't ready to trust him with that.

I woke before the first lightening of dawn reached the lake, just as I did every morning. But this was the first morning when it actually mattered that I had a final few waking moments in possession of my voice.

I crossed to the edge of the lake to refresh myself, and Gabe stood immediately, coming to join me. I didn't know if he was usually an early riser or if he had slept lightly given the circumstances. He certainly looked awake and alert in the remaining moonlight and the first gray hint of dawn. I couldn't predict the exact moment day would reach us, so I spoke quickly.

"I assume you can find your own way back to Brylee?"

Gabe regarded me with curiosity in his eyes.

"If I said no, would you guide me?"

"No. Any moment now I'll have the language of the swans again, and I'll ask one of them to accompany you and give you warning if you veer in the wrong direction."

"So they really do understand you? Like a person would?" He looked awed.

I glanced to the side where several of the swans lay pressed together, still asleep. "Not exactly like a person—sometimes the complexities escape them. But certainly far more like one than I can imagine is natural for a group of wild swans. I suspect they've been trapped and transformed by the curse just as I have, even if Leander didn't intend it."

Gabe looked at them consideringly before turning back to me.

"You really don't mean to accompany me? I thought you spent your days in the town?"

"I spend some of my day there," I said shortly. "And I have no interest in being seen emerging from the forest in the early hours of the morning in your company. The townsfolk already see me as odd—and therefore suspicious—enough as it is."

I also had something else I needed to do before heading for Brylee—but I didn't intend to tell Gabe anything about it. Not yet, at any rate.

He looked as if he meant to question me further, but a spear of light thrust between the trunks of the trees, significantly brightening the scene around us, and I grimaced. My hand rose instinctively to my throat, and Gabe cut off whatever he had intended to say. Conversation was over between us until night fell again.

"I will be here again tonight," Gabe warned—although perhaps he meant it as a promise.

I gave him a tight smile and a quick nod before turning to my sleeping swans. Several of them had woken, stretching and flapping their wings, and at my attention, they began to waddle toward me. I glanced at Gabe out of the corner of my eye, considering.

I had been thinking of sending Sammy with him—she was one of the steadiest and most reliable of the birds. But irritation at his intrusion welled inside me, and when I bugled to the swans, I found myself directing my instructions elsewhere.

"*Eagle,*" I said. "*Can you make sure he gets back to Brylee safely?*"

Let Gabe deal with the most ornery of the swans. And Eagle would probably be at her most cantankerous, too, since she wouldn't like being left out of our usual morning task. But she had been the one to bring him to the clearing, after all, so it was a fitting punishment for them both.

The black swan gave a strange sound almost like a chortle and glided over from where she had been floating on the far side of the lake—a dark patch almost lost in the still dim scene.

I hadn't expected such an amenable response from her, and I felt an irritating moment of concern on Gabe's behalf.

"*And promptly,*" I added in a warning squeak. "*Don't let him spend half the day wandering around the forest lost.*"

Eagle trained one beady eye on me, and I could sense her disapproval. I didn't need words to know that the task had lost its appeal for her if she was to be denied the right to make mischief.

Shadow gave a commanding honk from behind me, and Eagle

ruffled her feathers, regarding us all with weary resignation from the edge of the water.

Gabe looked warily from the swan to me.

"She's the one you want me to follow? Why do I feel like I just missed something?"

I shrugged and pointed toward the trees in the direction he should begin.

Eagle stared at him for a moment and then in one big movement, lifted her body from the water, her wings unfurling and holding her just above the surface as she ran along it for some way before breaking free and soaring into the sky. She disappeared above the level of the trees in the direction I had pointed.

I raised both eyebrows and indicated with my head that Gabe should go after her. He hesitated for only a moment before wishing me farewell and breaking into a jog. Within moments he had disappeared between the tree trunks.

All of the swans had now taken to the lake, searching for breakfast and calling to each other. When I didn't move, Shadow looked back in my direction, honking at me. I couldn't tell whether she meant it as inquiry or instruction, but I shook myself and returned to my shelter.

Digging out the food supplies I kept there—provisions from Cora combined with fresh berries from the clearing and surrounding forest—I ate quickly. I was already late leaving, and I needed to get going.

When I set out, I ignored the stretch of forest Eagle and Gabe had departed into and headed instead for the trees that had emitted Leander the night before. I moved quickly, almost as familiar with this path as I was with the one that led to Brylee. The stretch of forest looked much like all the others, and yet I could never shake a feeling of foreboding when I passed through it. Once again I tried to tell myself that it was entirely my own imaginings, and that the lingering shadows were no darker here than elsewhere, that the trees creaked no louder, and the undergrowth grew no thicker. But the feeling remained, grown stronger on this occasion when combined with the burden of my new worries about Gabe's arrival.

I tried to draw strength from the knowledge that my wedge accompanied me—bar its black member. But they flew high above the treetops, out of sight for now. Still, I forced myself onward, toward the growing feeling of menace. I owed it to my friend.

The trees didn't thin, as they did around Brylee. Instead I stepped directly from the thickness of the wild forest onto the fringes of a vast lake. Only the thinnest verge of clear land allowed me to walk beside the shoreline, skirting the short stretch of water between me and my target.

I kept my eyes on the ground, but all too soon, I had reached a stretch of jagged rocks that climbed steeply to the base of a broad wall. The ancient, rough stone soared into the air above me, a deserted battlement at the top. No gate broke the gray expanse— I had reached the rear of the curtain wall as intended.

I forced myself to look up and take in the whole of it, my eyes quickly scanning the surrounding area for any movement. In all the mornings I had come here, I had never seen any, however, and—true to form—nothing stirred around me now.

Instead, my eyes were drawn magnetically back to the stone structure. In vain I reminded myself that it was small compared to the home in which I had been raised—the vast palace at the heart of the Palinaran capital. It was even small compared to the heir's castle where my mother had often taken my brother and me during the years of my childhood. But it made no difference —still the walls and tower seemed to loom above me.

Leander's Keep.

CHAPTER 7

a splash drew my attention back to the water, as my six swans landed gracefully on the lake. They paddled over toward me, climbing free to press against my legs. I brushed my hand along their feathers, drawing courage from their presence. We were later than usual which meant we would have to work quickly.

"You know the drill," I bugled. *"Look for any change in routine, any way inside, and any sign of Audrey."*

We had been doing this for enough mornings that I no longer needed to describe my friend—the same age as me but distinctive thanks to her bright copper hair.

All six of them took off, their wings beating, and their legs pumping as they ran along the surface of the water before gaining altitude and wheeling toward the Keep. I watched them go with a swiftly beating heart, just as I always did. If Leander saw and recognized them, if a hunter from the Keep took note of their presence, if one of them swooped too low and put themselves within reach of one of the Keep's large pack of hounds—

I cut off the thoughts. There was a reason we came only in the early hours of the morning and left once the full activity of the day began.

I strained my ears to hear any unusual sounds, but nothing stood out. Soon the beat of wings sounded, however, and Sunny came back into view. She flew in a direct line toward me, angling down to land in the water as near to me as possible.

Each of my swans had an individual role—something specific to observe. For Sunny it was the gate.

"Was the gate closed?" I bugled.

She thrust her beak down into the water once before raising it again and watching me, drops of water sliding down toward the surface of the lake. I waited hopefully for several seconds, but she made no extra movement.

I sighed. A single tap of the water meant yes. Two taps meant no. In all the mornings we had come here, she had never tapped the water twice for that question.

"How many guards?" I asked next.

This time when she bent her neck, she kept it near the water, thrusting it down six times in quick succession.

I sighed again. The opposite answer to what I hoped to hear. Six guards manning the only gate was an increase, not a decrease, on the usual number. Because of the crown prince's arrival in town?

Not that the reason mattered. I had no more hope of sneaking past the usual four guards than I had of six.

On your own, at least, an insidious voice whispered in my mind. *But you aren't on your own anymore.*

I thrust the thought away. Two people weren't enough to force their way past six guards, and even if I had more forces, the whole point was to make a surreptitious entry. I couldn't put Audrey at risk with an open assault even if it had been within my capacity.

More flapping presaged the arrival of two more of my swans.

When I saw it was Snowy and Sweetie, my mood lifted slightly. If they were back already, they must have seen something.

"Did you see Audrey?" I bugled.

Snowy tapped the water once. Yes.

"Did she look well?" I asked.

This time Sweetie was the one to give a single tap.

I let out a small breath of relief. Audrey was rarely to be seen in any of the Keep's courtyards at this time of the morning, so I didn't get regular updates on her condition. I wished I could ask what she had been doing, but the spy system I had set up didn't extend to that sort of detail. It had taken me long enough to get the swans to understand the simple questions I asked them.

The rest of the birds swooped in one by one, reporting nothing more out of the ordinary. According to Shadow, the guard patrols looked normal for that time of the morning, Sammy had detected no potential new avenue for breaching the Keep's outer walls, and Stormy had seen no sign of Leander.

Like Audrey, the local lord was rarely to be seen out at this time. Stormy had occasionally spied him through a large window at the top of the Keep, however, and we had managed to determine that it was his study. But that information would do me no good if I couldn't find a way inside the walls.

An angry hissing broke the stillness of the morning, and movement flashed across the corner of my eye. I swung around to see Eagle flapping toward me. As soon as she saw me looking in her direction, she bugled loudly, swinging around in a tight circle. She circled twice while I scrambled into motion and then took off in a direct line back the way she had come.

I raced after her, my heart pumping and my body shaking. Eagle had only one role—to look for threats and sound the alarm. But she wasn't urging us away from the Keep—she was urging us toward it. Audrey. I ran faster.

We weren't making a direct line for the front gate—rather re-entering the trees at an angle that would bring us close to it. And as I wove between the trunks, I remembered an important point. Eagle hadn't been with us this morning. Eagle had been given a different task.

Gabe.

I let out a strangled groan of frustration but didn't slow down my pace. Eagle wouldn't have sounded such an alarm unless time was short.

The road from Brylee to the Keep appeared ahead of me, and I swung my head, my eyes searching it. There. I angled my run, bursting out onto the road and directly into the solid bulk of the prince.

His head was turned in my direction—no doubt due to the sound of my approach—but he was otherwise unprepared. He staggered backward, and I drove both of us off the road and into the trees on the far side.

For a moment, I thought we would fall, but Gabe managed to keep his feet under him and me upright as well. He continued to clasp me close, however, even after we had both steadied, blinking down at me in surprise.

"*Idiot!*" I cried, not caring that the word came out as a hiss that sounded almost identical to the ones Eagle had been making as she flew.

"Adelaide?" He seemed to realize suddenly that his arms still encircled me, and he let go abruptly, stepping back. "What are you doing here?"

I could ask you the same, I said in my head, putting my hands on my hips and giving him two raised eyebrows combined with a glare that I hoped conveyed the sentiment without words.

He had the grace to look guilty, at least. I followed his eyes upward to where a flash of black showed in the air above the road. Eagle must be flying large circles around our position.

"I suppose I know who is to blame for your arrival," he said, a hint of humor in his voice.

I just narrowed my eyes and continued the glare.

He shook his head. "Don't be angry with me. I found you, Adelaide! I actually found you! And you're enchanted, unable to leave Brylee—something you don't want me to tell your brother. Which means it's up to me to free you. And I'm not going to do that by sitting around at the local inn."

I opened my mouth, closed it again, and let out a grunt of frustration. I needed words.

Gabe gave me a smug look. "I did, however, have time to swing past the town and pick up certain essential supplies." He rummaged through a small pack he carried on his back alongside his bow and quiver and produced a parchment and pen, complete with a small, stoppered inkwell.

I took them from him, but then hesitated, trying to think of the most efficient way to express myself.

"You can write, can't you?" A shadow of concern crossed Gabe's face. "The curse doesn't prevent it? I did wonder since you didn't seem to have any writing tools with you at the haven."

I took several steps over toward a large rock with a small flat section that only required me to stoop a little. Placing the paper against the stone, I pressed the pen down.

<I can write.>

"But you don't?" Gabe frowned over my shoulder.

I hesitated again before scratching out a longer reply.

<Writing takes too long. At the haven it's faster to use hand signs, and I don't talk to anyone else. Plus Vilma and Gregor don't have the eyesight to read anymore, and Juniper doesn't know how. It all just gets too complicated.>

I bit my lip, annoyed with myself. Too much detail. This was the problem with writing. I wanted to say too much, and then it ended up taking forever to write. Usually the other person got impatient and had already moved on to say something else by the time I got my full reply out. It was impossible to have any sort of normal conversation.

Gabe, however, had remained silent while I took the time to

write out the longer reply, turning to survey the forest, and only turning back when my pen stopped moving. He took in the lines I had written at a glance and nodded his head. His eyes fixed on me.

"But something tells me that's not all. Let me guess. You don't like to talk to people this way because they might ask questions you don't want to answer."

I flushed, surprise overtaking my anger. Was I that transparent?

His expression told me he disapproved of my secrecy, but I wasn't wrong. I knew that for certain. Looking pointedly at him, I turned to look in the direction of the Keep, and then back at him before leaning to write again.

<Giving people information isn't safe. Leander is dangerous.>

"All the more reason he needs to be stopped," Gabe said. "But I don't get the impression Cora is the type to go charging off, so I don't think you would have any need to..." His voice trailed off as he examined my face.

I didn't write anything, but I saw a question bloom across his features.

"That girl. The one at the castle—Cora's sister. What was her name?"

Shame pulsed through me, and my hand shook slightly as I pressed my pen to the paper again.

<Audrey. And she's not Cora's sister, she's Wren's.>

"You told her what was going on, didn't you?" Gabe asked. "And she ran off to the castle, to...what? Find some way to free you?"

<I don't know for certain. I would never have let her go if I had known anything about it.>

I paused in my writing to fight back tears. I refused to cry in front of Gabe.

<Six months ago, she had a fight with Wren. She took off into the forest in a huff and crossed paths with me, returning to the

lake. I should have sent her back, found a way…> My pen pressed too hard against the paper, almost tearing it, and I paused before continuing. <I let her come to the lake. I spoke to her when darkness fell and told her everything. She was my best friend, and I—>

Gabe placed a gentle hand on my arm.

"You were lonely and trapped and given the opportunity to speak to your friend again. You didn't do anything wrong, Addie."

I shook my head. I had known Audrey's impulsive nature—Gabe reminded me of her—and I should have known better. It was *my* moment of weakness, but Audrey had been paying for it for six months. Because there was no way she would have gone so long without communicating with Wren and Juniper. Not by choice.

<When I woke up in the morning she was gone, and when I got to the haven, she'd left a note saying she was going to seek work at the Keep. She'd never even mentioned such a thing before. And no one has heard from her since.>

Gabe gazed in the direction of the Keep. I could guess what he must be thinking, so I wrote again, having to flip the page over as I had filled it already.

<I know she's alive. My swans have seen her.>

Gabe looked at the words and then at me, brows raised.

"So that's what you're doing here."

I worried at my lip, wondering how much to tell him.

"Addie." He took my left hand in both of his. "I can understand how you feel given the situation with Audrey. But I'm not her. I'm the crown prince of this kingdom. I guarantee that I'm not going to walk up to that gate, disappear inside, and never be heard from again. And just to be sure, I took the precaution of letting the innkeeper know where I was going. Leander won't harm me, and he won't imprison me. He wouldn't dare. We need to know what's going on in there, and this is our best chance."

66

<We need a proper plan.> The words looked dark on the page from the pressure of my pen.

"What sort of plan? As in, you're willing to see what your brother can do to get you out of this enchantment?"

I stiffened at the suggestion and shook my head vehemently. For a brief second, Gabe looked a little too satisfied with my answer. I suspected he was already invested enough in his adventure to not like the idea of sitting back and waiting for others to arrive.

"In that case, we could talk for a week, and we're not going to come up with a better plan than my walking up to the gate and demanding entry," he said. "And if I'm going to do it, I might as well do it now."

I frowned. I didn't like the plan, but I couldn't think of any arguments likely to sway him. After a reluctant moment, I sighed and put pen to paper again.

<If you're going in, then I'd better tell you everything I've learned about the Keep.>

"Everything you've learned?" Gabe sounded surprised. "Just what have you been doing here? How often do you come?"

I kept my words as brief as possible, but he still had to retrieve another piece of paper before I had finished explaining my daily mission with my birds and what we had discovered—from the number of servants and guards, to their daily movements, and the rough layout of important rooms and buildings. It was an incomplete picture, but hopefully better than nothing.

When I finished, Gabe looked impressed.

"I would never have dreamed swans could be so useful," he said.

<I doubt they could in the normal course of things.>

He nodded, but his attention was already on the distant Keep. He glanced back my way and threw me a smile.

"Don't worry about me. I'll be fine. And don't wait here—you should go to the haven, and I'll come straight there once I'm finished. But don't worry if that's not anytime soon. This Lord Leander will no doubt feel obliged to host a meal and offer me a bed for the night."

I didn't like the sound of that, but I reluctantly nodded. There was nothing else for me to do, especially since there seemed no point in telling him that my concerns were less for him and more for Audrey. Who knew how Leander would respond if he realized Gabe had some interest in her?

Gabe smiled again, oblivious to my thoughts, and strode back onto the road, moving quickly toward the Keep. He had almost disappeared from sight when I remembered one small thing I could do.

"Eagle?" I bugled the name, and the black feathers swung back into sight. Tipping my head, I called up to her. *"Will you stay here? Keep an eye on him? And come and fetch me if you see him get into trouble?"*

She bugled back to me, sounding pleased enough with the request. She must have decided she liked him then, after all. I watched her turn and flap in the direction he had disappeared, remaining in place until she also left my sight.

Then, with a sigh, I began the trudge back to Brylee.

CHAPTER 8

Quiet greeted me at the haven's entry, so I headed straight back toward the kitchen. Sure enough, I found Cora there, enjoying a moment of quiet before the lunch preparations began. For the second day in a row, Wren was here as well, although this time there was no sign of her daughter.

"Do you really think he'll—" Wren's quiet voice broke off as I walked in, resuming when she saw it was me. "Oh, it's just you, Lady. We've received word that the prince has gone to the Keep today, and I was just asking Cora if she thinks he really will keep an eye out for Audrey."

I kept my hands still, ignoring the instinct to reassure her. As far as Cora and Wren knew, I had no more knowledge of Prince Gabriel than they did.

"I wouldn't go raising your hopes," Cora said, caution in her voice.

My eyes strayed over to the table where a number of bread loaves and rolls were piled haphazardly. So the baker had been here, despite it not being the end of the day. He must have someone else watching his shop. No doubt he had been the source of the news regarding Gabe's movements—perhaps the gossip had been his excuse for the early visit.

I looked pointedly between the bread and Wren, raising an eyebrow.

"Yes," said Cora in a wry tone, "Ash is here. He wanted to be sure we had heard the news of His Highness, and thought he would bring some fresh bread while he was at it. Claims he feels bad about only giving us the leftovers at the end of the day." She paused, her mouth edging up on one side. "I can't imagine why."

Wren studiously ignored us both.

"It's very considerate of him to think of the haven's residents," she said. "He even brought a small cake for Junie. In fact, he's off fetching her from Selena now."

I snorted. Yes, very considerate of him.

Juniper burst through the doors, cutting off further conversation. Ash and Selena followed more sedately behind. The tall, muscled baker looked out of place beside the young girl and slim youth, but he carried himself easily and with a comfortable smile.

"Mama! Mama!" Juniper cried, throwing her arms around her mother's legs before spotting me and giving me the same treatment.

She looked up at me with shining eyes. "Ash brought me a cake, Lady!"

"Ash said it was fine for her to leave the lesson, but I thought it was best if I come and check with you directly," Selena said to Wren. Her responsible tone was somewhat belied by the way her eyes kept sliding toward where Juniper's cake rested on the table.

"Thank you, Selena," Wren said, hiding a grin. "Junie, perhaps you could share the cake with her."

Juniper pulled free of me and rushed over to the table, climbing onto a chair and eagerly beginning the process of dividing the cake. Selena dropped all pretense and hurried over to join her, the two of them discussing a fair division without further reference to the adults in the room.

"I had thought Juniper might share some with her Mama," Ash said, looking slightly crestfallen.

Wren smiled. "Selena will enjoy it more than I could. One of the delights of youth. It was very kind of you to think of Junie."

He brightened at her gratitude and moved over to talk to her quietly. I watched her face as they spoke. Her smile and laugh seemed genuine, and the two of them always got on so well, but she made none of the little encouraging looks and movements I had seen other young ladies in Brylee use when they wished to show a courting man that they returned his interest. And I knew she always denied that Ash even was courting her—although it was obvious to everyone else.

Did she think she had nothing to offer a man with a prosperous business and respected position in the town? Or was it grief still for the woodsman husband she had married young—the one who had died in a tragic accident while Juniper was a small baby?

I could still remember how shattered she had been by her grief when they first arrived—holding herself together purely for the sake of her child and younger sister. Without her husband and the income he brought in from chopping wood, the three of them had been left with nowhere to turn but the haven.

She had come a long way since then, however. And while she never forgot, she had regained some of the joy for life that Audrey said she used to have. Juniper always gave her a reason to smile, despite her grief, and lately Ash seemed to be giving her another reason to smile despite her protestations. I hadn't worked out yet whether she was being deliberately obtuse to his interest, or if she was truly blind to it.

Juniper interrupted them, running over, her face covered in patches of icing sugar.

"Thank you, Ash! It was *delicious*. Will you bring me another one someday?"

The adults all chuckled. He reached down and put his hands

under her arms, hoisting her up and setting her legs swinging around in crazy patterns. She squealed with delight, laughing and calling for more. When he finally put her down, he was smiling almost as hard as she was.

"Ash can't be bringing you cakes every day," Wren said, although she had the same smile on her face.

"Awww. Why not?" asked Junie, scrunching up her face.

"I don't mind," Ash said quickly. "I just wish all my customers were as enthusiastically grateful." But his eyes were on Wren, not Juniper, and they looked wistful.

"You're far too kind, and your actual paying customers might be wanting your delicious cakes," Wren said lightly.

My heart stung a little in sympathy at Ash's crestfallen look, but Wren didn't seem to notice, ushering Juniper back out of the room under Selena's supervision. Ash watched them for a moment before his eyes fell on me.

He gave me an easy smile until his brow crinkled slightly, the expression changing into one of concern. He took several steps in my direction.

"I'm glad you're here, Lady," he said. "I've been worried about you."

I stared at him in surprise. Most townsfolk had taken little note of me when I was a quiet thirteen-year-old sheltering at the haven. I had come and gone among them, running errands for Cora, without occasioning any particular notice. People were friendly enough, assigning me to the background tapestry of town life—as they did anyone who found their way into Cora's care. Not even the most frightened of residents could look at me as I was then and see a threat.

But then everything had changed. I had disappeared into the forest and come out different. I no longer spoke, no longer attempted to barter at the market or exchanged the friendly greetings they had barely noticed before. Soon enough, I stopped frequenting the market at all. And, worse than any of that, I spent my nights alone in the forest. Not even Cora would think of doing such a risky thing, and my continued reckless behavior only cemented the idea that something was terribly wrong with me.

Now they shunned me, whispering among themselves if they saw me pass and hurrying their children away. It had long since ceased to bother me. Those at the haven had taken my changes in their stride, their initial shock and questions giving way to acceptance when they realized that I truly did not intend to give any answers.

Ash was different, though. He continued to be friendly, even if I often read confusion in his eyes. At first I had thought it was purely because of my close association with Wren, but moments like this reminded me that his concern was genuine, and for my own sake. The knowledge warmed me and unsettled me in almost equal degrees, although I didn't understand why.

I tried to smile reassuringly at him, but his expression only deepened.

"I don't like to pry," he said, and I flinched. Ash had never asked me intrusive questions, but everything in me tightened now—I should have been prepared for their inevitable arrival.

"I'm sure you have your reasons," he continued. "I just wish you would consider staying at the haven tonight. And for a while. I worry about you out there on your own."

I frowned. That hadn't been quite what I expected.

I signed toward Cora, and she stepped closer. She had already been listening, her own face beginning to mirror his concern.

"She says that she cannot," Cora said, interpreting for me. "But she thanks you and says you needn't worry about her."

Ash gave a wry smile. "If only it were so easy to turn off such feelings." His eyes glanced briefly toward Wren, who was now talking to the newly arrived cook, but he turned back to me. Apparently we weren't finished with the conversation.

"As I said, I know it is none of my business, but I've been

hearing some disturbing rumors, and it keeps me up at night sometimes to think of you out there in the dark."

I smiled and shrugged. I wasn't alone, of course—I had my swans with me—but I wasn't going to attempt to explain that to him. He seemed disconcerted by my calm response, but I knew Brylee too well to take any real fear from his words. The towns-folk seemed to feed on frightening rumors these days, although I couldn't remember the last truly frightening thing to happen in the area.

Excluding Leander, of course. He was frightening enough to fill all my nightmares, but he was cloistered away in his Keep, and unlike me, the townsfolk knew no real reason to fear him. They resented that he no longer did business with Brylee, sourcing his supplies elsewhere, but the now-absent servants didn't cause them great alarm. Those who served the local lord had never come from among the townsfolk—most of them had been born and raised at the Keep, taking over the roles of their parents before them.

Cora, however, took his words more seriously. She frowned and stepped even closer, dropping her voice low.

"What sort of rumors?"

"Not the good kind." Ash threw me a look that suggested he was concerned about being more explicit.

I rolled my eyes and gave him a pointed look, and reluctantly he continued.

"There are fewer woodsmen than there used to be." Once again, his eyes flicked sideways to Wren, but he didn't stop. "Fewer men are willing to brave a solitary life in the forest. But those that remain have been telling strange stories in the tavern. Stories about animals behaving in odd ways. Ways that aren't...natural."

Cora pulled back slightly, her eyes going wide, while I tried to keep myself as still as stone, my face unmoving. An icy chill trickled down my spine.

Animals behaving in odd, unnatural ways? I knew some animals like that...and I could only imagine what the terrified townsfolk would make of them. Would they be frightened enough to finally be goaded into action? What if they sent a hunting party out into the forest?

It took all my self-control not to run to the lake to reassure myself my friends were unharmed. But I suppressed the foolish impulse. I needed more information.

Before I could sign my questions at Cora, she jumped in, asking them for me.

"Animals acting unnaturally? How so? What sort of animals?" She looked at me, and I could see Ash's worry had taken root in her. "Dangerous ones?" I hated the thought that she would fret now when I left each evening.

I held my breath as I waited for Ash to answer. He seemed reluctant still about going into detail.

"I'm afraid so. I hear talk of wolves and bears and large packs of hounds that no one has claimed."

Cora looked confused. "I thought we could all stop worrying about such animals coming across the border now that Palinar has been healed?"

I bit the inside of my cheek, still struggling to keep my expression calm, but no one looked at me this time. They had no reason to do so. The curse had already begun when I arrived in Brylee, and I had never wanted to draw attention to myself by owning up to being Palinaran.

"That's the thing," Ash said, finally warming to the topic. "They're not coming from the border region. Most of the reports have been on the eastern side of the town."

Cora and I shared a look. The border lay to the west of Brylee and the capital to the south. North was only uninhabitable mountains, and to the east lay two things: more forest and Leander's Keep. Cora never complained, but I knew her dislike for Leander ran deep.

Unlike his father, he did nothing to care for his people, and the absence of the old lord's gifts made the haven's existence a struggle. Even worse, Leander had taken the Keep's business away from Brylee, meaning that the whole town suffered, and fewer of the locals had excess supplies to send to the haven, either. Cora worked hard every day and never expected anything for herself, but she relied on the help of the community to keep the haven open. Without donated supplies, we wouldn't be able to keep accepting those in need, and I knew the thought kept Cora awake at night. When Audrey disappeared to his castle, it had only deepened her existing dislike of the current lord.

But I knew something Cora did not. Every morning, seven swans behaved very strangely indeed in the woods to the east of the town. And it wouldn't be the first time a story had been exaggerated as it spread—made more terrifying than had any basis in reality.

"Dr Jenkins's housekeeper came into the bakery this morning," Ash continued. "Yesterday the good doctor had to patch up one of those woodsmen. He came into town with several nasty wounds—says he barely got away with his life and is swearing up and down that he won't return to the woods for anything."

The first stirring of genuine fear for my own safety uncurled in my stomach. I shivered. Both Ash and Cora turned to look at me, and I managed to summon a smile for them. I didn't suspect the housekeeper of making up the story, but it was possible she had exaggerated it. Possible also that the woodsman had been injured in some normal way—none knew better than us that felling trees wasn't the safest way to earn a livelihood. Perhaps the two stories had become merged at some point.

Still, I couldn't entirely shake the feeling of unease. How much help could a wedge of swans be against a pack of wolves or a bear? My enchanted lake might keep me safe at night, but I still had to walk there and back each day.

But no matter how much I disliked it, my only other option

was to remain at the lake and never come to the town at all, and that was out of the question. So there was nothing to be done except to thank Ash again for his concern, try to avoid Cora and her newfound anxiety, and do my best to keep my thoughts away from the sort of wounds a wolf might inflict on a woodsman.

All of which was quite enough to keep my mind busy without the added layer of tense alert as I waited for Gabe. Every sound made me twitch and look to the door. It was going to be a long day.

CHAPTER 9

I fled the kitchen before lunch had even begun—offering to take the trolley full of food trays to the wing that housed the more elderly residents. I had too much stress of my own today to cope with Cora's gaze lingering on me wherever I went, the slight crease between her eyes telling me that she was trying to decide if it was worth raising the issue of the forest with me.

She hadn't tried to talk me into spending my nights at the haven for at least eighteen months, and it would be the worst of timing for her to start again now.

The large sitting room shared by the older haven residents had none of the buzz of the kitchen or the chaos of the opposite wing which held the schoolroom and the children. Some of the calm sank into me, taking the edge off my tension. As I handed out the meals, I smiled and greeted each person. Most of them were women, and most of them had knitting or crochet to lay down at my approach. They kept themselves busy supplying clothing and blankets for the children.

One lady, however, had no such gainful occupation in her hands. Instead she rested them on her hips as she stood over the largest and plushest armchair in the room. Her eyes were narrowed as she stared down at the chair's occupant.

"Don't you give me any of that nonsense, Gregor," Vilma said. "No one has taken your favorite cushion." She grinned triumphantly. "I saw you with my own eyes. You hid it behind that potted plant. Wanted something to complain about, no doubt. I daresay you're planning to get Lady in here to fuss over you."

"I don't know what you're talking about," said Gregor, but his guilty eyes slid over to the plant in question where a corner of blue plush could indeed be seen.

"Ha! I know your tricks." Vilma laughed suddenly. "And a good thing, too, because no doubt you'd forget you ever put it there and then it would be missing for a week."

Gregor stared at her for a moment before letting out a rough bark of laughter.

"Ah, right you are, lass," he said. "No doubt I would. Which is why I need you around to keep me straight."

I left their food on the trolley and slipped over to retrieve the cushion in question. When I approached them, holding it out, both of their faces lit up.

"Ah, Lady!" Gregor leaned forward, inviting me to place the cushion behind his back.

When I did so, Vilma shook her head.

"You spoil him, Lady dear." Her tone was affectionate rather than accusing, and I smiled back at her.

When I turned to get their trays, she took over from me, adjusting Gregor's cushion with hands that were still gentle despite their age. Only when she was satisfied that he was comfortable did she take the seat beside him and accept her lunch from me.

Gregor hunched forward over his bowl, but she sat straight-backed, bringing her fork carefully from plate to mouth. One thing I had discovered about being silent was that people tended

79

to confide things in me—filling my silence with words of their own. And Vilma had admitted to me once how proud she was of her straight back. Not for vain reasons, though, or even physical comfort. No, instead she considered it a daily reminder of her husband's love and care, and a sign to the world of how well he had provided for her.

"He worked hard every day of his life so that I wouldn't have to be bent before my time—broken by too many days and nights hunched over unending labor or carrying heavy loads. He provided for his parents and mine, as well, you know—along with our two children. No one could ask for a better husband— you should find yourself one just like my Gregor, Lady."

I always smiled and nodded, although I suspected Gregor's breed were few and far between these days. Their own son had married a merchant's daughter from another town and left without a backward glance. Their daughter seemed to have married a nice enough fellow based on Vilma's comments about him, but they had married for love, not wealth, and couldn't afford to take in her parents. I knew it grieved her, and she visited them as often as she could, bringing any excess she had to contribute to the haven's supplies.

When all the food had been distributed, Vilma patted a seat beside her, inviting me over, and I went willingly enough.

"You seem sad today, Lady. Is it a young man?"

I grimaced. It was, of course, but not in the way she meant. She patted my knee.

"Not having a voice might present something of a problem, but he'd be a fool not to see your value," she assured me.

I couldn't help smiling back despite her mistaken assumption.

"And I know it's not easy," she continued. "Trust never really is. But it's harder to come by in a place like this. Still necessary, though, you know."

I frowned at her this time, my eyes asking the question my lips could not.

"I see it every day, you know," she said. "Fear is more natural for most of us who have found our way here, but love can't thrive in a garden of fear."

I blinked at her, no longer sure what we were talking about.

"My water!" Gregor called abruptly, interrupting our rather confusing tête-à-tête. "Does anyone know where I set my water down?"

Vilma turned to him. "Did you ever have it to begin with?"

He frowned, thinking, and then let out a guffaw, striking his knee.

"Why, I don't think I did. What a duffer I've become. It's a wonder you ladies put up with me."

I hurried over to a cabinet against one of the walls and removed a large clay jug. Several mugs sat beside it, and I took two, filling them both with clear, cool water. Treading carefully, I returned to the elderly couple and gave them each one. They drank with murmurs of enjoyment, remarking to each other on the superior and refreshing qualities of the water.

Vilma and Gregor had been forced to give up everything, leaving their life behind to move here when age and infirmity overtook them. But Gregor had insisted that the one thing he could not give up was the water of their home. His daughter, filled with contrition at not being able to take them in herself, had been more than happy to oblige, and every week she refilled the jug at least twice from the small, ancient well that sat just inside the forest behind their old house.

The new inhabitants didn't use it, and I could hardly blame them. I had accepted a taste from Vilma once, and the water had a slightly unpleasant, musty flavor compared with the water drawn from the local river. But apparently after more than five decades in the home the two of them had become accustomed to it. It had often made me wonder what the water of my lake would taste like to someone else.

Gregor began to tell me the story of his discovery of the well.

I had heard the tale at least five times, but I nodded and smiled and clapped as needed because I knew he loved to tell it. And I didn't mind hearing it again. It was all wrapped up in the story of how he had built the house so he could propose and have somewhere to bring home his young bride.

As I listened, it hit me suddenly that they didn't cling to the water because it reminded them of their old home and independence. They refused to let it go because for them it was the taste of love. Moisture filled my eyes. If I could summon up the warmth and love of my mother every time I took a sip of water, wouldn't I hold onto that, too?

Gregor had just finished the sweet finale of the tale when a slight movement caught my eye. I looked toward the open door that led out to the hall. A newcomer had arrived and was watching us from across the room, his eyes fixed on me in particular.

I jumped to my feet, shocked enough to emit a loud squeak. A rustle ran through the residents as they looked from me to the prince. I rushed over to him, waving a quick farewell and giving no chance for any of them to start asking questions.

He was back already! I couldn't quite grasp it. I had been preparing myself to wait days to hear anything further and here he was already.

I bustled him out of the room, shutting the door firmly on the interested spectators before giving him a piercing glare.

"It's lovely to see you, too," he said, a laugh in his voice.

"Well? What happened?" The words burst out of me, bugling senselessly down the hall. I clapped both hands over my mouth and glared at him again. He had caused me to forget and speak more words since his arrival than in the previous year.

His smile did not abate, an infuriating dimple appearing as it deepened. Whipping out a fresh piece of paper and a pen, he held them out to me.

With a sigh, I scribbled the words out. He leaned over to read them before clapping a hand to his heart.

"What, no words of concern for my welfare or relief at my safe escape? I'm wounded."

I narrowed both eyes at him. I'd wound him indeed if he didn't get on with the story.

"Come on," he said instead. "I've got something to show you."

He grabbed my hand and began to tug me down the corridor. His grip was strong and sure, his hand rough and callused in a way I hadn't expected—although I shouldn't have been surprised. Gabe might be an expert archer, but he was too impetuous to remember gloves half the time. Dominic and I had once heard Gabe's instructor chiding him on it—I could still see my brother's smirk.

How long had it been since someone held my hand like this? I couldn't remember. I pulled it free, ignoring the way the warmth of his fingers seemed to linger.

All thoughts of hands, archery, and even our childhood, disappeared as I stepped through the door into the kitchen.

"LADY!" Audrey's scream filled the silence where my own cry wanted to be.

I had barely absorbed that she was real and here before she bounded over and enclosed me in an embrace. I squeezed her back, tears springing to my eyes.

"Auntie Audrey!" Juniper tugged at her skirt, and my friend let me go abruptly, reaching down to swing her niece up high.

"You're so big!" she said. "When did that happen?"

Juniper frowned at her. "You went away and left me."

"Oh, precious, I'm sorry. I had to go."

I winced, my eyes searching out Wren. I knew what Audrey meant, but her sister didn't.

Ash must have departed sometime before Gabe and Audrey's arrival, but Cora and Wren were both here. Wren's eyes didn't leave her sister, following her mercurial passage around the room as if she didn't dare lose sight of her. Cora looked pleased but also thoughtful, her eyes flitting between each of the occupants of the room.

"It smells delicious in here," Gabe said in a meek, plaintive voice that didn't deceive me for a second.

Cora immediately offered him leftovers of the lunch, however, and Wren came forward to scoop up Juniper as Audrey laughed and declared her intention to serve both herself and the prince.

"I drove him at a shocking pace," she said as she gathered two plates and cups. "I couldn't wait to get home here to see you all."

"An absolute slave driver," Gabe assured us all with a solemn expression. "Not even a morsel of food was to be permitted."

Audrey giggled as she served their meal and put her favorite herbal tea in a mug to steep. Wren wrinkled her nose at the smell of it—just as she always did—and it felt almost as if Audrey had never left and the last six months had never happened.

Audrey ordered Gabe to take a seat and pushed a plate toward him from the other side of the table.

"Audrey," Wren hissed at her sister. "He's the prince!"

"And thank goodness for that," Audrey said, not bothering to keep her voice lowered as her sister's had been. "I wish I could do as I liked and go where I pleased."

Wren's wry voice said, "You mean that's not how you live your life?" at the same moment as Gabe said, "It's not quite like that," the laugh back in his voice.

I rolled my eyes at all of them, and leaned over Gabe, waving the piece of paper still clutched in my hand in front of his face. I didn't bother holding it still so he could read the words—he already knew what it said. Audrey, however, leaned across the table and snatched it from me, absorbing the request for information. For a brief second our eyes met across the table, and I saw the first hint of seriousness beneath her bubbly, joy-filled energy. We had more to talk about than could be said in this room. And whether I liked it or not, Gabe was now a part of that conversation.

"It was a very short visit," Cora said. "Don't tell me our local lord turned away the crown prince?"

"Of course he did," said Audrey, wrinkling up her nose in apparent distaste for Leander. "I don't think he's had a proper visitor there in his life."

"Don't tell me he has improper visitors," Cora muttered.

Wren gave her a warning look, her eyes flicking to Juniper who was racing around the room, too excited to contain herself.

"You know what I mean—noble people, paying social visits," Audrey said in a voice of exaggerated long-suffering. "Not people like you and me."

I frowned. What commoner visitors had Leander been having at the Keep? None that I knew of. Or did Audrey just mean the servants who all lived there?

Gabe had begun eating, although his eyes kept track of the conversation. He struck me as half-amused and half-bemused by Audrey's exuberance.

She came around the table, approaching Gabe from the other side and sliding onto the bench awfully close to him.

"Go on, Gabe," she said. "Put Lady out of her misery and tell her what happened."

She tore the hunk of bread she held in two, offering the slightly larger half to him. He took it with a warm smile—not seeming in the least offended by her casual treatment of him.

It was a point in his favor, so I wasn't sure why it made my stomach clench uncomfortably. If anything, I should be feeling relief. My friend had returned—seemingly unharmed and in good spirits—and the prince was accepting her as if the two of them had the same long-standing friendship as both had with me. Not that I counted Gabe as a true friend—more like a child-hood acquaintance.

As if he could read my uncomplimentary thoughts, the prince

85

glanced my way. I met his eyes, gesturing toward the piece of paper that Audrey had discarded.

He flashed me his signature grin and finally began talking.

"When I announced my arrival and identity at the Keep's gates, I was naturally invited inside," he said. "Unfortunately, a number of the staff are laid low with a contagious illness, and Lord Leander couldn't countenance any risk to my person." Gabe stopped short of actually rolling his eyes, but I could hear it in his voice.

I glanced at Audrey, but she had her head down and was shoveling food into her mouth. Clearly she knew better than to contradict the official message in our present company.

"He sent me away with many apologies and promised that as soon as it was safe to do so, he would hold a party in my honor to welcome me to the region."

"A party?" Astonishment laced Wren's voice. "Who does he intend to invite? We're a little isolated out here."

"All of Brylee, I believe were his words," Gabe said.

"All of Brylee?" This time it was Cora echoing him in surprise. "That would be a first."

"Well, it's also the first time a member of the royal family has visited the town," Audrey said, finally chiming in.

I stared at her. Did she honestly find that a compelling reason for such odd behavior, or was she merely trying to keep Wren and Cora from asking too many questions?

"Who's having a party?" Juniper piped up. "Am I invited?"

"Definitely not," said Wren firmly. "Parties at castles aren't for four-year-olds. You'll stay here if such an occasion ever eventuates."

"With me," Cora said, smiling at the girl. "I'm sure it will be a very boring party with a great deal of talking, and I'd much rather be here with you."

That seemed to satisfy Junie, and she began attempting to worm her way onto Audrey's lap.

I had reluctantly seated myself on Gabe's other side, and I now poked his shoulder. When he looked my way, I gestured questioningly toward Audrey.

"Ah yes," he said. "Since the good proprietress here," he paused to give a half-bow to Cora, "mentioned how much her sister was missing Audrey, I thought I would request that she accompany me back to the town so that she might spend time with her family. I don't think Lord Leander could deny such a simple request after being forced to turn me away from his gates. It is merely fortunate that she was untouched by the illness rampaging through the Keep."

I glared at him for his final quip. He should be taking his cue from Audrey and not inciting Wren and Cora into asking questions we didn't want to answer. But it was just like him not to take the situation seriously. Had he truly just asked Leander to turn Audrey over? Even mentioned her family specifically?

Fear churned in my stomach, and anger made me long to jump to my feet and put distance between us. We had discussed how dangerous Leander was, and yet not only had he brought Audrey to his attention, he had extended it to her family and the haven as well. While I didn't think Gabe would be purposely malicious, it had been heedless in the extreme. We weren't all of us princes. One day Gabe would leave, returning to the capital, and Audrey, Wren, Cora, and everyone at the haven would remain, exposed to Leander's ill will.

I thought I had escaped that sort of careless thinking—kings and princes who believed their kingdoms existed only to be bent to their own whims—but apparently it had chased me down even here. Or one of those princes had, anyway. I could only hope not too many people would pay the price when he was gone.

PART II
THE KEEP

CHAPTER 10

$\mathcal{I}$ waited among the trees, far enough from the road to be out of sight, but not so far as to be hard to find. As the light began to fade, I fidgeted, throwing glances at the sky and the increasing shadows around me. How much longer should I wait? If they didn't appear soon, I would have to leave without them.

The crunch of leaves underfoot reached me, and I jumped, visions of bears and unnatural wolves filling my mind. If I was honest, I was twitchier than the increasing hour demanded.

But it was a human figure that stepped into sight, the prince soon followed by Audrey, only a few steps behind him.

"Sorry!" she called as soon as she saw me. "It was a little hard to get away."

I wasn't sure how she had managed it at all. I had expected her family to cling to her given her unexpected return.

"I told them I was exhausted and needed to go to sleep early," she explained without my having to ask. "They currently think I'm holed up in my bedroom. I had to climb out the window and everything."

It was one of the things I liked best about Audrey. Once she had accepted the fact that I wouldn't be providing any answers, she had adjusted quickly to my lack of speech and answered most of my questions without me needing to voice them.

She flashed a smile at Gabe. "Thankfully I had a handsome prince to catch me."

"Did you hear that, Adelaide?" Gabe asked. "Some people think I'm handsome and appreciate having me around."

I grunted and took off walking. I didn't have time for their silly flirtations—and I doubted either of them wanted a visit from Leander tonight any more than I did.

Sure enough, they quickly fell into step behind me. I increased my speed, and they both kept pace. I didn't want to cut it fine if I didn't have to.

We broke through the trees around the lake well before the final light leached from the sky. A chorus of honks and bugles greeted us, my birds all swarming toward me. Even Eagle came over—albeit more slowly than the others. The way they clustered around gave me the impression that each one wanted to reassure herself that I was fine. I greeted them all by name, murmuring reassurances, surprised by how much their presence and affection warmed and calmed me. After the upheaval of the last twenty-four hours, the stability of their presence was unexpectedly comforting.

"I saw them this morning, didn't I?" Audrey said, watching us from several steps away. "At the Keep." She sounded subdued, none of her earlier high spirits in evidence now.

I flashed her a concerned look, but she quickly shook her head.

"I didn't mention it to anyone, and I don't think anyone else noticed them. I'm sure no one else would have thought anything of it if they did."

Without thinking I turned to share a concerned glance with Gabe. We both knew that at least one other person at the Keep had a particular reason to take note of any swans.

"I'm sure he hasn't seen them," he murmured, but he didn't sound entirely convinced.

Now that I stood here at the lake with nightfall so close, my enforced silence irked me even more than usual. Sighing, I walked away from the others, talking softly to the swans as I crossed over to my shelter. The two of them let me go, turning toward each other and beginning their own conversation. From the way they kept glancing around them, I suspected they were discussing my strange prison sanctuary.

I took several long breaths, facing the water and attempting to block everything else out. I struggled to absorb anything of the tranquility of the setting, however. A weight pressed on my shoulders. After six months with almost no progress, I had Audrey back—I should have been feeling elated. Instead I had the dizzying sensation that everything was spiraling rapidly out of control. I had been the one to stumble into Leander's trap, and my one hope had been to avoid ensnaring the others at the haven —but now they had all come forcibly to his attention. And the prospect of a party at the Keep—if he did indeed mean to keep his word—only filled me with more dread. I couldn't fathom his plan, but that it must be nefarious I was sure.

Nothing in my strange history had prepared me for this, and it was all too tempting to turn and throw the burden onto someone else's more capable shoulders.

So many times I had nearly poured it all out to Cora. But she had taken me in, and loved me, I believed, when I had no one else. She owed me nothing now and had many more than just me looking to her for support.

No doubt Gabe would have happily received the burden. But I shuddered to think of the mess he would make of it. No, I knew better than to trust him with such an important task. Despair swirled in my belly.

As my thoughts consumed me, the last of the light faded. I felt the change in me, like a slight release of pressure that I never noticed until it disappeared each night. Turning with a soft sigh of relief, I spoke.

"So, tell me what really happened."

Audrey and Gabe both looked up at the sound of my voice, hurrying toward me as my swans scattered for the lake. They looked comfortable together, smiles lingering on their faces. Did they not feel the same burden I did?

"It truly did happen as I described," Gabe said. "I arrived, the guards at the gate fetched Leander, and he would allow me no further than a few steps into the courtyard." His tone turned darkly satirical. "For my own protection, of course."

"And what about you?" I turned to my friend. "What happened, Audrey?"

She didn't smile or laugh or turn my question aside, and I got a glimpse of something in her eyes that looked even more suffocating than my own dragging weight. But then she turned to Gabe with her usual smile, and I could only assume it had been a trick of the light. She seemed so much her normal self despite her six-month absence.

"Prince Charming here rescued me, of course."

Gabe snorted. "It was all very heroic. I inquired after her—on her family's behalf, of course." I winced at his words, but he didn't notice, his attention on Audrey. "Given I'm the crown prince, Leander could hardly refuse my request to have her accompany me back, so he fetched her and just about pushed us both out the gate."

"And glad I was to leave that dreary place," Audrey assured us both.

"So you *were* a prisoner," I said.

She nodded slowly. "Not in the dungeon and chains sense, of course. But it turns out Lord Leander doesn't allow his servants to take leave, and he has commanded that rest days are to be spent inside the Keep's walls. For our own protection, of course." She threw a wry glance at Gabe as she mirrored his words. "The guards are commanded to open the gates to no one. Short of throwing myself from the top of the walls, there was no obvious way out."

"We were worried about you," I said slowly. "How did Wren and Cora take the news that you were trapped in there?"

"Oh, I didn't tell them that," she said. "I did patch things up with Wren, though." Her face dropped, her voice turning sad. "I never meant for her to think I had run from her. I just told them that I did it to try to earn my keep for once. Lord Leander does pay his servants—although only the visiting merchants give anyone an opportunity to spend it." She wrinkled her nose.

"Visiting merchants?" I asked, astonished. So those were Leander's common visitors.

"None that I recognized," she said. "They must come purely for the Keep because I'm sure they don't visit the town. And very odd sort of merchants they were, too. From the look of them, you'd be more likely to conclude they were soldiers."

I frowned. Perhaps they were the only sort of merchants still willing to venture through the forests? But I had too many questions to linger longer on that one.

"And they believed you?" I asked. "Cora and Wren, I mean."

She shrugged. "I just explained that Lord Leander gives the opportunity for his servants to earn more coin by working through rest days. I'd left the note, so I knew they had no reason to worry over me."

I stared at her. Could they really have bought such a story? I worried at my lip. Audrey loved her family, but she had always been a little heedless and rather foolhardy. So perhaps they had found it believable.

"What were you thinking?" I asked, the words bursting out of me. "Why did you go there?"

"I had to, Lady," she said, full of earnestness now. "I couldn't abandon you to such a fate. I'd heard that young Tom went to the Keep looking for work a year ago, and they didn't turn him away.

I thought if I infiltrated his servants, I could get information on how to free you."

"And did you?" Gabe asked, eyes alight with curiosity and interest.

I frowned at both of them. "It was a dangerous thing to do! Tom may have found work there, but did he ever come back out again? You should have thought it through more carefully. If Gabe hadn't arrived, you would have still been stuck there."

"But he did come along," she reminded me, and my jaw clenched at such a hare-brained—but somehow unassailable—argument.

"Is she always like this?" Gabe asked Audrey with a grin.

"Oh, sometimes even worse," she assured him with mock gravity.

"Do neither of you intend to take this seriously?" I asked.

All humor instantly dropped from Gabe's face. "I can assure you I take it utterly seriously. No nobleman is permitted to keep his servants trapped in his castle in such a way. And I do not doubt for a second that he has brazenly lied to my face about this illness. I have every intention of getting to the bottom of what is going on in that Keep and then removing him from his position entirely." His voice became almost a growl. "At the very least."

This serious side to him took me by surprise, easing some of the frustration that had been filling my chest with pressure.

"Don't they threaten to rebel?" I asked Audrey. "How does he keep them in line?"

"Oh no, there's no threat of that," she said. "If you think the people of Brylee are bad, you should see this lot. Meek doesn't even begin to describe them. They were almost as determined to keep me safe inside with them as Lord Leander was not to have anyone leave. I couldn't even get them to do something so *adventurous* as to try my tea—I took a whole bag with me and had plenty to share. There's no way any of them would have wanted to step outside the walls. Especially not with all the wild tales of deadly animals roaming free." She rolled her eyes.

I shook my head. "You know they might have a point when it comes to that tea. You do know the stuff smells vile, don't you? It's not just Wren who thinks so."

"If you mean the stuff you were drinking at lunch, then I'm afraid it's true," Gabe said apologetically.

For half a second, I forgot I was angry and actually grinned at him. "In an act of true friendship, I actually tried it once. She's right that it doesn't taste nearly as bad as it smells. It was almost nice, in fact. But hard to enjoy with that stench in your nostrils."

Audrey just rolled her eyes. "Can we focus, please?"

"What I want to know, is what is this talk of dangerous animals?" Gabe asked. "I heard them talking about it at the haven, and I thought I heard someone saying something similar yesterday when I was lingering around town waiting for Adelaide to emerge."

"Yes," I said slowly. "I only heard about it today." I repeated the gossip Ash had delivered, while Audrey nodded along in agreement.

"They had the most outrageous stories inside the Keep, but I had been in the forest recently enough to know they weren't true. I've never encountered such an animal in my life."

I nodded. It was true that Audrey was one of the few towns-folk still willing to enter the forest—thus how she had followed me in the first place. Plus, I also had never seen any such thing.

"If the rumors are worse inside the Keep, it makes me wonder if Leander is the one spreading them," I said. "But why would he do such a thing?"

"Why, indeed," Gabe said. "And you can be sure once he has been exposed and arrested, I shall ask him. But in the meantime, we are in something of a difficult situation. As long as Leander insists he's protecting me by refusing me entry to his Keep, there's nothing I can do to force the issue. Not without a couple of squads of guards to back me up anyway."

I half expected him to make a case for going for help, but he said nothing about it. Whether he was respecting my wishes to keep my location and identity hidden, or whether he was driven by his own heedless desire to be the one to personally bring down Leander I didn't know and didn't ask.

"What would you do if you could get inside?" Audrey asked. "I've been in there for six months and was unable to find anything that seemed of any use in freeing Lady."

Gabe explained our theory about the godmother objects, and an intrigued look crossed her face. For a brief moment hope filled me that she might have seen one in her time in the Keep. But her next words dashed it.

"It never occurred to me to go poking around for strange objects. But even if they do exist, I'm not sure I could have reached them. Lord Leander spends an awful lot of time in his study, and no one else is allowed in there—not even the maids for dusting or to deliver food to him."

"Well, that would be the place to look then." Gabe sounded far too excited for my liking. "But the question is how to get in there."

Audrey leaned forward. "Do you really think if you could find and destroy this object that it would free Lady?"

"Actually, I'm hoping we might be able to free more than Adelaide." He looked my way, as if checking for permission to share the rest of our thinking with Audrey.

I nodded slightly. At this point, she was as wrapped up in all this as either of us.

"It's very interesting that you say Leander's servants are even more timid than the people of Brylee," Gabe said. "It would seem to confirm another theory of ours." He proceeded to outline our idea that something insidious had infected Talinos, and that it seemed to emanate from this region—and quite possibly from Leander and his mysterious Keep.

"I knew it!" she exclaimed. "I knew something awful was going on. Everyone acts so strangely. But do you really think you could break it—whatever it is? That you could completely defeat Lord Leander just by gaining entry to the Keep?"

"It's a place to start at least," Gabe said.

Audrey looked between us, a gleam in her eyes. "Then I think I might be able to help."

CHAPTER 11

*I*t turned out Audrey had spent a lot of time around the oldest of the servants—those who had been at the Keep the longest. She figured they were most likely to know its secrets, and, as it happened, she was right.

Some ancient owner of the Keep had built a hidden escape passage out into the forest. And while some of the oldest servants knew about it, they weren't sure if Leander had ever been told by his parents. His mother had died when he was young, and his father could be absent-minded at times.

When I asked why she hadn't used this passage to get out of the Keep herself, Audrey explained that while she knew the place it let out into the forest, she didn't know where it began inside.

"The problem was that I only heard the end of the conversation," Audrey said. "And they refused to answer any of my questions about it." She rolled her eyes. "They were all convinced I was a danger to myself and likely to do something *reckless*."

"I can't imagine where they got that idea," I muttered and then grinned apologetically when she threw me an accusing look.

"I spent so many hours searching for it," she said with a sigh. "I can tell you a great many places where the entrance *isn't*."

"Well, we'll know soon enough," said Gabe. "From this side, all we need is the exit—the tunnel itself will lead us to the entrance."

"You know I just escaped from the Keep, right?" Audrey said. "I can't say I'm excited to be sneaking back in there the next night."

"You're not going at night," I said quickly. "Because you're definitely not going without me."

Gabe grimaced, looking as if he wanted to argue, but refrained from actually doing so. I wasn't sure if he was frustrated at the limitation or just wanted to keep me away from potential danger. Either way, I didn't intend to budge on the matter.

"In the morning, then," Gabe said. "And you don't have to actually come in, Audrey. We just need you to show us the exit to the passage. It's probably better that way, anyway, since Leander won't be able to do Adelaide or me any great harm even if he does find us. He can instruct his guards to bar me entry under the guise of keeping me safe, but he won't dare actually harm me if he finds me already inside."

"Not that we want to be seen," I said quickly.

We might be safe, but our friends were not. And in truth, I didn't have the same faith that Leander wouldn't be willing to cross a line of no return. Knowing I was a princess hadn't stopped him from entrapping me.

I didn't mention any of that, though. Something had to be done about Leander—and for more than just my sake. Going into the Keep seemed to be our only option. I agreed that Audrey didn't need to come, though.

"But what about Lady?" Audrey asked. "She's not the crown prince."

"No, but she's close enough," Gabe said, before I could think of a reply of my own. "And he seems to want to keep her alive." He gestured around us at the lake and the clearing, not seeming to notice my wide eyes and tense expression. "I've been wondering if perhaps he's scared of her brother."

"Why would Lord Leander be scared of Lady's brother?" Audrey asked. "You know Lady's not from around here, right?"

Gabe finally picked up on the confusion coming from Audrey and the tension radiating from me. He looked quickly between us, his eyes settling on me.

"I thought you said you told her everything."

"I told her everything about my situation and the trap or curse or whatever this is." I glared at him. "Not everything about *everything*."

"Wait, what's going on?" Audrey's eyes darted back and forth. "What don't I know?"

Gabe looked more uncomfortable than I'd ever seen him, having just stepped into the middle of something he clearly didn't want to be involved in.

"I'm sure I mentioned that Adelaide sent me to get you," he said. "Didn't you wonder how I knew her?"

"Well…" Audrey bit her lip. "I guess I was just so relieved to be out of there and to see my family again. Plus, Lady is a damsel in distress and you're a prince, so I guess it just seemed like the kind of thing that would…"

She trailed off at my unimpressed look.

"Sorry, Lady." She gave me a cheeky grin before scooting over to sit closer and gazing at me coaxingly. "You know whatever it is, you can tell me, right? We've been friends for years now. I even went to the Keep for you!"

And how could I resist that? I sighed. "Gabe thinks Leander might be concerned about my brother because my brother is Prince Dominic of Palinar."

"King Dominic now, actually," Gabe cut in.

I winced at the reminder.

"King Dominic…" Audrey barely seemed able to squeeze the

words out, for once actually robbed of speech. "But that would make you…"

She stared at me.

"A princess, yes," I said with another sigh.

"You're a princess!?!"

I winced at Audrey's shout, so close to my ear.

"She is, indeed," Gabe said. "The missing Princess Adelaide, no less. We've known each other since we were small children." He frowned. "You know, come to think of it, I'm surprised none of you ever considered the possibility. She must have turned up just after the curse fell, and it's not like she changed her name."

"I was thirteen," I said. "I had other things on my mind than creating a false identity."

"I didn't mean it as a criticism," Gabe said with a smile. "It made my job easier in the end."

"I don't think many people in the village even know my name is Adelaide," I added. "Most of them just call me Lady. And I'm not sure if word of a missing princess ever reached the haven. Brylee is fairly insular—and the haven even more so."

"I'm sure I would have remembered news of a missing princess named Adelaide who disappeared at the same time as our Lady turned up," Audrey said, apparently having regained her voice.

She fixed me with a betrayed look. "You're a princess, and you never told me? How could you not tell me? I thought we were best friends!" An even more horrified look came over her face. "You didn't tell Wren and Cora and not me, did you?"

"Of course not." I said. "I haven't told anyone. And I still don't intend to tell anyone, so keep it to yourself, please."

"A princess. You're an actual princess…and I'm the only one who knows." Her voice sounded a little dreamy.

"Apparently I don't count," Gabe said under his breath to me.

"Of course you don't," I murmured back. "You don't live at the haven, and you're a man. A prince, in fact."

"The worst crime of all," he said gravely.

I rolled my eyes but couldn't help chuckling.

"Did you grow up in a palace?" Audrey asked, clutching at my arms. "And go to balls? I bet you did. And I bet your palace was bigger than that stuffy old Keep."

"A great deal bigger," Gabe said. "The Palinaran capital—and its palace in particular—is famed for its grandeur."

"And I much prefer the haven," I said, injecting some reality into the dream-filled fantasy that seemed to have overtaken Audrey. "Plus I was only thirteen when I left. Not exactly the age for balls."

"Why did you leave?" Audrey asked. "If I'd grown up in a palace, I would never have left."

Gabe said nothing, but I recognized the curious glint in his eye. He was as interested in the answer as Audrey. Apparently my brother had failed to tell him the full story of how he ended up cursed. What a surprise.

"I wasn't given a choice," I said shortly, "but I was more than happy to leave. And that's all I intend to say on the matter."

I stood up. "I think that's enough talking for tonight. You both need to get back to your beds before anyone starts asking questions, and I need to get some rest. In the morning, we'll meet back here and Audrey can show us this hidden tunnel."

I expected one of them to protest, at least, but neither did. I asked Shadow to guide them back through the darkness, and she took off into the air. I might not have my swan language, but she knew me too well to need specific words for such a simple request.

I watched them leave, their unintelligible murmurs drifting back to me. Loneliness tried to claw around my heart, but I made myself turn away toward my pallet.

~

They arrived together late the next morning without help from my swans. So one, at least, of them had memorized the path.

"Good morning, Your Highness," Audrey said, sweeping into a deep and extremely wobbly curtsy. "How were your slumbers?" She threw a playful look at Gabe. "Did I do that right?"

"Perfectly," he assured her.

I raised an eyebrow, and he quickly amended his words to, "With perfect enthusiasm, at any rate."

Audrey just laughed at the correction, coming over to give me a quick hug. Just as usual she began to chatter away, answering all of the questions I couldn't ask.

"I thought I would have such a time trying to get away at a decent hour this morning. Wren and Cora were watching me like hawks after I emerged from my room this morning. But it turns out having princes in on your plotting is a great advantage in more ways than one. When he turned up and asked if I could show him around the town, neither of them even protested once. You could have knocked me over with a feather."

She bent a comical eye on Eagle who had sidled up right beside us and was eyeing her suspiciously.

"Please don't, though," she said to the swan. "I'd much rather stay on my feet."

She leaned in close. "I'm sorry, Lady, but your pets rather terrify me."

Eagle honked and snaked out her neck, and Audrey only just jumped away in time.

"*Eagle!*" I pointed an arm toward the water, and she slunk away not looking in the least repentant.

"I don't think they like to be called pets," Gabe said, clearly trying to smother a laugh.

Audrey sighed. "I suppose they mean to come with us, too."

I bristled slightly, annoyed that I couldn't argue on their behalf, but to my surprise, Gabe stepped in to defend them.

"I actually think it would be a good idea, if they don't mind. It seems they make excellent scouts." He explained how I had set them to watching the Keep each morning, looking for a way to rescue her.

The news clearly softened Audrey and also gave me an idea.

"Snowy!" I called. *"Sweetie! Come over here and meet Audrey."*

The two sweetest of my swans responded instantly to my call, paddling over and approaching us. Audrey pulled back, but I pushed her forward, and the two of them pressed up against her, raising their heads on their long, elegant necks to get as close to hers as possible.

"Are these the two?" Gabe asked.

I nodded, and he turned to her.

"These two are the swans who had the role of looking for you every morning and reporting back to Adelaide if they saw you."

"Oh?" She reached out and ran a tentative hand down Snowy's neck. "That's very kind of you, ladies."

Sweetie reached up and nipped gently at one of the long strands of her copper hair. Gabe grinned.

"I'm guessing your hair made the job a bit easier for them."

Audrey grinned, her usual confidence returning as she adjusted to the close presence of the swans.

"I'm glad it came in useful for something since it's generally been a great trial for me."

"Thank you," I said to the swans, and they both bugled happily, coming over to nudge me in turn.

"We should be moving," Gabe said, his eyes focused on the trees in the distance.

He looked eager and alert, every inch the forester he had seemed when he first arrived at the haven, his bow and quiver on his back, and his tall leather boots and archer's gloves soft and worn. Hopefully the tunnel wasn't a tight squeeze because his bow seemed excessively long. I didn't think of asking him to leave it behind, though—even though I didn't think arrows would do him much good in the Keep. Gabe's bow was almost as much a part of him as his arm.

"I'm confident I can find the spot once we get near," Audrey said. "But you'll need to get us to the Keep first, Lady."

I nodded and took the lead. The swans, restless after the delay to our usual morning departure, began to take off from the lake. I called out, reminding them that we were on a different mission this morning, and one-by-one they dipped slightly in the sky, acknowledging they had heard me.

"They're elegant creatures," Gabe murmured softly, and I couldn't disagree.

And then we were off, moving as fast as the forest undergrowth would allow us.

CHAPTER 12

I didn't hesitate, familiar enough with the way not to need to, and at first no one tried to talk. Even Audrey fell into an uncharacteristic silence, yet another hint that she wasn't entirely unaffected by her six-month ordeal.

But Gabe began to ask questions, and since I wasn't able to answer them, she was soon chatting away.

"It's a great pity Lord Leander's father died because he was much nicer than Lord Leander. We didn't live in Brylee back when he was still in charge of the Keep, but all the servants there talked about him affectionately."

"What do they say of Leander?" Gabe asked.

She frowned, hesitating. "That he's very different from his father. They don't criticize him directly, but given how they praise his father, it's rather implied. He doesn't mistreat them, exactly, but they don't much like the merchants he brings in. Apparently he and his father always clashed—they were so different—but it got worse after he returned from studying in the capital eight or nine years ago."

"How so?" Gabe asked.

"I don't know, exactly," she said. "But I think he hates how remote we are out here. I guess his father hoped that letting him go off to study would help him settle down, and that he would come back ready to take on his responsibilities here."

I snorted.

"Yes, exactly," Audrey said to me. "Instead he just came back with an even stronger desire to get out of here. He wants to conduct experiments of some kind, but the servants didn't know any details about them since he spends all day locked away alone in his study. I guess he hopes they'll help him make a name for himself? Apparently he always used to complain that his father made no effort to improve the family fortunes and earn a higher rank and more important estates."

"It sounds like a good thing that the people of this region have Cora," Gabe said, his gaze distant and voice thoughtful.

"Oh yes, everyone around here knows to send those needing care and shelter here to Brylee," Audrey said, her voice proud.

"However did she come to start the haven?" Gabe asked.

"She doesn't talk about it much." Audrey sighed. "I think it was all very sad. She was orphaned when she was a year or two younger than I am now, and her remaining relatives sent her to live with her Aunt Florinda."

She wrinkled her nose. "She sounds like a perfectly horrid old lady. She owned the haven's building but tried to run it as an inn —not too successfully, since Brylee is hardly big enough to need two inns. Plus everyone says she was miserly and miserable, so who would want to stay with her?"

"Who indeed?" Gabe sounded slightly amused at Audrey's narration.

"Well, Wren told me that Cora made a vow that if anyone ever turned up at her door, she would give them a better welcome than her aunt gave her. Thankfully, her aunt died a long time ago, and the haven went to Cora. And she's stayed true to her promise ever since. It's all a bit beautiful and romantic, really."

I bit my lip. Except for the parts where the roof leaked, and I'd overheard Cora talking about watering down the soup. With Leander as lord, Cora might have to finally break that promise. Unless we could take him down first.

When flashes of the Keep began to appear ahead of us through the trees, Audrey stopped abruptly. Gabe and I also slowed to a halt, going back to join her. With narrowed eyes, she gazed ahead at the building, and then to either side.

"This way," she said, her voice low.

We followed, eventually stopping in the trees to one side of the Keep. I could just see the road to our left, and occasional glistens from the sunlight hitting the lake at the back of the Keep to our right.

"I could see the spot from the top of the walls," she told us. "I looked for it especially after I overheard about its location. I thought maybe I could trace it back, but of course that didn't work." She frowned at a tree in front of us, craning her head back to look up toward its crown. "I used to spend a lot of time on the walls when it all began to feel a little claustrophobic."

My heart seized in sympathy, but she kept murmuring, almost to herself. "It all looks a bit different from down here, but I think...Yes...That must be the one."

A number of large boulders, some taller than us, broke up the trees in this section, and she stepped toward one of them. Circling around it, she began to pull down the various creeping vines which trailed over it.

We both hurried to help her, sweeping them away rather than completely removing them where possible. We wanted to avoid advertising our presence here.

A small door appeared, made of stone a similar shade to the rock itself. With the vines trailing over it, we would never have noticed it without Audrey's prior knowledge. But having now uncovered it, we all stood there, staring at it with varying degrees of perplexity. It had no handle or latch—at least not on this side of the door.

Gabe set his shoulder against it and pushed, but it didn't move even slightly.

"I suspect it opens outward," he said. "Which means I'm not likely to get far pushing like this."

I wasn't sure how it had been built into the rock, but it must have required either a magical tool or incredible workmanship because we could find no weakness. Our attempts to wedge our fingers around the edges and pull met with utter failure, and attempts to lever it open with a sturdy branch were equally unsuccessful. Eventually, even Gabe had to admit defeat.

"I'm sorry," Audrey said. "It never occurred to me it couldn't be opened from the outside. I really thought you would be able to get in this way."

"Don't feel bad," Gabe said. "I should have thought of it too. It makes sense, since it was designed as an escape hole for the castle inhabitants, not as a means to allow uninvited guests in."

And yet, we all lingered, as if hoping a solution would somehow magically appear. Nothing did. Instead an eerie howling sounded. We all took an immediate step closer together, each peering out into a different section of the forest.

"What was that?" asked Audrey.

No one answered, but Gabe swung his bow around, nocking an arrow to the string much more quickly than I would have thought possible. All traces of his usual good-humor had disappeared, replaced by a serious gleam that suggested trouble for anyone who tried to cross him. I gulped and looked away, just in time for another howl to shatter the forest.

"That sounds like a wolf," Audrey whispered.

"Wolves don't usually hunt during the day." Gabe's voice sounded tight as he scanned the forest around us. "And neither the townsfolk nor Leander would allow a pack to establish their territory so close to the town or Keep."

I made a soft honking noise, and he glanced swiftly in my direction.

"But, yes," he admitted reluctantly, understanding my meaning, "it did sound like a wolf."

Audrey gulped audibly. A streak of gray flashed between two trees, and I jumped, pointing toward it.

"I saw it," said Gabe.

"And there!" Audrey pointed to another.

I didn't bother to look because I had already seen two more. It looked as if we were surrounded. Audrey whimpered, and I reached back, groping for her hand. When my fingers found hers, I squeezed, and she squeezed back.

A moment later, my eyes fell on the long, sturdy stick we had used to try prying open the door. Letting her go, I grabbed it, turning so I could pass it to her. She accepted it, eyes wide, and gripped it in both hands. Scanning the area, I tried to find another one for me, but the only possibility was located too far away for me to risk running for it.

I had no time to do anything but press my back against hers when a wolf appeared in full view, racing toward us, teeth bared. This time the flash of movement in the corner of my eye was Gabe, his arm swinging up and an arrow releasing before I had time to do more than register the danger.

With a loud thwack, the arrow found its mark, the wolf breaking off its attack with a high-pitched whine. The other wolves immediately appeared from the trees, forming into a tight cluster around the injured animal, all of them advancing on us, their growls filling the air.

Gabe stepped in front of us, his bow raised again, but something made him hesitate. I could just see the side of his face, his brow furrowed as he stared intently at the terrifying sight.

"Something isn't right here," he whispered.

That much was clear, but right now I was more concerned with the fact that we were about to be eaten by a pack of angry animals. Unfortunately I didn't have the words to say so.

Gabe must have come to the same conclusion on his own,

however. Without prompting, he drew the string back, preparing to fire. And this time, he wasn't aiming to wound.

But a loud wolf's bark sounded from somewhere in the trees, and he hesitated again. The growls immediately cut off, the wolves all stopping their advance. The bark sounded again, and they turned their noses toward the trees, racing away as quickly as they had appeared. Only three remained behind—the injured wolf, flanked by two others who helped their wounded pack mate along. And soon even those three had disappeared.

For a long moment we all stood frozen, Gabe with his string still drawn and Audrey with her branch raised. But no further animal sounds disturbed the forest, and we caught no more glimpses of gray between the trees.

"What just happened?" Audrey asked, voicing my own question.

Gabe gazed into the trees in the direction the animals had disappeared. "Wolves like to run after their prey. They don't attack groups of stationary, armed humans."

"And they generally hunt at night, as well," Audrey reminded him. "I think we can safely say that was not a normal situation."

I pulled out the paper and pen which I had kept from the last time Gabe handed them to me. When I finished writing, I angled my paper toward Gabe.

<Remind you of anything? Or rather, *anywhere*?>

Much of my home kingdom had been filled with unnaturally aggressive wolves and other such creatures—starting from the descent of the curse.

"I think it's time we investigated these rumors of strange beasts in the forest," Gabe said in reply.

None of us much liked the idea of lingering in the forest to talk or plan, so we hurried directly back to town. Gabe walked in front, his hand tight around the grip of his bow, and I kept my eyes firmly fixed on his back. It was better than looking at the trees and wondering what might be lurking in them.

My swans flapped above us, quiet after the strange encounter. I was only glad none of them had been on the ground with us. Gazing at them as they soared silently through the air, I wondered if I should assign one of them—Sammy, maybe—to keep a watch on Gabe.

All we needed was for the impulsive prince to go rushing off on his own—as he had done the day before—only this time looking for wild wolf packs. I didn't much like the idea of having to take the news of his death to the king and queen. And although Gabe himself discounted the idea, I couldn't shake the feeling that Leander would be quite pleased if a wolf removed the crown prince for him.

The more the idea grew in my mind, the closer I watched Gabe's back, as if I could keep him tethered to us by a stare alone. Audrey walked beside me, her own gaze flicking between the road and the trees. Her breathing had returned to a more steady rhythm, but she still hadn't relinquished her hold on the stick. Only when we reached the outskirts of Brylee did she reluctantly leave it behind. Her subsequent suggestion that we not mention anything of our recent encounter to the others at the haven explained her willingness to cast it aside.

Gabe held onto his bow longer, but once we were firmly ensconced among the houses of the town, he returned it to his back.

"I think we should all avoid wandering around in the woods any more than need be," Gabe said, just before we reached the haven's doors.

I pulled out my paper again.

<Does that include you?>

"As much as it can be avoided, certainly. But don't worry, I won't leave you to return to and from the lake unaccompanied. Not now."

Because, yes, *that* was my concern. I rolled my eyes but didn't attempt to refute him on paper. As Audrey opened the doors and stepped inside, he gripped my arm, holding me back for a moment and dropping his voice.

"We'll make sure we head back to the lake with plenty of time this afternoon. And not just for safety. I need to talk to you while the sun's still up because I need you to talk to your swans."

He let go and stepped through the door without waiting for a response, and I was left blinking at an empty doorway. After a moment he reappeared, looking at me questioningly, and I shook my head and went inside.

~

Cora had launched a comprehensive spring clean, muttering the whole time about the building falling down around us. Somehow she even managed to draw Gabe into her efforts, the prince ending up on the roof, patching leaks. The woman was formidable.

Consequently, we were once again hurrying through the forest, having left later than we intended. I had insisted that we not leave the town together, waving the paper with my request in front of his nose until he at least agreed. If any wolves appeared on the fringes of the forest, I would throw awkwardness aside and honk at full volume to bring him racing to my side. But I didn't want wild rumors filling the town about me leading the prince off into the forest.

As we walked, Gabe asked if I thought the swans would be capable and willing to complete a scouting assignment. When I looked surprised, he outlined all the reasons why they were the best candidates for the job and reassured me earnestly that he had no thought of them landing and putting themselves at any sort of risk.

"But it's a big forest," he said, "and wild animals aren't the easiest to track. From the air the birds could cover a lot of ground, though—and who better to recognize beasts behaving strangely than other animals? If the swans could pinpoint a location—find a den for the wolves even—it would make our job a lot more manageable."

Dark hadn't fallen yet, so I had no words to tell him that his explanations and reassurances were unnecessary. My surprise had been at his suggesting such a reasonable and measured approach—one that didn't involve exposing himself to any unnecessary danger. Actually, on second thought, it was probably a good thing that I couldn't tell him the true source of my shocked expression.

When we reached the lake, I gathered my birds around me, explaining our request to them. They listened with interest, heads cocked to the side, only responding when I mentioned our morning's encounter with the wolves. Then their feathers ruffled, and they honked and bugled in chorus.

"Yes, we know there was something unnatural about them," I bugled. *"And that's why we need to find them. All we want you to do is to fly around and see if you can find any animals acting strangely. Especially predator animals."*

They clearly understood me, their feathers ruffling at the mention of predators. For a moment they seemed to be communing among themselves until Shadow gave a decisive bugle, cutting the rest of them off. She then dipped her head and tapped the ground once before looking back at me. Yes.

Shadow, with Sunny, Sammy, Stormy, and Eagle behind her, waddled into the water and took off, wings flapping and feet running. I looked at Snowy and Sweetie who had made no move to leave. It seemed I was to be left with some company. My eyes moved to Gabe. Extra company, that was.

He had already told me on the walk that he intended to spend the night in the forest again. He claimed it was to be on hand for the swans' return, but I suspected he was motivated by some misguided notion that I needed protection.

After two years, I trusted whatever enchantment kept my lake free of dangers. But despite still having my paper on hand, I made no move to dissuade him. After all, it was possible it was actually a sensible precaution—if there was something unnatural about these particular animals, the enchantment might not work against them.

It seemed like a perfectly valid reason for wanting him to stay, so I made no further effort to delve into the possible reasons for my somewhat out-of-character acquiescence.

CHAPTER 13

There was nothing to do but wait for their return—and worry, but that hardly seemed productive—so I used the last of the light to show Gabe where he could find sweet, ripe berries. It wasn't a difficult task as little bushes of them were tucked in odd spots all over the clearing.

When he commented on the strangeness of harvesting berries in spring, I shrugged. If I had my voice, I would have told him that at my strange lake, you could harvest berries all year round. It was one of the elements that fit into the idyllic, rather than villainous, aspect of my forest home.

The arriving dusk made it difficult to find the sweet treats, but it seemed to take an agonizingly long time for the last of the light to leave. Finally, however, I felt the familiar sensation of lightening pressure, and sighed with relief.

"Do you ever have a fire at night?" Gabe asked.

"No, I have no reason to light one." The words flowed smoothly from my throat. I sighed again with the pleasure of it.

"Do you think the lake would be angry if I lit one tonight?" he asked.

"The lake isn't alive, Gabriel. You can do as you please."

I led him back to my shelter in the meager moonlight. The clouds were out tonight, and I could see why he wished for some light.

His voice in the dark sounded rueful. "It's such a strange place, I can't shake the feeling that it's living somehow. That someone is watching us."

I shivered. "I live here, remember? Please don't go putting that idea in my head."

I turned toward where I remembered seeing a small pile of branches earlier and collided with a solid figure.

"Oomph," I said, elegantly, but his hands reached out instantly to grip me, so I remained steady on my feet.

He didn't release me immediately, speaking instead.

"You will never have to spend another night here alone, Adelaide. I swear it."

He kept his voice low—although there was no one here but my two swans to overhear us—and the darkness loaded it with depth and meaning. I shivered slightly, and his hands tightened around my arms.

"What a foolish promise," I said, struggling to keep my voice light. "I'm under an enchantment, remember?"

"I never make promises lightly."

And although I wouldn't have believed it earlier, somehow— here in the warm darkness—I didn't doubt his words.

His strong hands still held me, and the heat from his body radiated through the layers of clothing that separated us. I felt myself flush, the intimacy of the moment causing my body and emotions to betray me—giving in to the beguiling promise of his reassurances. How much I longed to know that I would not be alone again.

But here at the lake, surrounded by my swans, was not the place where I had been most alone. And the memory of that true isolation—filled with grief and terror—made me pull away from him.

"There should be some wood over here," I said, proud of the steadiness of my voice.

It was dark, and he said nothing, so no doubt I imagined that I could sense his disappointment at my lack of reaction. And whatever his emotions, he quickly shook himself free and came to help me, both of us fumbling in the dark as we gathered some branches.

"We should have thought of this earlier, while it was still light," I said, struggling to keep the moment light and impersonal.

His shoulder brushed against mine, and I made my hands move faster. We needed light, and we needed it soon—before my mind lost control again and forgot it was the reckless, heedless Gabe who worked beside me.

I wouldn't have predicted the prince would prove more dangerous without his gold-flecked eyes and charming grin—but the darkness likes to make fools of us all.

When the first flame sparked into life, I sucked in a relieved breath and stood back. Gabe worked quickly, coaxing it into full life and feeding the small blaze until we had a contained and respectable fire. He sat down in front of it, and I carefully took my place on the opposite side.

The light sent shadows dancing across his face as he gave me a rueful grin.

"I'm sorry, but I don't keep any food suitable for cooking here," I said quickly, to fill the gap. "I only eat cold food out here usually."

"No matter," he said. "I ate well at the haven. You have an excellent cook."

I agreed, marveling even as I did so at the surreal nature of the moment. I could never have imagined that I would find myself in such a situation, having such a conversation, with Gabe of all people. But, unbidden, the memory of all the other princes and princesses of our childhood flashed through my head, and I had to admit that I couldn't think of one who I would have wished here in his stead. If an adventure was going to be forced onto you, then Gabe was an ideal person to have along.

I didn't usually indulge much in reminiscences, but either this idle thought, or the flames themselves, put me in a strange mood, and I found myself reminding him of one of the funnier incidents that had occurred at Princess Daisy's christening.

She had been born not long after Gabe began his years as a ward of her parents, so he had naturally been there, and my mother had taken me to Trione for the event. My father had kept Dominic back with him, and I had missed him at the time, feeling nervous to be among the other children without my older brother to shelter behind. But I had soon relaxed—and Gabe had played a large part in that.

Back then, he was even more good-humored and full of fun than he was now, and in the absence of both my father and my brother, I had been free to run and laugh with the other children like a normal eight-year-old.

Gabe laughed heartily, supplying a number of details I had forgotten and shamelessly blaming the entire escapade on his foster brother Teddy.

"Next you'll be trying to say it was Teddy's idea to climb that bluff above the beach," I said.

Gabe just grinned. "You would have been up there with us, admit it." His eyes softened. "Except that you were too kind-hearted to leave my sisters alone, and they were too young to attempt it. You were always looking out for the younger ones."

"Not just the younger ones as I recall." I gave him a loaded look.

But even this reminder of the time he had injured his leg and been forced to stay abed for an entire week elicited no shame. It had been during an anniversary gala in Trione when I was twelve and he was fourteen, and he had attempted to sneak among a group of sleeping seals on the beach. He had been lucky to escape without worse injury. But he had merely laughed it off, saying he had not been able to resist the urge to have a closer look at them.

Personally, I suspected one of the other princes had dared him to do it, but he had never admitted to such a thing. Not even to me when I stayed by his side and read to him or played chess while the other princes and princesses participated in the various picnics and beach visits which had been planned for their entertainment.

The memories—of a life so different from my current one—rushed back faster and faster. I hadn't thought of Teddy or his twin, Millie, in years, but I had always liked Millie, who was only a year older than me.

"Did either of the twins marry any of the newcomers?" I asked. "I don't think I've heard any talk about a Trionian wedding."

He shook his head. "The Old Kingdoms only sent princesses, and Teddy was too obsessed with his ocean girl to give any of them a second look." He rolled his eyes, but there was a laugh in his voice.

"His ocean girl? That sounds ominous."

"It was two years ago now, and he doesn't talk about her anymore, but he sometimes gets this look in his eye that makes me think he hasn't forgotten. Poor fellow."

"Was it some Trionian girl? Did his parents not approve?"

"I don't know that his parents have a strong feeling either way —given there's a very real chance he dreamed her up."

"Oh no." I started laughing. "Oh, Teddy."

It was the sort of thing someone would say about the crown prince of Trione. The heir to the island kingdom had always been something of a dreamer.

"He somehow managed to fall off their ship on the way to the Princess Tourney, and he swears he was rescued by some girl. Apparently she swam through the waves of the storm and dragged him back to the ship where they could throw him a line. Oh, and I nearly forgot that she was singing while she did it."

"Singing?"

Gabe's lips twitched. "I'm sure you can imagine what he has had to put up with from all of us. But he holds firm to his story."

I shook my head. "It sounds ridiculous, of course. But then, I would have called our own morning's experience ridiculous before I experienced it."

My reference to the wolves sobered him immediately.

"Perhaps you're right," he said, quietly. "Maybe I'll find myself apologizing to poor Teddy one day."

Silence fell between us, and I gazed into the flames. Teddy must be more like a brother to Gabe than his actual brother, Percy. Gabe had been only nine when he went to Trione, Percy only six when he farewelled his brother. And in the end, he had stayed eight years, not returning until he was nearly a man grown and my own kingdom long-since cursed.

"Why did you go to Trione?" I looked back up at Gabe. "When you were a child, I mean. Why did your parents send you away?"

Gabe frowned into the shifting orange light. "They didn't send me away exactly. At least, I don't think they ever intended such a thing. But King Edward wished to strengthen his ties with our kingdom, and we were all much too young for a marriage alliance to be any more than a distant promise. So he invited my parents to send one of us boys to spend some time in his court as his ward instead."

"Why did they send you?" I asked, emboldened by the night, and our strange isolation—the only two living creatures within the circle of our firelight—and by the unexpected sense of camaraderie that had gripped us. "I'm surprised they chose to send their heir."

"I suspect King Edward expected them to send Percy," he said, still not meeting my eyes. "But he reckoned without a mother's heart. Percy was only six and very much a mother's boy. He was only two when the twins were born, and he used to cling to her after that." He paused and shook his head. "He would have hated being sent away, and I'm sure she couldn't bear the thought of making him go." His usual grin resurfaced. "Whereas I thought it sounded like an exciting adventure, so that no doubt eased her conscience. My father was likely convinced because it was only supposed to be for a year."

"A year?" I was surprised enough to interrupt him. "But you were there for eight."

He gave me an easy smile. "You've been to Trione—you remember what it's like. Palinar has always been the mightiest of our kingdoms, but Trione has always shone the brightest. It's an easy place to love, and a hard place to leave. And Teddy and Millie could keep pace with me when Percy and the twins could not. I begged to be allowed to stay, and my parents indulged me. And then one year rolled into another..." He shrugged.

"You must miss it," I said softly.

"I do," he replied after a thoughtful pause. "But I've been back for three years now, and I am learning to love my own kingdom as well. It's a different sort of love—one that has more to do with roots and responsibilities than freedom and wings and the sun shining on the sea. But I think it will grow to be a deeper love."

He laughed suddenly. "Listen to me. A bit of darkness and a few flames, and I'm turning into a philosopher."

"No, I understand," I said. "My mother always taught me that it is a ruler's role to serve their people and their kingdom. In caring for them we find our own satisfaction and joy."

"She was always a kind woman," Gabe said, his eyes fixed on me now, and a cold spear thrust into my heart, freezing the warmth of the moment.

I had let myself be lulled into forgetfulness, pulled into the past. I had allowed myself to become the person I used to be, and I had forgotten for an instant the tragedy that had destroyed that princess. I had no wish to be any kind of ruler now—my tasks at the haven were service enough for me.

"The swans will likely not be back until morning," I said, the ice coming out in my voice. "We should sleep."

Gabe frowned slightly, his eyes examining my face, but when he opened his mouth, I pointedly turned away, and he let it go, remaining silent. I lay down on my pallet and told myself firmly that I had nothing to feel guilty about. I had enough troubles today without his bringing up the troubles of my past.

We had woken, completed a cursory wash, and eaten a light breakfast before the swans touched back down in the lake. One, two, three, four, five, I counted them all, a small ball of pressure in the back of my mind easing at their safe return. I wished I could ask where they had spent the night, but I had no way to understand the answer to such a complicated question. Instead I welcomed them back and then limited my questions to the task at hand.

"*Did you find any strange animals?*" I bugled.

Shadow's head dipped down and struck the water once. Gabe and I exchanged a brief look. Success.

"*Wolves?*" I asked, and she struck the water once again.

"*Could you lead us to them, do you think? Were they in their den?*"

She hesitated this time, and I reminded myself to keep my questions simple. I re-asked just the first one, and this time she gave a confident tap of the water.

Once again I expected Gabe to go rushing off, but he showed no inclination to do so. After gravely thanking Shadow, he suggested we make our way into Brylee.

"We'll need more supplies before attempting our own scouting mission," he said. "And it would be safest if we speak with Audrey, at least, first, and let her know our intentions."

I issued no objections, so we were soon on our way. When we arrived at the haven, however, we were only steps behind Ash, so it was impossible to pull Audrey aside. The baker exclaimed over her return, and insisted she eat one of the cakes he had brought—a task she accepted with great enthusiasm. He also showed great interest in the inner workings of the Keep, asking her a number of questions.

When she had answered them, he confessed his interest was not without selfish motive.

"I have some news," he said, "and have been hoping I'm the first to bring it to you." He looked hopefully at Wren as he spoke, and she drifted nearer, curiosity on her face.

"Lord Leander is to host a party at his Keep!" he announced, once she reached his side. "Can you imagine? And all of Brylee is invited."

"So he really means to do it? I'm astonished," Cora said.

"You had heard of his intention?" Ash looked a little crest-fallen. "I have to admit, it took me utterly by surprise. Who could have imagined such a thing after so many years?" He straightened slightly, a proud smile on his face. "But that is not all. His servants have finally appeared again—or at least a couple of them—and are busy procuring supplies for the event. And guess who has been asked to bake the cakes? It will be an enormous order."

"Oh, Ash! How wonderful." Wren laid a hand on his arm. "And such a compliment since they must have a chef of their own."

"No doubt she will be otherwise occupied with the savory dishes." Ash couldn't hide the pleasure in his voice at Wren's praise. "I'm to attend the castle in three days with samples for us to discuss the menu."

"Three days? That's quick," said Cora.

"Well the party is to be in only a week. I imagine they must be in a flurry of preparations up there, it's no wonder they had to turn to Brylee for supplies. It's to be in honor of Your Highness, of course." Ash bowed his head in Gabe's direction, and the prince nodded in return.

Although he was taking it in stride now, the baker had looked nearly as surprised to find the crown prince here at the haven as he had been to find Audrey returned.

"His servants seem to have recovered from their illness rather swiftly," Cora said in an aside to the two of us.

"Indeed." Gabe's voice was unusually serious.

I glanced up at him quickly. What was he thinking? That such haste on Leander's part—after so many years without hosting so much as a simple reception—seemed ominous?

Because I was certainly thinking that.

After all our efforts to gain entry to the Keep, in one week, we were all to be invited through the front gate. And yet, I felt nothing but dread.

CHAPTER 14

*C*learly news of the party had filtered into the haven from multiple sources because while Ash hadn't left the kitchen, the children soon came streaming in en masse, exclaiming about it and begging to be allowed to go. Even Selena and Frank abandoned their dignity to join the pleading.

Cora, however, announced that as far as the haven was concerned, it was an event for adults only. After that, it took the combined efforts of Wren, Audrey, and myself to soothe and placate the devastated children. But I didn't once waver and consider speaking to Cora on their behalf. I didn't want children anywhere near Leander.

It wasn't until after the children had been consoled with Ash's cakes that we were able to herd them all back into the large room designated for their schooling. Wren remained behind with them and, after three escape attempts, managed to keep Juniper with her as well.

In the chaos, I caught both Gabe and Audrey's attention, gesturing for them to extricate themselves and follow me. I led the way to an empty room I had recently cleaned out after the departure of its resident. When Gabe closed the door behind him, we all took a moment to simply breathe and enjoy the calm and quiet.

But our minds inevitably turned to the various problems confronting us, Gabe and Audrey speaking at the same time.

"We sent the swans on a scouting mission, and they say they can lead us to the wolves."

"I don't like the sound of this party." Audrey cut herself off and blinked at Gabe. "The wolves? You really want to go looking for them?"

"We have to," said Gabe. "I cannot leave wolves rampaging around my kingdom attacking people. Especially not when such behavior is so far outside their usual ways. Something has affected them, and I need to know what it is."

Audrey didn't look entirely convinced, and I had to admit I understood her hesitation. But I also understood Gabe's determination. He had a responsibility to Talinos that she did not.

"I wasn't thinking that you would come along, Audrey," he assured her. "We just wanted to inform someone of our intentions." He turned to me. "But, in fact, there's no reason for you to come either, Adelaide. It would no doubt be safest for me to go alone."

I frowned and pulled out my paper. He might have deluded himself into thinking he was safe in Leander's Keep, but he couldn't possibly think he would be safer alone while scouting a pack of unnaturally aggressive wolves through a forest known to contain at least one pocket of enchantment. He was trying to protect me. But while I might not have his skill with a bow, I did come with some advantages. My wedge of aerial scouts being the main one.

Various arguments and recriminations filled my mind, and I considered how best to condense them down to the most efficient number of words. In the end, I gave up and kept it to two words.

<I'm coming.>

I trusted in my glare to convey the rest of my feelings on the matter, and to my relief, it must have been a speaking one because he didn't attempt to argue further. I then switched subjects.

<I agree with Audrey. This party—and its haste—seems highly suspicious.>

"Perhaps." Gabe's voice suggested he wasn't greatly concerned. "But it also presents us with the perfect opportunity to get inside the Keep."

"Yes, but Lord Leander will know we're there," Audrey said, "which is a major difference. I think it would be much better if we snuck in." She looked quite agitated as she continued to enumerate her arguments. "Plus, there's no way he's throwing everyone a party out of the goodness of his heart." She looked between us. "If it fits with his plan to have us all inside his Keep in a week's time, then surely we need to get ahead of him. You've said you think this is about more than Adelaide—that he might have enchanted the whole kingdom—so who knows what he's planning?" She was working herself up into a crescendo now. "Perhaps he even means to use the party as an opportunity to assassinate you, Your Highness!"

Gabe looked like he was about to laugh until he saw my face.

"You can't really think that's a danger?" he asked.

I bit my lip and slowly shrugged. I didn't know what to think. But it was certainly something I feared—and something he would do better to have a healthy fear of as well.

"But if he wanted to do that," Gabe argued, "why throw a party and invite the whole town? It seems like he would have far better opportunities. I did show up at his gate and invite myself in, after all."

<But if you were killed while staying in his reclusive castle, that would be highly suspicious.>

Audrey peered at my words and nodded vigorously, grasping onto my thoughts and taking them further.

"He won't want to risk the guilt falling on him. He probably intends to have a whole host of witnesses to your *accidental* death."

Gabe didn't look entirely convinced. "As you both already know, I have no qualms about gaining illicit entry to Leander's Keep, but we have yet to work out a way to achieve such entry. And, in the meantime, I must go after those wolves. The swans managed to locate them, but we have no way of knowing how long they will remain in one place. We have to move quickly or risk losing them."

I nodded. I agreed we needed to leave—and soon. But an idea had struck me.

<What about Ash? He said he's been invited to the Keep in three days' time.>

Audrey gasped, her eyes growing round. "It's perfect! He said he has to take samples, so I'm sure he intends to drive in with his wagon. We could be hiding in the back!"

Gabe arched an eyebrow. "And Ash would be amenable to the three of us turning up and asking to secrete ourselves among his baked goods?"

Audrey grinned. "From what I've seen this morning, not much has changed in the six months I've been away. Ash is sweet on my sister, and I bet she could convince him to do anything."

"I don't like the idea of putting him at risk," Gabe said slowly.

"He won't be at risk if Lord Leander never knows anything about it," Audrey countered. "And even if something went wrong, you're the crown prince. Ash can just say that you ordered him to do it."

I worried at my lip. It had been my idea, but I kept thinking of ways it might go wrong.

<He'll be terrified, though. He might give us away without meaning to.>

Audrey paused for a moment, her eyes trained on the oppo-site wall, before turning and giving me a grin.

"I might have an idea about that. I think this idea could work, but..." She trailed off, giving me an apologetic look.

My heart sank.

"I'm going to have to tell Wren the truth," Audrey continued, just as I feared. "Because I'll need her to help me."

I took a slow breath. Everything was unraveling, but it was far too late to try to stop things now.

<I should be the one to tell her.>

"There's no time," Gabe interrupted. "If you still intend to accompany me, we need to leave now."

"I think it might be better coming from me, anyway," Audrey said. "And it will give me a chance to tell her why I really went to the Keep—something she should really hear from me."

I didn't like it, but I also couldn't deny that the sisters should have a chance to speak in private. And Gabe had already crossed over to the door, eagerness to be gone clinging to him. Reluctantly I nodded my agreement.

Audrey and I joined Gabe at the door, and he gave her a list of supplies he needed. While she explained where he could purchase more arrows, I thought about what I wanted to take for myself.

They split, Gabe going out for the arrows with a promise that he would be back to collect me and the rest of the supplies Audrey had promised to gather. If it wasn't for the supplies, I might have suspected him of meaning to slip away without me. But I couldn't shadow Gabe—I had something of my own I needed to take.

Everything Gabe had requested fit into a single sturdy bag, and I was waiting out the front of the haven for him when he returned. Only when he actually appeared did I realize that suspicion about his intentions had still been lingering in the back of my mind.

For his own part, Gabe wasn't entirely pleased with my appearance.

"Is that a sword?" he asked.

I had hoped he wouldn't notice it beneath my cloak, but it wasn't the easiest object to conceal, especially since I had strapped it firmly around my waist. I met his gaze squarely. I wasn't going to face wolves without a weapon.

He frowned, and the many objections my father would have made to the sword ran through my head: that it was beneath my dignity, unladylike, unbefitting my station, and an insult to Palinar to suggest that its princess would ever need to lift a finger to defend herself.

And it had been true, in a way. The only time I had ever needed to defend myself had been against him—and someone else had stepped in to do it for me.

I strode over to Gabe's side, handing over the bag when he reached to take it from me. He took one look at my face, sighed, and led the way out of town. But clearly he wasn't quite willing to let the matter drop.

"Weapons can be extremely dangerous in unskilled hands. If you don't know how to use it, it can end up doing more harm than good."

I had intended to ignore any arguments he put forth, maintaining silence rather than getting into a ridiculous paper argument. But his unexpectedly reasonable objection surprised me enough to deserve a response. As soon as we entered the forest, I paused to quickly write a sentence on the paper I carried with me.

<My brother gave me some training when I was young. I'm no expert, but I won't cut off my own hand.>

Gabe looked a little surprised, but he accepted my competence without further question and made no more objections to the weapon. My swans flew above us, urging us to continue on the road, so we did, moving as fast as we comfortably could.

As we walked, I watched Gabe out of the corner of my eye. He had looked surprised to hear that my brother taught me such a thing, and I couldn't blame him. Dominic had always been haughty and arrogant, especially to outsiders—he didn't seem the type to bend the rules and take the role of tutor to a younger sister.

But I had begged and begged, and he had always had a soft spot for me. When we spent time at his own personal castle, with only our mother in attendance, I had often managed to convince him to do things he wouldn't otherwise have done.

The memory should have been a pleasant one—I had loved those times—but instead it felt more akin to pressing my finger against a bruise I already knew was tender. It hurt, but sometimes I couldn't help myself doing it anyway, as if I needed to check if anything had changed. I had loved my brother despite his faults and felt as if it were the two of us against the world. I had never doubted that he would do anything for me. Until I needed him the most—and our kingdom with me—and he had withdrawn, consumed by pride and anger. I realized then how misplaced my trust had been. I was better guarded now.

I snuck another look at Gabe as he strode along, his bow already in his hand, though he carried it loosely. He had younger sisters himself. Did they love and trust him? Had he ever let them down? From his question, I suspected he would be far more willing to teach them the basics of swordsmanship than my brother had ever been to teach me.

No proper conversation was possible, given the daylight, but if I had been making the trek with Audrey, she would have chattered the whole way. Gabe, however, remained mostly silent, speaking only when he wished to point out something of note about our surroundings or to check for directions from the swans.

It was a companionable silence, though, rather than a cold one, and I had to admit I much preferred the journey to my usual solitary trips through the forest. Having his solid presence at my side was reassuring and somehow comforting in a way I hadn't expected. Although it was possible that was due to what awaited us at our destination. When you knew you were facing an unknown number of wild animals, it was bound to be reassuring to have an expert archer with you.

We walked for two hours before stopping in a clearing several steps off the road to eat some of the food from the bag. I had started to grow nervous by that point. I would have to turn back if we didn't reach our goal within the next couple of hours. And we would have to move fast on our way back if it took that long.

Thankfully we hadn't been moving again for long when Shadow flew down, honking assertively as she glided past our heads.

"Do we need to leave the road now?" I asked.

She dipped her head once in agreement.

"Is it far?" I added, thinking both of the awkwardness of following them through the forest and the fact that the sun had now moved past its noon day zenith.

This time she dipped her head twice before bugling loudly. The other swans swooped over to join her, forming themselves into their usual v shape and flapping away across the top of the trees.

"Did they just form an arrow?" Gabe asked, a laugh in his voice.

I shrugged. It was their usual flight formation, but it did work well for our purposes.

We left the road, striking through the trees in the direction the swans had indicated. They disappeared from sight before we made it half a dozen steps, the forest canopy blocking out our view of them. But they must have circled back several times because we continued to see the occasional flash of white through the leaves, letting us know we were heading in the right direction.

"We must be getting close," Gabe said, voice low. "I think it might be a good idea to move a little more cautiously from here."

As if to punctuate his words, loud barking broke out. We

looked at each other. That hadn't been far away. I wasn't sure what worried me more—that it had been so close, or that it had been the sound of a dog, not a wolf. What were dogs doing out here?

"Stay back," Gabe whispered and began to creep forward through the trees.

I stuck close behind him, carefully watching my feet so I didn't step on anything noisy that might give away our approach. He looked back over his shoulder and met my eyes. For a second I thought he meant to argue, but then the ghost of a smile crossed his face before he shook his head and continued on without comment.

He probably thought me as brave and foolhardy as him, and I was glad my lack of voice spared me any guilt at not telling him the truth—namely that I had no intention of finding myself alone in the woods at this juncture.

The barking continued with occasional pauses until it was split by an eerie howl. The sound sent shivers up and down my back. That one had sounded like a wolf.

My heart beat fast and every noise around us seemed impossibly loud and startling. My muscles would ache in a few hours from all the jerking I was doing. Assuming I was still alive, that was.

A smell hit me—a mix of wood smoke, animal droppings, and something like wet fur. Every instinct in me suggested I start hurrying in the other direction, but I forced myself to continue onward.

We reached a thicket with thick knobby branches twining through glossy green bushes. Something pink and flowering had gotten caught in the mix, and small, elegant blossoms peeked out from the mess of green and brown.

Gabe paused in front of it and frowned for a moment before tipping his head backward. I followed his gaze toward a tall elm just behind the tangle of bushes. When he glanced back at me, I nodded.

He leaped up, grabbing the first branch and swinging himself easily up to squat on it. I could tell he had plenty of practice, with neither his bag, his bow, nor his quiver causing him any grief. He stopped there and reached his arm down to help me scramble my way up, my skirts tucked up as far as they could go and still maintain some propriety.

In that manner, we managed to climb up several more branches, eventually finding ourselves sturdy nooks where we could wedge without danger of falling. In winter, the position would have left us completely exposed, but the thick foliage of spring surrounded us, effectively hiding our presence.

And when I finally managed to find an angle that let me peer through the leaves, I could only be glad to be safely out of sight. On the other side of the thicket, the ground became clear, sloping down to the shores of a lake. Any grass or flowers that had once grown there had been trampled, the area a morass of mud and tracks.

It took my mind a moment to process the reason for the mangled ground because the patchwork of leaves made the unbelievable sight even harder to absorb. But the more I stared, the clearer the picture became. We had found the wolves.

CHAPTER 15

a wolf pack drank at the lake—despite the sun high in the sky above us—and what must have been an entire second pack lay to one side of the cleared ground, in a small patch of shade. A little further around the shore, a shifting mass of legs and heads and ears and furry wrinkles appeared to be a large group of mastiffs. Some drank, while others nudged at each other or stuck their noses in the air, questing for a scent.

I drew back instinctively, as if that could prevent their smelling us. It must have been these dogs we heard barking earlier, although I was sure none of them had given the bark that called away the wolf pack the day before. That one had been unmistakably wolf.

"Adelaide," Gabe breathed, and I didn't need to ask him what he meant.

Three enormous, shaggy bears ambled into the clearing and approached the water. All of the dogs and both packs of wolves looked up, the wolves' ears perking as they watched the bears' progress. None of them moved, however.

The shivers now ran over my body in an unceasing wave.

Nothing could be less natural than such a grouping of animals or such behavior toward each other.

As if the scene needed to get stranger, all seven of my swans appeared, gliding down to land gracefully on the water of the lake. Fear gripped me, and I had to suppress the urge to call out and warn them to leave. But unlike with the bears, only a few ear twitches and a handful of head turns marked their arrival. The birds seemed equally unconcerned at the presence of such a large number of predators. Their honking calls added to the grunts, splashes, and yips—the latter coming from a litter of wolf pups I hadn't initially seen. They leaped, tumbled, rolled, and climbed over the wolves who lay in the shade.

"What *is* this?" Gabe whispered.

Our eyes met, him on a slightly higher branch than me, and I could see a fear there that I had never seen in him before. It wasn't so much the fear of a man who felt concern for his immediate well-being as it was the instinctive fear of someone confronting something utterly unnatural.

A deep rumbling growl flooded the clearing, drawing my eyes toward the trees to one side of the lake. Another dark brown head appeared, but this one seemed to have some sort of strange protuberance.

Several more steps brought the new bear fully onto the cleared land, and I gulped. He wore a harness that had been rigged across his back, over his shoulders, and down his chest. With it, he pulled a cart filled with several large terra cotta jars. A bear. There was a bear pulling a cart.

A second bear followed the first, his cart filled with what looked like sacks of food. Just as I was wondering who could possibly have attached a harness to a bear, five men stepped from the trees. Three of them broke off—one to greet the wolf pack by the trees and two to wade among the mastiffs.

The animals welcomed them, the mastiffs showing the most animation, several of them lifting their front feet into the air in a partial jump. Another growl ripped through the space, but the animals seemed too distracted by the newly arrived humans to notice.

The harnessed bears came to a stop, and the two remaining men freed the carts and began removing their harnesses. None of the men called to each other, the two with the bears working with smooth, efficient motions that suggested they had completed the task many times before. The bears seemed a little irritated, but neither made any aggressive movements toward the men, accepting their efforts with equanimity.

I was so entranced by the sight that it took me a moment to notice Gabe's attention had turned elsewhere. Following his gaze down through the branches, I sucked in a startled breath, wobbling for a terrifying moment before I clamped onto a branch and regained my balance.

Apparently the five bears around the lake were not the only ones in the area. In my absorption, I had failed to listen to the sounds of the forest around me, and a sixth bear had approached on our side of the bushes. He whuffed an audible breath through his nose, his great head swinging around before slowly turning upward—straight into the branches of our tree.

I froze in place, even my breath stopped, but clearly the bear had caught our scent and decided to investigate. He loped toward us as Gabe abandoned any effort at quiet.

Clasping the trunk in a hug, the bear gripped the bark and began to pull himself up. Gabe swung down from the branches far faster than I would have thought possible—more a controlled fall than a climb. I lurched into motion, trying to follow him, but in my haste, my foot caught in my skirt. I grabbed wildly at a branch but couldn't save myself.

My hands reached out, blindly grasping at anything they touched, but I couldn't catch a secure hold. I fell, whacking against branches and leaves.

Instead of hard ground, I fell into strong arms. For half a

second, Gabe cradled me like a baby. But before I caught my breath, he dropped my legs and pushed me away to stand on my own. Clasping my hand, he took off running, dragging me behind him as I struggled to get my feet under me.

Rustling and huffing sounded behind us. How long had it taken the bear to descend from the tree? As soon as I gained my balance, Gabe let go of my hand, and I risked looking behind us.

The bear was only steps away, and I barely held back a small scream. We were running at full speed, but Gabe's hands still managed to reach for his bow and quiver. He knew we weren't going to be able to outrun the bear now that it was on the ground again, but I wasn't sure he could take it down with just his arrows either. Certainly not when it was so close. And I couldn't imagine my borrowed sword would be any help at all.

I willed my legs to move faster, but my breath was already burning in my lungs, my muscles straining. At any moment I expected to feel claws raking down my back.

We burst from between two trees into an area where they grew more sparsely. We flew across the space, moving faster over the open ground, but had only made it half way when a loud bugling sounded. Feathers filled the air, white with a flash of black.

"*No!*" I shouted as my swans interposed themselves in a wall of wings between us and the pursuing bear.

I stumbled to a stop, turning back, but Gabe grabbed at me, dragging me onward.

"We can't stop," he panted. "We have to put some distance between us and that creature."

"*But my birds—*" My bugle did nothing to slow him down, and he continued to tug me along.

I twisted as he pulled me, peering back at the open area behind us. I couldn't see past my swans, but I heard the bear give a roar that sounded more like a loud grunt. He must have waved a paw toward them because their line seemed to ripple and bulge as they pulled away from him.

He didn't seem to have made any real attack on them, however, and Eagle let out a squeak that was more like a screech —the one that had earned her the name—and dove toward him. I squeaked myself, pulling back on Gabe, but somehow she wasn't swatted down.

Gabe threw a glance back over his shoulder, taking in the scene behind us.

"We need to keep going. Please, Addie. I have to get you to safety. I don't know how those birds are keeping him back, but they are, and we need to take the opportunity."

Reluctantly, I nodded. The swans did seem to have escaped harm so far—almost as if the bear wasn't interested in hurting them. Like how at the lake the other animals had ignored their arrival.

I latched onto that thought and took off running again, Gabe keeping pace beside me. After a while, the silence behind us made it clear the bear wasn't pursuing us, but neither of us slowed until we broke through onto the road.

Gabe wheeled around and stared at me, his breath coming fast and his eyes wide. I was in worse shape, sucking in ragged breaths after the headlong flight.

"What in the kingdoms was that?" Gabe asked.

I shook my head. Even if I'd had words, I wouldn't have known where to start. Instead, I tipped my head up and scanned the sky, hoping to catch sight of my swans, winging their way to meet us.

Still looking up, I stepped backward and onto a small stone. My ankle rolled, my trembling legs not able to catch me as I tipped backward.

Gabe lunged forward, grabbing at my shoulders and pulling me back forward, just in time. He drew me in against his chest, holding me there for balance. I gasped out my breaths, my heart beating raggedly against his.

"You're all right, Addie," he murmured against my hair, apparently sensing it wasn't just the near trip that had me in such a state. "You're all right."

I let him hold me for a moment, drawing strength from his solid presence. I could feel his heart beating a slowly descending rhythm, but he otherwise seemed unaffected by our adventures.

I told myself that I should pull away, but my body didn't obey my directive. Instead I let my head rest against his chest and felt myself relax.

It was a revelation.

I wanted to be held by this bold, reckless prince. Despite all the sensible strictures of my head, my heart was trying to convince me that here was safety and security—combined with the sort of heady thrill that kept my heart from completely returning to its normal pace.

Apparently my heart hadn't learned its lesson after all. I pulled back sharply, forcing my body to obey this time. If Gabe noticed any oddity in my behavior, he didn't comment.

"We need to get you back to the lake," he said, instead. "I think there's been enough excitement today without running late for that."

I nodded slowly. That was something we could agree on, even if it wasn't late enough to have me worrying yet. But as we started the walk back, I realized he was right. It had been years since I led the pampered life of a princess, but even with my time spent helping at the haven and the twice daily trek to the lake and back, I wasn't used to so much physical exertion. My feet hurt, my legs ached, and I could already feel bruises forming in various places from where I had hit branches as I fell. It was going to take longer to get back than I had been anticipating.

At least my swans had reappeared, although they flew too high above us for me to question them. I cast frequent glances upward as we walked until they flew out of sight. No doubt they knew we could easily find our way back now that we were on the road.

None of them looked injured, as far as I could tell, and with that worry abated, my mind turned inescapably to our encounter with the bear and the strange sights in the clearing before that. I went over and over them in my mind, trying to make sense of it. And I didn't like anything that occurred to me.

In unspoken agreement, we bypassed Brylee, making straight for my lake. I didn't have time to stop at the haven anyway, and Gabe seemed determined to see me all the way back. I wished he would break off and return to the town, but I didn't bother suggesting it. His presence might make me uncomfortable, but even I had to admit we needed to talk about what we'd just seen. And my lake was the only place we could do that.

I would just have to make it clear he wasn't welcome to spend the night. It was far too dangerous now that I realized how much I wanted him near me.

We reached the lake just as dusk was falling. Despite Gabe's gentle coaxing, my pace had slowed considerably, and only the fear of falling short drove me the final distance. I was utterly exhausted and everything hurt.

My swans were already on the lake when we arrived, and they all swam for the shore, waddling up to crowd around me.

"Thank you," I told them, stroking each of their heads in turn. *"You saved us."*

They honked and squeaked, sounding pleased with themselves. Stormy went so far as to preen, until Eagle nearly nipped her wing. I laughed and knelt down to wrap my arms around them.

"Please thank them for me, too," Gabe said from several steps away.

"Gabe thanks you, as well," I diligently repeated, and Snowy and

Sweetie broke off from our little huddle to approach him, bumping against his legs.

He smiled and knelt on one knee, running gentle hands down their necks and along their backs.

"Aren't you elegant ladies?" he said, and they both butted him gently with their heads in response.

He grinned up at me, and for an unthinking moment I grinned back at him. But I turned my head away quickly. I couldn't let myself be lured into dropping my guard just because he was kind to my friends.

CHAPTER 16

J continued to murmur to the swans until darkness fell fully, and I felt the subtle pressure inside me lift. Then I stood, turning reluctantly to Gabe as the swans dispersed back to the lake.

He had been busy with something, but I had been keeping my head averted. Now I could see the small fire he had built by my shelter. He blew the first small spark into life and soon had it burning merrily. My body pulled me toward it, and I sank onto my pallet, sighing with relief at both the warmth and the release of being off my feet. My mind fixated on the flames for a moment before being drawn inexorably back to a different lake. I looked up and found Gabe watching me.

"What was that today?" I asked, breaking the silence. "I can't say that's what I expected to find."

"No." Gabe gave a rueful smile. "I'd like to think we would have been smart enough to avoid being chased by a bear if we'd realized ahead of time what we were walking into."

I slowly shook my head, reliving the terrifying moments.

"I didn't even get a chance to draw my sword." I smiled reluc-

146

tantly. "Which actually might be for the best—I'm a little rusty in truth."

"You brought a better defense with you, as it turned out," Gabe said. "I don't like to think what would have happened without your swans."

"I never expected them to intervene like that. I'm just so relieved none of them were hurt."

"Did you get the impression the bear wasn't particularly interested in hurting them?" Gabe asked. "Like there was...I don't know...some sort of connection between them?"

I frowned. "It did seem odd the way they just landed on that lake as if the whole area wasn't filled with predators. And the other animals didn't seem particularly interested in their arrival, either."

"And that's without going into the strangeness of dogs, wolves, and bears all inhabiting the same area—let alone the same clearing," he added.

"I feel like we would have an easier time naming what wasn't odd about that scene," I said.

Gabe chuckled. "Fair enough. I'm just thinking about the connection between all the animals—and the humans."

I shuddered. "Seeing those men taking harnesses off those bears and wandering around among the wolves..."

"Did you hear those growls?" Gabe asked. "The ones when the bears with the carts were arriving?"

I nodded slowly. I vaguely remembered some growls.

"Did you see where they were coming from?"

"No, I was watching the dogs at the time, but they must have been from the bears. Those weren't wolf growls."

"No, they sounded like bear growls, but..." Gabe bit his lip. "A week ago I couldn't have imagined suggesting such a thing but...I think they might have been coming from the men."

My eyes widened as I immediately grasped his point. When I

turned to look toward the distant black shapes of the swans on the dark lake, Gabe nodded.

"Exactly. It would explain how the men could move so freely among the animals. And how they could convince them to do unnatural things like pull a cart."

"You think those men have been enchanted in the same way I have," I said softly.

Gabe leaned forward, eagerness tinging his voice as he explained his theory.

"I've been thinking about it all the way back. It seems too great a coincidence for there to be two such similar enchantments in such a small area for them not to be related. Perhaps that's why the animals are willing to co-exist—some recognition that they are bound in the same way? I don't know, I'm just guessing, of course, but I would be willing to bet that some similar curse has been cast over them."

"You think those men were trapped as I am?" Nothing about their manner had given me that impression.

"No." Gabe sounded grimmer than I had expected, and my eyes flew to his. "They looked like mercenaries to me. I suspect they went into this arrangement willingly."

Sick dread filled my stomach. "So Leander has built himself an army of dangerous animals under the command of mercenaries who answer to him."

Gabe's mouth tightened. "That's the way it looks. And I suspect he's been slowly building it for most of the time you've been trapped. He can't create the creatures from nothing, so it must be taking him time to gather and enchant them."

A horrible thought struck me. "Do you think he has more than we saw today?"

"It wouldn't surprise me at all. We already know he gets his supplies for the Keep from somewhere other than Brylee—no doubt to isolate his servants and keep information of his doings away from anyone who might form a full picture of them—so who knows what type or quantities of supplies he's sourced? If he gets them from far enough away, no one would know to question why he needs so many."

"And what would he be planning to do with such an army?" I whispered, but it was a rhetorical question, and Gabe didn't bother to answer.

In a kingdom immobilized by fear, an army of wolves, dogs, and bears would wreak havoc and destruction. Breaking Leander's enchantment had just become about a lot more than just my freedom.

"We have to get into that Keep." I sat up straighter, my aches and pains forgotten.

"Let's hope Audrey has had success," Gabe said.

My mind was still reeling from the day and the conversation, but I saw my opening.

"Yes," I said. "We must hope she has. It's dark, but it's not too late. You could stop in at the haven on your way back to the inn and find out."

Gabe frowned. "I already told you I'm not going to leave you alone out here."

"You're not leaving me," I said, my voice coming out sharper than I had intended, "I'm sending you away. We've discovered the wild animals you were concerned about—and they're not so wild after all. They're also connected to my swans somehow, so I'll be fine."

Gabe's brows drew together, his eyes focused on my face. "But—"

"I'll meet you at the haven in the morning."

Gabe's face expressed his feelings on the matter, but he reluctantly rose to his feet.

"Very well." He paused. "Addie—"

I shook my head quickly. "Not tonight. I'm exhausted. I just want to sleep."

He paused again before sighing and nodding. "Tomorrow, then."

He fashioned himself a makeshift torch from one of the thicker branches before heading for the trees. He didn't look back, and I told myself that was a good thing. Hopefully he had received my message—we were both committed to stopping Leander, but that didn't mean I needed his protection and company. Even if a large part of me desperately wanted it.

~

The next morning I arrived earlier than usual at the haven. I had slept deeply, thanks to my exhaustion, but had woken early. I tossed and turned, unable to get back to sleep, until I eventually gave up trying. It turned out that knowing there were well-laid plans to ravage your kingdom with deadly animals—and that you were somehow caught up in them—wasn't conducive to sleep.

I stepped through the haven doors with trepidation. How had Audrey's conversation with Wren gone the day before? Would she hate me now that she knew the truth? And would she help us even so, if she knew the kingdom was at stake?

I hesitated inside the entryway, wondering where Audrey would be at this hour. Eventually I headed for the kitchen. It was still early enough that breakfast would be in swing.

Sure enough, I found food and dishes everywhere. The cook didn't arrive until lunch, so the capable residents took turns preparing the first meal of the day.

Audrey leaped on me before I had even seen her.

"You're alive! Oh thank goodness! I've been so worried!"

I frowned and signed out Gabe's name.

"Gabe? What about him? Is he all right?" Audrey asked.

I nodded, and gestured around the room.

"Oh, do you mean is he here?"

I nodded, and Audrey shook her head.

"I haven't seen him since you two left yesterday. I've been worried sick."

So he had returned straight to the inn instead of coming to see Audrey without me. I tried to tamp down the warm feeling that evoked. A second thought—that something might have happened to him—easily quenched the sensation. Before I could think of any way to voice my concerns, however, another voice spoke.

"Yes, worried so sick you only managed thirds at breakfast," Wren said from the back of the kitchen.

I turned to her, and she dropped into an awkward curtsy before I could get a good look at her face. "Your Highness."

I hurried toward her, shaking my head, and as she straightened, I winced. She might be giving me royal courtesies now, but she wasn't happy with me.

"I can't believe you're a princess." She wouldn't meet my eyes. "That you've been a princess this whole time."

So that was what was bothering her—not the curse, and the fact I hadn't told her about it.

"Personally, I was more surprised you can talk to swans," said another voice from the doorway.

I whirled around, my wide eyes flicking from Cora to Audrey.

"Sorry, Lady," Audrey said belatedly. "I had to tell Cora, too."

"I'm afraid I demanded answers after I saw you creeping off with my old sword," Cora said, her expression hard to read.

Sorry, I signed. *I should have asked.* I hurried forward and offered the weapon to her.

She accepted it, placing it on a bench by the door. When she looked back at me, she chuckled, and the band around my heart eased a little.

"No doubt you knew I would say no—since I prefer you avoid the kind of trouble that requires a sword to get out of." Her voice softened. "I wish you'd told me, Lady. I might have been able to help you."

I glanced across at Audrey, and Cora nodded slowly.

"That's exactly what you were afraid of, wasn't it? That we'd try to help you."

I nodded, glad for her ready understanding. If only that understanding was enough to remove the hurt from her eyes. Cora was the last person I wanted to hurt.

"Never mind all that," Audrey interjected. "What happened yesterday? What did you find in the forest?" She looked around the kitchen. "Where's that paper of yours?"

I pulled it out and placed it on the table.

<Leander is building an army of wild animals, and we're afraid he means to use it to destroy Talinos.>

All three of them had drawn close to read my words, but they all pulled back again, shock and horror on their faces. I leaned over the paper a second time.

<Will you help us, Wren?>

"How can I refuse?" She met my eyes this time, although she looked reluctant.

Did she mean because Gabe and I were royalty or because of Leander's threat to the kingdom? I wished I could tell her not to help unless she wanted to—to show her I wasn't that type of princess. But I didn't have that luxury.

This. This was why I had been happy to leave that life and all its luxuries behind. It was no easy burden bearing the responsibility for a kingdom, and I had seen firsthand what happened when that responsibility wasn't respected.

I'm sorry, I signed, but she had already turned away and hurried from the room.

"Wren!" cried Audrey, hurrying after her with an apologetic look thrown over her shoulder at me.

I turned to Cora, who sighed.

"Give her time. I don't know what else to say."

I hesitated. I wanted to ask her why Wren was so upset—or at least, why Cora wasn't equally angry—but I didn't quite know how to phrase it.

Cora must have seen the questions on my face, though. "If you're wondering about me, I'm far too old and tired to muster up the necessary righteous indignation."

I rolled my eyes at that, and she chuckled.

"Or maybe I just have the wisdom not to waste my indignation on the foolishness of youth." She gave me a sterner look. "And yes, I do consider it the foolishness of youth. Anyone with an ounce of experience would have foreseen that entrusting such a secret to Audrey—and Audrey alone—would lead to disaster. Wren is hurt because you let her believe for all those months that she was the one who drove Audrey to the Keep—but I think her pride is hurt a little also. You were always Audrey's friend, but Wren considers you a friend as well. And I don't think she likes that apparently you couldn't see how different she is from her sister. She wouldn't have run heedlessly into danger like Audrey. You could have trusted her."

I looked down into my lap. She was right about letting Wren believe she had driven Audrey away with their fight—that had been wrong of me. I would apologize again as soon as I had the opportunity.

But as for everything else...the last six months of anxiety was more proof than I needed that I had been right to keep my curse to myself.

CHAPTER 17

*W*hen I went looking for Wren to reiterate my apology, she was nowhere in sight among the children. Audrey extricated herself from Juniper's grip, however, and hurried over to me.

"She's already gone to speak to Ash. I'm watching the children until she gets back. But then we need to talk." She peered over my shoulder. "Is Gabe here yet?"

I shook my head at her casual way of addressing him and reminded myself to be grateful for it. The same attitude that led her to treat him as if he was another Brylee boy—rather than her crown prince—was the one that had kept her from reacting like Wren when she found out the truth about me. Still, she was fortunate she had never attempted to address my brother as she did Gabe.

Or maybe I had that the wrong way around. Maybe discovering she had spent years living and working alongside a princess had reduced the awe and respect Audrey might otherwise have felt for royalty. I was only glad she seemed to have had the good sense to keep her head down at the Keep. I couldn't imagine

Leander would have appreciated her particular brand of irreverence.

With nothing to do but wait for Wren's return, I stayed to help Audrey with the children. The older ones clustered around Frank and Selena—no doubt well aware that Audrey didn't have the patience to be of much use to them in their studies. The younger children, however, swarmed toward me, led by Juniper.

I lifted Junie up and swung her wildly around while she screamed in delight. Naturally I then had to perform the same service for each of the others. And once they had all had a turn, I had to submit to being the villain in their latest imaginary game. My presence appeared to give great satisfaction, and Audrey whispered that before my arrival they had been involved in an argument over who was to play the unappealing role.

I secured myself a comfortable seat and decreed that the villain watched over everything from the top of her mountain. The children seemed happy enough to accept my self-serving storytelling, and my poor, aching body appreciated the opportunity to rest.

At least an hour disappeared while the children wove me into their fairly nonsensical story. At one point, part way in, I looked up and spotted Gabe lingering in the doorway. To my frustration, I flushed at the sight of him, but I couldn't call out a greeting, and he had slipped away before I could gesture for him to come inside. And since Audrey had disappeared, I couldn't follow him either. I was stuck until Wren returned.

Thankfully she arrived not long later, pulling up short when she caught sight of me. I signed to her that Audrey had gone, and she gave a long-suffering sigh.

"Why am I not surprised? She always did take advantage of your good nature, Lady." She stiffened. "I mean, Your Highness."

Please, no, I signed, and then added, *I'm sorry. About Audrey.*

She regarded me for a long moment while I held my breath.

Finally, she sighed. Glancing at the children, she kept her voice low.

"Audrey is...Audrey. No one knows better than me that she's hard to control. I can't blame you for failing to do what I have never really managed." She gave me a hard look. "But you should have told me what happened."

I nodded my agreement, hoping my face sufficiently reflected my repentance, and her anger melted away. She glanced toward her daughter.

"I know you just wanted to protect me. I'm familiar with the feeling—I would do anything to protect Junie. But, Lady, I'm not a four-year-old. I just wish you'd trusted me."

I looked away, not sure how to respond, and was suddenly enveloped in a hug. Tears pricked my eyes as Wren held me close. She was a good friend—better than I deserved.

"Now get out of here," she said. "I saw Audrey on my way in and gave her my report. And I think I spied Gabe as well. No doubt they're waiting for you."

Although the children were busily occupied on the other side of the room, a cry went up from Junie when I moved toward the door.

"No! You can't go! The villain needs to stay on the mountain."

I hesitated, but Wren waved me on with a wry look.

"Don't worry, I'll sort them out. You be off."

With a smile for her and a wave at the children, I took the offered opportunity and slipped away. I paused in the corridor. No one was in sight. I couldn't hear anything either. So I did what I always did when in doubt and headed for the kitchen. The large room was the undeniable hub of the haven—its beating heart.

Sure enough, I heard voices as I approached the kitchen door, but something made me hesitate. Catching my name, I lingered outside. It only took me a moment to place the two voices—Cora and Gabe. The strange combination was enough to keep me outside, out of view, as I heard my name again.

"It's like she's two different people," Gabe said. "When I see her with the residents here—the elderly or the children—she's like the Addie of my childhood. Kind, gracious, gentle...But when she interacts with me—"

Cora barked out a laugh. "Let me guess. She's defensive, closed off, and generally prickly?"

I peeked through the gap in the door and saw Gabe give her a rueful look.

"It's that obvious, huh?"

"A number of things are obvious," she told him dryly. "Lady doesn't trust you—because she doesn't trust most men." She gave him an exaggerated look up and down, a smile tugging at her mouth. "And, given your unfortunate excess of charm and good looks, I'm guessing she doesn't trust herself around you either."

I stiffened. Cora knew me far too well, apparently.

"Doesn't trust herself..." Gabe trailed off as he grasped Cora's meaning, a surprising flush appearing on his cheeks. "Oh, I see." His gaze grew thoughtful.

"I've always assumed it had something to do with her past— and with how she turned up on my doorstep alone at thirteen. But it's my policy not to ask questions of those in need—they know my ears are open when they're ready to talk. And maybe Lady would have reached that point eventually—if her voice hadn't been stripped away."

Cora paused, frowning. "Of course, now that I know who she really is..." She shook her head. "There have been all sorts of rumors about old King Nicolas and Prince Dominic—King Dominic, I should say—so I can only guess at what she went through." She bent a piercing eye on Gabe. "You probably know more about that than me."

"I know something," Gabe said. "But I'm not exactly one of

Dominic's confidants. I suspect he doesn't have a great many of those. But I know he was far less at fault than his father, at least."

Cora sighed. "Which is not the same as being blameless, as I've no doubt Lady was. It's a pity because it would be nice to think she had some family worth finding."

"Dominic has been tearing Palinar apart looking for her," Gabe said. "Whatever his faults back then, he's changed."

"Changed, eh?" Cora raised an eyebrow. "It's not the most common thing, but I've seen it happen."

"To tell the truth," Gabe said softly, "I was hoping to find her first in case she didn't want to be found by him. But now that I'm here—and she doesn't want him to know—I just keep hoping she'll decide to give him a chance."

"And perhaps she still will," Cora said.

Footsteps down the hallway made me jerk away from the hinges, turning as Audrey came into view.

"Lady!" she cried, in her usual enthusiastic way. Linking her arm into mine, she dragged me into the kitchen. "There you are at last, Gabe! We need to talk."

"You've found a way for us to get inside the Keep?" Gabe asked.

She nodded excitedly. None of them seemed to notice I was doing my best not to meet anyone's gaze.

"Wren went round to visit Ash at the bakery and said she'd like to go and see his sample cakes before he sets off." Audrey rolled her eyes. "A nonsensical thing to want to do, but he's more than happy to accommodate any visit from Wren. Once he's shown her the cakes in the wagon, she's going to distract him, and we're going to sneak in." She beamed around at us all. "Easy."

We weren't quite as enthusiastic about the plan as she was, and it took some time before we could agree on the details. Cora wandered away not long into the conversation. She knew the whole kingdom might hang in the balance of our finding a way to defeat Leander, but she informed us tartly that she had better things to do than bear witness to our hare-brained scheming. Gabe looked slightly bemused, but Audrey and I knew it was just her way of expressing her worry for us.

One thing Gabe and I agreed on was that we would be the only two hiding in the wagon. Not only was it too small for three, but it didn't seem like a good idea for Audrey to return to the Keep in such a manner.

I had expected her to fight us on that point vociferously, but she agreed with only a little coaxing. I didn't like what that implied about the time she had already spent there, but nothing in her manner was pronounced enough for me to question her on it. Whatever trauma she had experienced, she was hiding it well.

Despite her planned absence from the excursion, she seemed determined for us to succeed, and she would no doubt have continued the conversation all day if unchecked. She even suggested that we reconvene at my lake, but I vetoed that. I was physically and emotionally wrung out, and the last thing I needed was Gabe invading my space again.

Eventually we had the plans straightened out. Audrey was downright enthusiastic, fully prepared for her role helping conceal us in the wagon. I think she was relieved there was still some way she could help.

My refusal to have them accompany me home to my lake didn't deter Gabe. He was waiting for me when I left the haven late that afternoon. For a brief moment I considered trying to send him away via a written message, but he looked determined, and I decided I didn't have the energy for it.

We fell into step beside each other, crossing into the trees without any attempt on Gabe's part to make conversation. Surrounded by the trees, and the strange tricks of light produced by the setting sun, I admitted to myself that exhaustion had nothing to do with it.

In just the few short days since his arrival, I had grown used to having him with me. The trees had never felt safe—and they felt less so now. My swans couldn't keep me company as I walked, and I felt the prickling sensation of eyes on me, even when there was none. But even my unease didn't fully explain it.

Before Gabe's arrival I had felt alone even when I was not. It had made the physical isolation easier to bear. But I didn't feel that way anymore. We shared a goal and a purpose, and he understood me—the background and forces that shaped me—in a way no one else here could. He knew my family and what they had been like, and he knew what it was to be raised royal. Having tasted that companionship again, the solitude of the lake now felt like a burden I wasn't sure I could bear.

I said nothing, but I acknowledged to myself that I wouldn't send him away again. If he was willing to brave the forest to keep me company, I would let him. But as soon as I was free from this enchantment, I would put some distance between us. My friends at the haven knew the truth about me now, and my life there could provide the companionship I needed.

Gabe didn't attempt conversation while the light remained, but neither did he make any move to leave me alone at the lake. And when darkness fell, he still lingered. When I didn't send him away, he took what had become his usual place by the small fire he had built. I could tell by the way he looked at me that he had a question, and I feared it was about his conversation with Cora.

Part of me wanted to do anything to avoid his questions—I even considered lying down and pretending to sleep. But it was better to talk here, where I had my voice and no one else could overhear. I sighed.

"What is it?" I asked.

He opened his mouth to speak, closed it, then opened it again. "There's no question that we need to get inside the Keep. We have to make this scheme with the wagon work. But do you really think Leander might be planning to assassinate me?"

My mind scrambled to adjust to such an unexpected topic.

But it was the first time I had heard him speak of the possibility with an utterly serious tone, and I wanted to answer him with equal gravity.

"Yes, I do."

He blew out a long breath. "I have to admit, after what we saw in the woods, it looks increasingly as if Leander must be responsible for the kingdom's strange timidity—and as if he must have violent plans to exploit it. There is some master plan here, and it's the work of years. But why call those wolves off the other day? If he intends to kill me, why not let them finish the job right there?"

I frowned. "I've been thinking about that. I don't think it was a targeted attack. I've been wondering if the wolves were wandering where they weren't supposed to be, and were called back into line. It was probably chance as much as anything that they found us."

I paused. "I also think Audrey might be on to something regarding Leander wanting to ensure you have a public death to avoid suspicion falling on him. If he has been laying this plan for years, then he won't want it to be overset before his planned moment has arrived, and he doesn't appear to be ready to march on the capital. So while I can easily imagine him wanting to take advantage of you falling into his lap in such a way, he wouldn't want to do it in a manner that brings too much attention to him."

"Thanks to whatever enchantment he's cast, I'm not so sure anyone at the capital would take action on any suspicions," Gabe muttered, wearing a look of discouragement that I hadn't seen on his face before.

I wished I could reassure him, but my experience of the inhabitants of Brylee made me wonder if he was right. Even so, however, Talinos wasn't the only kingdom.

"You're loved outside of Talinos," I said. "The other kingdoms wouldn't overlook your death—or allow Leander to get away with assassinating you if he appeared to have done so. And if

MELANIE CELLIER

your family didn't act, that might give the other kingdoms a reason to bring troops of their own in. They have to be suspecting that something untoward is going on here."

"So you think Leander means to engineer an accident?" Gabe asked.

I shrugged. "Or have it appear that someone from Brylee is responsible for the assassination. He may even set it up so that he appears to be defending you. He'll have plenty of witnesses—and pliable ones, too. None of them are likely to take any unexpected action to upset the drama he has planned."

Now Gabe looked decidedly uncomfortable.

"I have to admit, you make a compelling case," he said.

CHAPTER 18

The next day passed with agonizing slowness, and I could only keep half a mind on the talk around me. Juniper managed to winkle two cookies out of me just before lunchtime, and I somehow promised Vilma that I would come and parade my finery for her before attending Leander's party at the end of the week. Only afterward did I realize what I had said. If we had success in the morning, no one would be attending any festivities—and regardless of what happened, I had no intention of celebrating with Leander.

Ash turned up at lunchtime with fresh rolls for everyone, and the glow in his eyes sent fresh guilt surging through me. He thought Wren had sought him out yesterday of her own volition, and I was sure that was what had brought him back today. After so long spent attempting to win her over, she finally seemed to have opened up to him.

I watched them out of the corner of my eye, observing as he solemnly listened to one of Juniper's stories before producing a cake which he had decorated with speckles of pink sugar just for her. Wren's eyes lit up, and she certainly looked genuinely pleased. He made an aside to her, and she laughed before asking him to lift something down from one of the higher shelves for her. I made myself turn away.

As the day wore on toward night, my guilt for involving Ash grew. Only the memory of my terror as the bear chased us kept me determined to follow our plan. We weren't just doing this for me—we were doing it for everyone.

As the last of the afternoon slipped away, Audrey stuck to my side. She was determined to come to the lake for a final conversation before the attempted entry to the Keep first thing in the morning, and I didn't attempt to dissuade her this time.

None of our plans had changed, but it was a relief to be able to speak and participate properly in the conversation as we went over them one last time around our little fire. The swans, perhaps sensing that something momentous was about to happen, left the lake and came to lie around us.

I rested my hands on their springy feathers, fighting back tears at the sight of them all. I had been so focused on winning my freedom, I hadn't given any thought to what I would have to give up.

For all it was a prison, my lake was both peaceful and beautiful, and—far more importantly—my swans had been my friends, companions, protectors, and comforters for two years now. They had shown me unswerving loyalty, and I struggled to imagine life without them. What would happen when Gabe and I destroyed the object that bound us together? Would the loosing of the enchantment return them to their wild state? Would they simply fly away, never to be seen again?

I went to sleep as I had done on the terrifying first nights of my curse—with my feathery friends settled around me, pressing against me on both sides. The fear, anticipation, hope, and unexpected sense of loss mingled together to create a strange dreamscape that left me wrung out and poorly rested when I awoke the next morning.

Audrey looked like she hadn't slept much better than me, but

Gabe looked elated. He had an extra spring in his steps, and I could see the shine that the prospect of the day's activities had put in his eyes. Gabe wasn't daunted by anything he considered an adventure.

He soon had Audrey in high spirits, the two of them proposing more and more outrageous suggestions about how the day might go, their chuckles seeming to lighten the gray and brown of the trees as we made our way back to Brylee. But just as I began to feel a hint of concern, Gabe met my eyes and gave a slight nod. Beneath the levity, I glimpsed a serious layer that told me he knew what we were about to walk into—or roll into in this case.

Audrey led us through the streets, ducking down a side alley to bring us out at the back of the bakery. She gestured for us to stay around the corner against the wall of the building while she peeked into the open courtyard. A moment later she was back at our side.

"Wren is already here," she whispered. "She saw me, so if we just give her a moment, she'll find an excuse to draw him back into the shop. I'll keep watch."

She disappeared, and Gabe and I exchanged a look. This was the established plan, but I had never been quite comfortable with this part. The prince's expression and body were drawn in serious lines now, however, and I tried to draw confidence from him.

When Audrey popped back into view, eyes wide, and waved for us to join her, we both reacted instantly. Together the three of us dashed out into the courtyard, Audrey gesturing for us to hurry in exaggerated movements that would have earned her a teasing in normal circumstances.

As we approached Ash's wagon, his horse swished his tail, making no other protest to our presence. But I eyed the vehicle with misgiving. I remembered seeing it around the town previously—but I could have sworn it was bigger. I glanced sideways at Gabe, but he didn't seem in the least concerned or uncomfortable, so I pushed the thought away. We would make it work somehow.

Audrey pulled back the canvas that covered the bed of the wagon, revealing a number of boxes. Straw stuck from various cracks in the rough crates, the baked samples it protected hidden from view inside. Several blankets appeared to have been shoved haphazardly to the back to make room for the boxes.

"Get in," Audrey hissed. "Up the back."

Gabe leaped up into the wagon, turning to help me in behind him. I heard Ash's voice approaching and scrambled ungracefully up, nearly landing on one of the boxes.

Wren's voice called from further inside the shop, and Ash's footsteps receded again. All three of us let out simultaneous breaths of relief, and then Audrey had to choke back giggles—the tension apparently starting to get to her.

Gabe dropped onto his hands and knees and crawled under the canvas covering, right to the back of the wagon. Pushing blankets out of the way, he lay down with his back against the front of the wagon bed. Beckoning for me to join him, he held out his arms. Misgivings filled me, but I hesitated only a moment before lying down and allowing his reaching arms to firmly grasp me around the waist and pull me tight against him. I curled into a ball, only my back resting against his chest.

"Quick, Audrey," he whispered. "Cover us."

She scrambled up into the wagon herself, crawling around the boxes to retrieve the discarded blankets. Weight and darkness settled over me, bringing with it the smell of dirt and animals and the musty remnants of ancient baked goods. I gasped and gagged.

"Breathe, Addie." Gabe's warm breath brushed against my ear, his arms around me tightening slightly, and I managed to even my breathing.

The wagon creaked, moving beneath us as Audrey climbed out.

"Audrey! I didn't expect to see you," said Ash a moment later.

His tone was welcoming, and he made no mention of her being in his wagon, so presumably she had made it off just in time.

"I thought I would come down to wish you the best and walk back with Wren," Audrey said.

"How kind!" I could easily imagine Ash beaming at the two sisters. "I know Wren is glad to have you at home again, Audrey. As am I."

They murmured various other pleasantries while I silently pleaded for them to hurry up. We were committed now, and I wasn't sure I could bear much more waiting.

At long last, Ash climbed onto the bench seat at the front of the wagon and called to his horse to get moving. The slap of the reins sounded, and Gabe jerked into me, both of us sliding forward slightly before he managed to brace us.

We rolled around, whacking against each other and the walls while Ash made two tight turns. The wagon hit the main road and straightened just in time to bounce over an enormous pothole. Gabe gave a tiny grunt in my ear as both of us lifted into the air and whacked down hard against the wood. I winced silently—more practiced at verbal restraint than him. That was going to bruise.

I tried to calculate how far we might have traveled, but both time and distance had disappeared inside the stale darkness of the wagon bed. Every now and then Ash called gentle encouragement to his horse, but otherwise the only sounds were those made by the clop of hooves and the wheels of the wagon.

I tried hard not to think about the fact that I lay pressed up against Gabe, his strong arms around me, but it was a difficult situation to ignore. Thank goodness the dangerous aspect of our mission was enough to account for the speed of my heart rate. I didn't want Gabe thinking his proximity made me uncomfortable. My only surprise was that his pulse beat against my back at nearly the same pace. His manner this morning had suggested he was inured to the excitement and fear of such dangerous undertakings.

We lay there together for an indeterminate amount of time, and I was lulled into a strange sort of peace. When we finally did begin to slow, I gasped softly, caught off guard. The Keep—it had to be.

Guards called down to Ash, and he called back a reply, explaining his purpose. Soon the creak of the great wooden gate sounded, and the wagon rolled forward again, lurching to another stop inside the Keep's external walls. Now came the complicated part. We hadn't been able to make specific plans since everything depended on what happened with the wagon, the cakes, and Ash.

A voice I didn't recognize welcomed the baker, and from the rocking of the wagon, Ash had climbed down to greet the speaker in person. Various sounds of boots, animals, and unidentified thumps made it harder to hear than before. I strained to catch the words exchanged and decided this must be the Keep cook, come to meet and direct the baker.

Sudden light filtered through our wool covering as someone thrust back the front of the canvas to expose the boxes of cakes. The cook called loudly for a number of assistants to remove the crates and carry them to the kitchen, berating anyone who didn't treat them gently enough for her liking.

I held my breath while Gabe did the same behind me, neither of us making even the slightest movement. If someone pulled the canvas all the way off, or came poking toward the back of the wagon, there was every chance they would notice the strangeness of our shapes beneath the blankets.

"Six—that's the lot of them," Ash said, and the darkness returned, the canvas over the wagon dropped closed again.

I gave a silent breath of relief, but Gabe's arms around me didn't relax. Several long moments stretched out, and then the wagon lurched again. No one had climbed up, so someone must be leading the horse.

A loud voice soon confirmed the impression, calling for a stable boy to lead the vehicle to an out of the way spot behind the stables. I could almost hear and feel Gabe's grin.

The wagon stopped again, and the horse was unharnessed. The slow clop of hooves retreated.

"Give it another minute," Gabe breathed into my ear, and I remained still.

When I thought I would burst with the tension of the wait, his arms moved, disentangling themselves from me and giving me a gentle push. I twisted around, scrambling up onto my knees and crawling to the back of the wagon. The way was clear now, the boxes all removed, and I reached the edge as Gabe pulled himself up beside me.

Cautiously, he lifted the canvas, sticking his head out just enough to see.

"All clear," he whispered, slithering out the back and disappearing.

I followed as quickly as I could, clambering down to stand beside him. We both looked around, taking in our surroundings as fast as possible.

We stood in a thankfully shadowed corner of the large space inside the Keep's walls. A stone building that must be the stables sheltered us, and I could see a number of other outbuildings scattered around. Inevitably, however, my eye was drawn to the Keep itself—an enormous round stone tower, reaching far above us.

That was where Leander's study was, where we would find anything of importance—and where Leander himself would be. An icy trickle counteracted the flush that had gripped me.

"We need to get in there," Gabe whispered, and I realized his eyes were trained on the Keep as well. "We need to find Leander's study."

I pointed toward the big window near the top.

169

"Is that the one Stormy saw Leander through?" Gabe asked. "If only we had wings to fly up there ourselves."

The sound of footsteps made us both draw back, retreating around the side of the wagon. They passed without pausing or moving in our direction, and I let out the breath I had been holding.

"We need to move confidently, as if we belong," Gabe said. "But heads down, so our faces can't be clearly seen."

I gave a single, quick nod. I didn't like this part of the plan either, but I could see no other alternative.

CHAPTER 19

*G*abe produced a cap and a scarf from nowhere, handing the scarf to me and gesturing for me to tie it over my head while he pushed the cap over his own curling locks. And then he stepped out into the open, and I had no option but to follow.

We stuck to the edge of the vast courtyard, moving along the buildings rather than drawing attention to ourselves by walking through the middle of the open space. Every muscle strained at being held back, urging me to sprint to the distant door of the Keep, but I held myself in check.

At any moment I expected to hear someone hailing us in accusing tones, but somehow we made it into the shadow of the Keep itself. We avoided the main doors, making instead for a simple wooden one some way around the curve of the building.

Gabe pulled it open and strode confidently inside. I followed on his heels, closing the door quickly behind us. I turned to find myself in a small, plain antechamber.

I didn't have time to do more than absorb the shape of the room before Gabe grabbed me by the shoulders and spun me through a second narrow door. It swung shut behind us just as the antechamber filled with voices and tramping feet moving through and out of the Keep.

"That was close."

I stared up at Gabe, my eyes wide. Why did he sound amused?

"I'm fairly certain the door on the other side of the room led through to the kitchen," he added. "And I imagine that's a busy place this morning, particularly. I bet as many of the servants as possible are finding reasons to swing past in the hope of participating in the taste testing."

He was actually smiling, the mad prince, as if he found the extra challenge exciting. I pulled away and looked around us. We had hidden ourselves in the bottom of a stairwell, worn stone stairs spiraling up away from us, the narrow walls closing in on them. A servant's stairway, no doubt.

"Upward then?" Gabe asked behind me, and with a sigh, I put my foot on the first step.

Every time we approached a landing, I held my breath, but no one appeared. This must not be the only set of servant's stairs in the Keep, then.

We continued heading upward. Leander's study was somewhere near the top, and we'd agreed to start there if we could. Thanks to Audrey, we already knew we weren't likely to find the enchanted objects anywhere else.

I didn't think we'd climbed high enough to reach the top level when the stairs ended, spitting us out into a large central space ringed with doors and broken by the top of a large, formal staircase. I frowned at it. I must have misjudged then, if even the main stairs ended here.

"Over there," Gabe said quietly, pointing at one of the doors.

It didn't look any different from the others, but a tray sat on the floor in front of it. Jumbled on the tray were the remains of a large meal, the dirty crockery now containing only a single crust of bread and the dregs of a cup of tea.

"Breakfast," Gabe whispered. "Left outside the door, so the maids have no reason to enter, just like Audrey said."

I turned my head to look up at him, raising an eyebrow.

"Yes," he murmured back, "that is the question, isn't it? Is he still in there?"

I frowned. That was a good question, but it wasn't the one I had been thinking of—namely how we were to get in there ourselves. But now that he had raised the question of Leander's current location, I couldn't think of anything else. What if we somehow broke into the room, only to end up face to face with the lord himself?

I stared at the door in question, as if I could somehow see through the wood to the room beyond. Steps sounded behind us, coming up the servants' stairs as we had done, and this time I was the one to pick a door and pull it open.

I peeked inside before stepping through and gesturing Gabe to follow. He whisked himself in but didn't close the door completely behind us, instead leaving it open a crack and setting his eye against it.

I left him to his spying while I looked around. We stood in what looked like a guest suite—once lavishly decorated but now looking old and worn. I couldn't see any dust, however, so the maids, at least, must visit it regularly. My eyes flew to the door, but no one had appeared, so this must not have been their destination on this occasion.

Hurrying back over to Gabe, I tapped him on the shoulder and made a questioning gesture. He turned his head to look at me, and I took a quick step backward. I hadn't been prepared to find his face so close to mine, the gold flecks of his eyes standing out as he grinned at me.

"It was two maids collecting the tray," he said. "And talking about how Leander will be back in his study soon and probably wanting an early lunch. Which means he's not there now."

He stepped away from the door, leaving room for me to peer

through the gap myself. No one was in sight. I pulled out the piece of paper I had tucked inside my dress. A bad feeling kept snaking up and down my spine.

<We've been awfully lucky so far not to be seen by anyone.>

"Not at all," Gabe said. "We were seen by at least two people outside in the courtyard, and I'm fairly certain at least one person saw us before I got you into the stairwell."

What? I stared at him.

He shrugged. "I would have been a great deal more concerned about attempting something like this under normal circumstances, but we have a decided advantage here. With everyone so meek, no one is too inclined to investigate anything. As long as we mostly stay out of people's way and don't cause a ruckus, anyone who sees us will gladly look the other way and assure themselves there's some legitimate reason for our presence."

I gaped at him. Of course. I didn't know why I hadn't thought of it myself.

"Sorry," he said. "I should have mentioned it. I just assumed you'd be thinking the same thing."

I felt like a bit of a fool now. But in my defense, this was the first time I had done anything like this. Somehow I had the suspicion Gabe had spent a significant part of his childhood sneaking into and out of various places. And, of course, danger remained. There was one person here we still needed to avoid at all costs.

"Come on," Gabe said. "Now's our chance."

He headed directly for the door to Leander's study, reaching over once he got there to pull something from his boot. Bending, he began to fiddle with the door. I hurried after him. Was that...?

Yes. Yes, it was. Gabe had come equipped with lock picks— and apparently knew how to use them. Any lingering doubt about the activities of his youth disappeared.

When the door clicked, swinging open at the push of his hand, he gave a satisfied grin. "My foster mother—Queen Juliette

—always called me a reprobate, but you just never know when a skill like this might come in useful."

I put my hand in the middle of his back and gave him a push into the room. When we had found and destroyed any godmother objects, and I had my voice back, I could shower him with the praises he clearly desired. For now, we needed to move quickly.

I closed the door carefully behind him, re-locking it with the key I found on this side. At least it would give us some warning when Leander arrived. Turning quickly back around, I stood and gaped.

I wasn't sure what I had been expecting, but it wasn't this. The word study evoked a large desk and shelves of books—perhaps an armchair or two. And it was certainly possible there was a desk and armchairs in here—somewhere. There were certainly books, but they weren't lined up on any sort of shelving. Instead they were strewn around in haphazard piles or lying open as if they had been flung away at some point and never touched again.

Everywhere I looked was chaos, mismatched items in a wide range of sizes scattered around on every available surface. The books competed with various items of clothing, innumerable sheets of parchment, several inkwells—one of which had tipped over, spilling its contents over nearby objects—and a number of items that looked entirely out of place in a study. At a quick glance, I picked out several staffs of different lengths and types of wood, a number of glass receptacles—some with murky liquids clinging to their bottoms—several plants, both alive and dead, four large baskets, at least fifty spoons, two ornate mirrors, three combs, a brush, and a long, rolled up carpet.

Even Gabe looked daunted by the room.

"How are we supposed to find anything in all of this?"

In case the room wasn't strange enough, a heavy smoke rolled slowly from under a door on one side of the room. It clung to the carpet, drifting along the wall until it managed to float up and out of the large window Stormy had flown past. An ominous popping sound came from behind the door. I glanced around the cluttered study again and then back at the door. *Please let the object be in here and not in there.*

"Do you think he remembers where everything is?" Gabe asked, pulling my attention away from the smoke. "Because I don't see how we can search through this without moving things. I was hoping to keep our presence here concealed."

I bit my lip. I didn't know enough about Leander to hazard a guess as to how well he knew his room. It didn't look like the detritus of someone who paid attention, but people could be tricky like that.

"Maybe we should look for something that's locked?" Gabe suggested, still sounding a little lost.

He walked toward a large, cedar chest, and I cast around for anything else with a lock. The first thing I saw was another door, almost directly opposite the one still emitting the strangely heavy smoke. This one looked more like the door to a cupboard than a room, however, so I went to investigate.

It opened easily, but I stuck my head in anyway. The small, square storage room, lined with shelves, appeared far more ordered than the main room. It had a pungent, musty smell, and I recognized various dried herbs tied into small bunches. There was nothing that looked like it could possibly be a godmother object, however, so I had just started to pull my head back out when I heard the ominous sound of the keyhole.

"*Gabe!*" The hiss that emerged caught his attention as easily as his name.

I gestured frantically inside the cupboard, my other hand still gripping the door. In four strides he had reached me and brushed past into the space. I threw myself after him, forcing myself to take the time to close the door silently behind us.

My heart beat rapidly as I held my breath, the darkness allevi-ated only by a thin line of light along the bottom of the cupboard door. Movement sounded from the room on the other side, and I stepped back without thinking, colliding with Gabe.

He steadied me, and for a moment we froze, both at awkward angles, our heads turned toward the door.

Please don't need any herbs, I thought. *Please don't need any herbs.*

Some other door opened and then closed again, but I was fairly certain it hadn't been the door into the study. The smoke door, then.

I looked up at Gabe, but it was too dark to make out his face. He must have sensed my movement, though, because he quickly dropped his hands from my arms, stepping back as far as possible to put a little distance between us. I could still hear his whisper clearly, however.

"If he's gone into that other room, then this might be our only chance to escape this cupboard."

I reached out and fumbled down his arm until I found his hand, bringing it up to place it against the side of my face. I wanted him to feel that I was shaking my head. He took one tiny step closer.

"I know we haven't found the object yet, but who knows how long we'll be trapped in this cupboard if we stay now? Ash will leave, and then we'll be stuck inside the Keep." He sounded afraid, and it wasn't like him.

"We have to get you back to the lake before dark," he whispered, and it burst on me that his fear was for me.

I had already been determined to stay, but a new courage formed inside me at his fear—as if rising to meet the gap where his used to be. He feared for me, but I would be brave for us both.

I pulled out my paper and dropped down onto my knees, placing it on the ground in the strip of light from the bottom of the door. Gabe crouched down beside me, the two of us pressed side by side and brushing up against the herbs on the shelves.

<We can't leave now. We might not get another opportunity. We just have to find and destroy the object before night. And

177

then we'll find the entrance to the tunnel and get out that way. Audrey couldn't find it in all those months. I bet it's in here somewhere.>

It took me a long time to write, but Gabe waited patiently. When I finished, he nodded slowly, the gesture visible now that my eyes had adjusted. I could even make out something of his expression. He looked torn—half proud, half worried.

I looked away to hide a smile. It would no doubt do him good to be worrying about someone else's bold actions for once.

Several hours later, my back was regretting my brief foray into recklessness. Sitting comfortably was difficult in such a cramped space, and the shelves on every wall made even finding a back rest difficult. After the first twenty minutes I had abandoned my efforts to keep from touching Gabe, and we were now positioned on opposite sides of the cupboard, our legs stretched out in varying positions, often against each other.

But even if I had wanted to do so, the chance to change my mind was long gone. Ash would be back in Brylee by now, and Leander had returned to the main room of his study quickly. He had lingered there ever since, moving around, throwing things, and muttering inaudibly. Gabe had spent some time pressed up against the door, trying to hear what he was saying to himself, but had eventually given up.

I tamped down on my mounting fear, forcing myself not to endlessly calculate how much time might have passed. Instead I tried to review everything I had seen in the room and consider what the godmother object might be and where Leander might be keeping it.

My mind kept reliving the first time I had stumbled onto the lake. I had been following a voice calling my name. I knew now it must have been Leander, although it hadn't sounded like him. He had been waiting for me, however. The image formed behind my closed eyelids, made more real by the low murmur of his voice through the cupboard door.

He had been kneeling by the lake, although he had stood up as soon as I arrived, smiling a smile that did nothing to put me at ease. I wouldn't have accepted a drink from him if I hadn't been so thirsty, and if he hadn't given me a small, empty glass bottle that I had filled myself from the lake.

The bottle stuck in my memory, catching on the images of all the items scattered around his study. There had been several glass receptacles, although none that were an exact match for the bottle he had offered me that day. What had happened to it? I strained to remember. I had handed it back to him, I was sure of that. And he had claimed to be thirsty as well, so I hadn't drunk it all. But had I ever actually seen him drink from it?

I didn't think so. And when I recalled the image of him strolling out of the clearing, my mind included a flash of light from something in his hand.

I straightened, the movement sudden enough to produce a similar response from Gabe.

"What is it?" he whispered, almost inaudibly. "Did you hear something?"

I shook my head. Pulling my paper back out, I flipped it over so I could write on the back.

<I remembered something. Those glass bottles in the study reminded me. I think the object we're looking for might be a small glass bottle. Similar to the ones out there, but slightly more rounded, with a narrow neck and a small cork. And I think it would have clear water in it.>

I didn't attempt to explain anything of that day by the lake— writing and reading in the low light was a strain, and I didn't want to run out of space in case I needed it later.

Gabe read the words twice through and nodded. As if to punctuate our renewed enthusiasm for the search, we heard the sound of the main door opening. We waited while it closed again and the key scraped in the lock.

I stood nearest the door, so I pulled it open a fraction, peering out. I could see no sign of Leander, so I didn't hesitate, moving out into the room and starting to scan the mess. My eyes latched onto any sign of glass or anything reflective, passing over both of the mirrors and a number of glass jars and bottles that were too large.

Gabe, however, had crossed directly to the window.

"Adelaide." He sounded strangled.

I looked over and felt my face pale, then warm. Even more time had passed while we were in the cupboard than I had feared. Already the sun was setting, the round ball of light passed below the level of the trees.

"Quick," he said. "Can you sketch the bottle we're looking for?"

I grabbed an empty piece of parchment at random from the various stacks lying around and drew a rough outline of the bottle as best I could remember it. Gabe gripped it in his hand as he rushed around the room, examining everything he passed.

Clearly he had abandoned any idea of stealth. Anything that caught his attention he snatched up, discarding it when it didn't match my sketch.

I watched him for only a moment before hurrying into action myself. Following his lead, I thrust aside piles of papers and clothes heedlessly, searching for anything that might be lurking underneath. The room darkened, and a tightness gripped my limbs, stress making my hands fumble when they had been steady before. I could already feel the first pinpricks of pain, although some light still lingered in the sky. Apparently my mind was producing it in anticipation.

"Addie! Over here!" Gabe called dangerously loudly, and I flew to his side.

He held out a small bottle, rounded, with a long neck, just as I had described. It was a third full of what looked like clear water, a cork stoppering it. Behind Gabe, a small display cabinet rested beside the window.

I nodded, suddenly nervous. It looked like the bottle I remembered, but it had been two years, and I hadn't taken particular note of it at the time.

I clasped it in my hands, feeling the familiar shape. Then, with a sudden movement, I lifted it over my head and threw it hard at the stone floor. It landed with a splintering crash, the water splattering out in all directions.

Almost simultaneously, the darkness descended, even the lake outside the window ceasing to reflect any lingering rays of light. Gabe and I stood facing each other in the gloom.

"Well?" he asked, his voice full of trepidation. "Did it work?"

I took in a slow, deep breath and then another.

"I feel fine—no pain at all."

Even the anticipatory pinpricks were gone. I was free.

Gabe swept me into his arms, spinning me around blindly before dropping me back onto my feet where I staggered and nearly tripped over some discarded object on the ground.

"That's excellent news," he said. "Now we just need to check if there's anything else of interest here. And then we should probably find that tunnel before Leander returns and decides to kill us both on the spot."

PART III
THE PROMISE

CHAPTER 20

*T*he meager moonlight that filtered in wasn't sufficient for any sort of search. Gabe went looking through the mess for an unbroken lantern while I examined the display cabinet where he had found the bottle.

It looked to be in slightly better condition than most of the other furniture in the room, and I could see why it had drawn Gabe's attention. Unfortunately it was now empty. If Leander had any more enchanted objects, he didn't store them inside it. My eyes were drawn irresistibly toward the smoke door.

"Adelaide," Gabe called softly, and I turned toward him.

He had located a lantern at what appeared to be the main desk, although both its surface and the chair beside it were littered with a variety of objects, rendering them unfit for regular use. The lantern's glow lit up the room, but Gabe hadn't moved, instead bending over something at the desk. I hurried over to join him.

A small desk drawer had been pulled most of the way out, hanging haphazardly. Whatever it had divulged now held Gabe's full attention as he bent over it on the desk. Apparently in his search for a tinderbox to light the candle, Gabe had discovered something of greater interest.

I peered over his shoulder at a small, leather-bound book, its blank pages full of scribbled notes. It looked like a journal, although small sketches and diagrams broke up the words.

"Is that Leander's journal?" I asked. "Does it say anything about my enchantments?"

"I've only read a couple of pages, but—" Gabe broke off, his eyes fixing on the locked door.

I froze as well, straining to hear. Were those footsteps? Gabe moved fast, scooping the book off the desk and thrusting it inside his jacket. With one hand, he lifted the lantern, while the other swept around my shoulders herding me back, away from the door.

For a moment I thought he was trying to push me toward the ominous smoke, and my body instinctively resisted. But instead of approaching the door, Gabe swept aside a long tapestry which hung on the wall beside it. As soon as he touched it, I could see why it had attracted his attention. It undulated in the breezes of the room in an unnatural way and, sure enough, when he pulled it aside, it revealed a hidden alcove.

We nearly tripped over each other both rushing into the small depression. Only when I was almost shoved up against it, did I notice that the space held a simple wooden door. I fumbled with the handle, expecting to find it locked, but a simple latch was all that held it closed.

A key scraped against the lock of the main door as I ripped open the one in front of me and threw myself through. Gabe followed behind, so close he was stepping on my heels, before pulling the door closed behind us as silently as he could.

The door—and tapestry in front of it—might hide the light of our lantern, but it didn't filter out all sound. A muffled roar of anger sounded from the room on the other side. Apparently Leander was able to distinguish his own chaos from the mess we had created. I looked around frantically for something to barricade the door, but the space around us was empty except for one thing. I tugged at Gabe's sleeve.

"Stairs," I breathed, pointing downward.

His eyes lit up, reflecting the orange light of the lantern, and he moved toward the hole in the floor without hesitation. I let him go first, taking the light with him, but followed close behind, casting several anxious glances over my shoulder.

The narrow stone stairs wound downward in a tight spiral. No openings or landings punctuated the endless turns, although we must have passed several levels.

"The escape tunnel," I whispered, hope filling me.

Gabe nodded. "It makes sense. We thought it must open from the locked study, and it certainly wasn't in that cupboard." He chuckled. "I'm now intimately familiar with every inch of it, and there wasn't a secret passage to be seen."

The spiral meant there was no way to see back up to the top of the stairs, and not even a distant glow would give forewarning if the door behind the tapestry was opened. But I kept looking back over my shoulder anyway. If there was any pursuit, it was silent, and I could no longer hear whatever angry noises Leander was making in his study. Had he found the fragments of glass and worked out what they meant? Did he know I was free?

The stone around us turned colder, as if we had descended below the bottom level and under the ground. Or was that just my imagination? We had been descending long enough that it felt as if we must be underground by now.

Sure enough, the steps ended, the stone beneath our feet abruptly turning to packed dirt. Rough stone walls bordered a short, narrow tunnel that disappeared into darkness ahead of us. Gabe had to stoop to avoid hitting his head against the roof, although I could stand straight.

His pace didn't slow, however, and I kept close behind him. My mind was now helpfully supplying images of the lake bursting through the ancient walls of the tunnel and flooding us. I pushed the thought away. This tunnel had stood for unknown generations—there was no reason for it to collapse now.

At long last, Gabe reached the door at the other end, nothing but another simple latch standing between us and freedom. This passage had been made for free access from the Keep to the forest, all the protections focused on travelers coming the other way.

A moment later and the fresh night air hit me directly in the face. I breathed it in deeply, stepping forward eagerly. But as I moved through the doorway, it occurred to me that there might be a way to secure the latch so that we could open the door from the outside. I turned back, intending to catch it before it closed, and stumbled over a twisted root.

"The door!" I cried, but Gabe reached for me instead, catching me before I hit the ground. It swung shut with a bang.

"I'm sorry!" I rushed over to see if there was any chance of opening it again. It didn't budge.

"Don't worry," Gabe said. "Eventually Leander's going to work out that's how we got out, and I would bet he's going to do something to secure the door at the top. At the very least, he'll be watching the passage. I don't think we can use it again."

I nodded slowly. "Perhaps we shouldn't linger here." I grimaced. "Just in case he works it out sooner rather than later."

Gabe nodded his agreement, and I took the lead, directing us back to the road. It felt utterly strange to be traversing the forest in the dark. The moonlight, combined with the lantern Gabe carried, provided ample light, but it had been two years since such a thing was possible. On instinct I had nearly directed us toward the lake before realizing it made more sense to head for Brylee.

Brylee. A smile grew on my face. For the first time in two years, I could spend the night in a proper bed and speak aloud to my friends again. It still didn't seem real.

"I wish we'd had time for a proper search," I said. "Who knows what else he has in there?"

Gabe reached into his jacket and pulled out the book. "This might tell us something about that."

I peered at it. What secrets did it hold? I wished I could stop and read it right now, but it looked thick, and I didn't much fancy the idea of tarrying in the forest, either. Even if Leander was unlikely to attack us out here, I couldn't help wondering about the other animals that would have been released alongside my swans. I didn't much fancy encountering a confused wolf pack right now.

Gabe must have seen something of my eagerness for the secrets of the journal in my face because he gave me a smile.

"I won't go to sleep until I've read it cover to cover—no matter how long it takes. And I'll give you a full report first thing in the morning."

Reluctantly I nodded. It made more sense for him to decipher it. We couldn't both read it at once, and I imagined I would have a lot of questions to answer from my friends when we arrived at the haven.

Brylee finally appeared on the road ahead of us, and Gabe insisted he would see me to the haven before returning to the inn himself. Except that when we actually arrived at the haven, I had no sooner touched the front door than it swung open and Audrey pulled me inside.

Wrapping me in a tight hug, she called for Gabe to come in as well.

"Thank goodness!" Tears streamed down her face. "I was fearing the worst. Wren and I were both waiting for Ash when he returned, and when you weren't in the wagon, I panicked. How did you get out?"

"The escape passage," I said. "No wonder you couldn't find the entrance—it was in Leander's locked study."

"Lady!" Audrey almost screamed my name. "You're talking! I

mean, you're here! I mean, you're not at the lake. I can't believe I didn't realize it straight away. So you did it? You broke the enchantment?"

"How about you come back to the kitchen before you wake the entire haven," Cora said much more calmly from behind us.

Audrey laughed and apologized, while Cora gave me a beaming smile.

"It's nice to see you here after the sun's down, Lady. It's been a while."

I smiled back. "Too long."

Wren appeared as we hurried into the kitchen, frowning at her sister and scolding her for disturbing Juniper. When she saw us, her irritated expression dissolved, however, and she ran forward to give me nearly as tight an embrace as Audrey had done.

"Oh, thank goodness!" she said, as Cora ushered us all into the kitchen, closing the door firmly behind us.

"How about we get the story from the beginning?" She bent a hard stare at Audrey. "Without questions."

I told the tale with occasional embellishments from Gabe, our appreciative audience gasping and applauding at the correct moments.

"So you're free?" Wren asked when we finished.

"As you can see," I gestured at myself and then at the kitchen around me.

"What happens next?" Audrey asked, looking suddenly uncertain. "With Lord Leander and everything?"

Gabe frowned. "That's a good question. And I think I'll have some more answers on that once I've read this. Hopefully it will provide the evidence we need to strip him of his title, lands, and freedom. Without his animal army, I don't see how he could put up much of a fight."

"Very reasonable," Cora said. "Best to read that book first and get everything in order before making any more moves. And for most of us, that means bed." She smiled in my direction. "We've always kept your old room open for you. You know that. And today in an act of faith, I even put new sheets on for you."

"It sounds delightful," I said with a small sigh.

She turned to Gabe. "And as for you, you're not going off to sneak into that inn. It's the middle of the night. I'll find a room for you here."

"I don't like to trouble you," Gabe began, but she cut him off.

"It's no trouble. We always have guest rooms set up and ready since we never know when someone might appear at our door. And truth be told, I don't think that these young things could bear to let you and that book go so far away. You just wait and see—they'll all be hounding you for answers over breakfast."

Gabe's lips twitched. "And I shall endeavor to have them."

"Youth," Cora muttered, with an upward roll of her eyes. "One day you'll learn the value of sleep."

We all dispersed after that, me hurrying as quickly as possible to my bed and sinking straight into its softness with a luxuriating sigh. Many of my things were still here, stored for me by Cora since I hadn't wanted them with me at the lake, and it was mere minutes before I was ready for sleep.

But despite the comfort of the bed, sleep didn't claim me. I kept reliving the moment of my imprisonment, as I had in the cupboard, and the moment of liberation when I smashed the bottle. Clearly my instinct about the bottle had been right—my pain-free presence here was proof of that. But something niggled at me.

My moment of liberation had come with no particular sensation, and the darkness had come only a second later. But I thought I had felt something as it fell—a lightening of pressure so familiar that I hadn't even noted it at the time. But now it had returned to bother me.

I knew I was free of the need to spend my nights at the lake, but was I truly free? I had always been able to speak at night, so my voice was proof of nothing. Had it only been the darkness and not the smashed bottle that released my voice? Would I lose it again when daylight came? Only morning would tell me that, and it suddenly seemed unbearably far away.

I tossed and turned for what must have been an hour before getting up. I kept thinking of my swans. Had they already flown away, abandoning our lake forever to return to their natural migratory habits? Or were they waiting there—still bound to me and wondering what danger had befallen me? On the nights when I had been late to return, they had always come to find me. Were they looking for me now?

I thrust my feet into my boots and pulled on my overdress and cloak. I couldn't lie here thinking such thoughts. If there was any chance my swans were still bound to me, I needed to know. And I needed to let them know I was fine. I could be there and back before Gabe delivered his report on Leander's journal in the morning.

I crept quietly from the haven, not wanting to disturb anyone else, and hurried through the deserted streets of the town. I had brought a lantern with me but almost regretted the decision. It illuminated the trees nearest me, but it cast the rest of them into even blacker relief, giving the impression that I and my pool of light traveled through a terrifying, hidden realm.

I kept the light burning, however, needing it to avoid all the roots and branches that lay in my path. Only when I reached the lake did I abandon it on the edge of the trees. I didn't need it here —the clear sky allowed enough moonlight through, while the water reflected it and increased its brightness.

I hadn't noticed I was holding my breath as I set the lantern down until it released in a long sigh. Seven sleeping shapes floated on the water. They were here and safe.

But they weren't searching for me. My breath caught again. So I had been wrong. The enchantment was fully broken, after all, my link with them gone. The release had happened as night fell, so it shouldn't be a surprise that they had chosen to spend the night on the familiar lake. No doubt in the morning they would depart.

"Adelaide!" Gabe's voice shattered the stillness of the scene as he came into view, illuminated among the trees by the lantern I had left on the ground.

The swans came awake, grunting, hissing, and snorting, their wings stretching as they looked for the threat. When their beady eyes landed on us, every one of them turned and paddled swiftly for shore, waddling up onto dry land and heading in my direction.

A relief I hadn't expected to feel overwhelmed me. Dropping to my knees, I welcomed them.

"Hello, friends," I murmured. "I hope I didn't worry you."

"They're still bound to you." Gabe cocked his head to the side, his gaze tracking between me and the feathered moat around me. He hadn't phrased it as a question, though.

I met his eyes. "It would appear so."

"I was afraid of that."

"The journal?" I asked, looking to see if he had it in his hands.

He nodded. "I came to find you, but you were gone. It terrified me for a moment before I realized you must have come here to see them." He pointed at the swans.

I flushed and slightly averted my face. He knew me too well.

Striding over, he offered a hand to help me to my feet. Reluctantly I took it, irritated at the way my heart leaped at his nearness.

"There's a second enchantment, just like I guessed on that first night. We destroyed the one tying you to the lake, but the one connecting you with the swans and stripping you of your voice remains." He didn't release my hand. "So please don't hit me."

"Hit you—?" My words cut off as he pulled me close, wrapped his arms around me, and lowered his face toward mine.

I knew in an instant what he intended. And I knew too that I should push him away—even hit him, perhaps, as he had suggested. But for all I told myself to move, a larger part of me refused to listen. In the suddenness of the moment, my heart and body took control, and I allowed him to press his lips against mine.

CHAPTER 21

*T*he kiss lasted too long and too short all at the same time, my heart singing as my mind screamed at my foolishness. It was too heady this kiss, too tantalizing. If I let myself, I would drown in it.

I regained control and pulled away. Gabe let me go with a reluctant sigh.

"Did anything happen?" he asked. "Do you feel any different?"

Yes! my heart said, *everything is different.*

"No. What do you mean?" my mouth said instead.

"Oh." He looked a little sheepish. "I thought maybe…I've heard a kiss of true love…"

"What?!" I shrieked, giving him a light shove. "You thought *what?* True love? That's a little presumptuous of you, don't you think?"

Before Gabe could respond, Eagle appeared in the air, gliding into the clearing, a black shape against the black night. I hadn't even realized she'd left.

She flew straight for Gabe, honking at him and flapping with her wings. He waved his arms around to defend himself, dancing backward out of her reach.

"I'm sorry! I'm sorry! I didn't mean to insult her, I swear."

"No," I hissed. "I can hear something. I think she's trying to warn us. Quick! Go hide in the trees."

He didn't hesitate, sprinting for the trees behind us, and a small warmth ignited in my chest at his trust in my judgment. My swans couldn't properly understand me at night, but I pointed at Eagle and then at Shadow—my two most assertive friends—and asked them to follow him and keep him among the trees. I could think of only one person whose approach would have such an effect on Eagle, and I didn't want him to know the prince was in such easy reach.

Both birds appeared to pick up on my intention, waddling away in the direction Gabe had taken. I resisted the urge to turn and check if he could be seen, and my restraint paid off a moment later when Leander stepped into the clearing.

He arrived as if he had just been out on a night time stroll and ended up here by chance. Nothing in his expression suggested he knew that I had spent the evening overturning his study and destroying one of his magic artifacts.

"Ah, Princess," he said. "I wondered if I might find you here. I take it you've realized that you're not entirely free yet?"

So he did know it had been me—or someone on my behalf, at least.

He gave me a snide smile. "I thought it behooved me to come and give you some relevant information before you made a fatal mistake. Because I would hate for something...untoward to happen to you."

I glared at him. "I have no idea what you're talking about."

"Oh, I think you do," he said, all of the casual friendliness in his voice disappearing, replaced by icy steel. "I'm talking about your little excursion this afternoon. No doubt you've been feeling extremely satisfied with yourself, but destroying that bottle merely put in motion a further layer of the enchantment. I had hoped not to need to take such an action, but I'm afraid you brought your fate on yourself."

I tried to keep my face impassive even as dismay filled me.

"You may not be tied to this lake at night anymore," he said, "but you are still bound to it. Pass more than a day's travel away from its shores, and you will quickly sicken and die—along with your feathered friends, who have spent so much time here they have become enmeshed in the enchantment."

He glanced at the swans and several of them honked rudely at him. I reached out to pat their heads and necks, shaken by the news that not only was my life in danger now, but theirs as well. Although Leander must want me alive for something, or he wouldn't have bothered to come and tell me this new stricture.

"How do I know you're telling the truth?" I asked, deciding on boldness. "Maybe there's no new enchantment at all, and you're just hoping to keep me here out of fear."

He didn't flinch—instead a new gleam entered his eyes. "Feel free to test it out. The weakness should overtake you slowly enough that you'll have time to crawl back here to die in a familiar place."

I couldn't prevent the shiver that shook me. One look at his face was enough to convince me not to put his pronouncement to the test—but neither could I meekly accept his words. I drew myself up straight.

"I'll find a way to destroy this part of the enchantment as well, and then I'll leave and never come back. There's always a way to undo such things."

"Naturally," he drawled. "And given the godmothers' foolish penchant for true love, you can no doubt guess what sort of thing is required. But that may be a problem for you, my dear." He grinned fiendishly. "For you to be free, the man you love must publicly declare his devotion to you and promise to marry you— an insuperable barrier from everything I have seen of you."

"What is that supposed to mean?" I asked.

"Why, simply that such a condition requires you to first give your heart to another. And I don't believe you are capable of such a thing. Perhaps on cold nights it will comfort you to remember that you are the cause of your own ongoing misfortune."

He gave a coughing sort of laugh and strolled away as casually as he had appeared. At the edge of the trees, he paused and looked back. "Oh, and you won't find it so easy to gain entrance to my Keep again. I have taken permanent measures against unnecessary bolt holes."

And then he was gone.

I struggled to breathe. At least he didn't seem to suspect Ash. From the sound of that last comment, he thought we had found a way to open the secret passage from the outside. Perhaps the locked door on his study had convinced him of it. But that provided little comfort for me. For several all-too-brief hours I had thought myself completely freed. Then one shackle had reappeared, and now a second. I was almost as bound as before.

Leander had disappeared for a full minute before Gabe emerged, striding quickly toward me, a surprising look of pleasure on his face.

"I suppose you couldn't hear him from over there," I said cautiously.

"Not at all, I caught everything, I think." His smile was still in place.

I frowned at him. "You seem awfully cheerful considering not even a full night has passed, and I'm already doubly cursed again."

"I'm sorry." He grasped both my hands. "Of course I would never want you to be cursed. I'm just enjoying the fact that Leander is so wrong. And when I free you, there's going to be nothing he can do about it."

"What do you mean?" I asked warily, trying to pull my hands free.

He just gripped them more tightly. "Adelaide, you were always the kindest of us as children. And I've seen you at the haven—you've somehow maintained that kindness despite everything. And now I've seen that you're brave and intelligent as well. And you care about my kingdom, even though you weren't born into it. I can't imagine anyone I would trust my people to more willingly—as well as my heart. It would be an honor to declare my love for you. And I will—tomorrow morning in the town square. And I will make any promise you want." His face broke into a cheeky grin. "And no one will dare gainsay it—you are Palinar's only princess, after all."

He smiled as if our families' approval were merely the icing on the cake. And he was right that they would approve of such a match. It was a strange thought after so many years without considering such matters. I could almost feel myself falling into this future he had painted, and only at the last minute did I jerk myself free.

"There is only one problem." This time I successfully pulled my hands free. "You're forgetting part of what he said. This isn't just about your love—it's about mine."

I half expected him to laugh off my comment with some quip about his charm and good looks—as he had been about to do earlier when I scolded him for the presumption behind his kiss. But instead he stepped forward, deadly serious.

"Leander is wrong about you, Adelaide. You have a big heart—the biggest I've ever known. You are more than capable of love. I don't doubt you for a second. The only question is whether you can love *me*."

I opened my mouth to disagree, to reassure him that it wasn't about him. But I couldn't say the words. Because it was him, wasn't it? His recklessness, his foolish insistence on bounding into danger—how could I trust my heart to such a man? But still it hurt to see him in pain, and I couldn't bring myself to say such a thing.

He looked searchingly into my eyes, paling slightly. I don't know how much of the truth he saw there, but it made him turn away.

"Of course." His voice sounded tight. "In that case we must believe Leander is wrong, and there is some other way." He swallowed. "Or someone else."

"There's no one else," I said instead, in a small voice.

He nodded once, but still didn't look at me, leaving us standing awkwardly beside each other. He pulled himself together first, turning to me with a carefully neutral face.

"We should return to the haven for the remaining hours of the night. At least this change to the enchantment leaves you free to do that."

I nodded. It was a significant reprieve even if I gained nothing else. Of course I would prefer to be freed from Leander completely, but I could make a life for myself within a day's travel of my lake. I would always have the haven.

The first part of the walk back was conducted in silence. And I tortured myself wondering what Gabe must be thinking of me. But eventually he cleared his throat and spoke, only a slight tightness in his voice giving any hint at everything that had just passed between us.

"I haven't finished the whole journal. It's rather difficult to wade through as he seems to mostly jot down short notes and thoughts without context. But amid all the railing against the shortsightedness of his father, and his frustrations at his failed experiments, I found several entries of significance. They're the reason I chased you down in the first place, and I'm afraid they're still of relevance now."

I didn't like the sound of that.

"Smashing the bottle only freed you from the lake—briefly, at any rate," he added, no hint of bitterness in his voice although I strained to hear it. "Like I said earlier, the tie to your swans—the one that gives you their language instead of your own—was worked by an entirely different enchantment. And we either missed that godmother object, or he doesn't keep it in his study."

"Oh no," I whispered, horror washing over me. I had been too happy at my swans' greeting to consider the broader implications of my link to them remaining intact.

Gabe nodded. "Yes, unfortunately that means we haven't managed to sever Leander's connection to his beastly army. And while his ramblings and bizarre notes on various experiments are hard to decipher, it's certainly clear that the enchantment on all the animals comes from him—and that he means to use his army to overthrow Talinos."

"We have to send for help," I said. "I don't see any other way. We probably should have done it before now."

Graciously Gabe refrained from pointing out that I had been the one to plead with him not to reveal my location.

"Yes, I think we must," he said. "Although I'm loath to pitch my men against wolves and bears. I fear it will be a massacre on all sides, and no one the winner, given the beasts are no more interested in attacking us than we are in fighting them."

The thought sickened me, but I didn't see any other way. "But Leander must be stopped."

"Yes, Leander must be stopped." Gabe sighed. "And apparently we are not the ones to do it. I'll send a message as soon as it's light."

Perhaps it was to aid in this task, or perhaps he merely wished to be away from me, but he only saw me to the door of the haven, saying he would spend the rest of the night at the inn after all. I didn't protest. How could I? I had turned him down, and there was nothing left to say between us.

CHAPTER 22

I woke Wren and Audrey just before dawn to fill them in on the new developments. I didn't mention Gabe's proposal, but I could see the question reflected in their eyes when I told them of how this new curse could be broken. Even Audrey didn't voice it, however—although I suspected that was due to a swift kick beneath the table from Wren.

"So we're bringing in the cavalry," Wren said quietly. "I must say, I'm relieved."

Audrey didn't look nearly so pleased about it—she shared too much of Gabe's thirst for adventure and glory.

"How long will it take for them to get here?" she asked.

"I'm not sure." I tried to work it out in my head. "I'm sure Gabe will pay someone to take the message express. He should probably have taken it himself, in truth, but—"

"He would never leave," Wren finished for me, and I nodded.

"But will they get here before the party?" Audrey asked.

"I hope so," I said. "There's still the better part of four days." Even with Gabe safely elsewhere, I didn't like the idea of all of Brylee's residents within Leander's walls.

The sun rose then, cutting off our conversation by stealing

my voice, and we busied ourselves over breakfast. Juniper wandered out sleepily, looking for her mother, but latched onto me instead.

"Lady! You're here so early! Come and see what I made." She started dragging me toward her small table, and Wren waved me away from the breakfast preparations with an amused smile.

As I played with Juniper, I attempted to calculate how long it might take Gabe to find and commission a reliable messenger. They would only have to make it to the closest royal way station where they could hand it over to a royal courier. Surely his task would be completed quickly.

But although I looked for Gabe all morning—alternately dreading and longing for his arrival—he didn't appear at the haven until lunch. When he did, he smiled and laughed with everyone as if nothing had happened the night before, whispering to me when he got the opportunity that the messenger was sent. Only once did I catch him looking at me with something deeper in his eyes, a whisper of all that had been said between us. I turned hurriedly away from him, and the moment passed.

I expected to see Ash at some point with fresh rolls, but he hadn't appeared by the time darkness fell. I sat with Wren and Audrey over a leisurely supper, long after everyone else had eaten and been settled for the night. It felt like a luxury, although we ate only bread and butter with a hearty stew.

"Ash didn't come past today," I said. "Is he already busy preparing the cakes for Lord Leander's dance?"

Wren stood abruptly, taking her bowl to the pot for another ladle of stew. Audrey watched her go, a guilty expression on her face.

"Didn't I tell you?" She looked back at me. "I guess we've been distracted. When you weren't in the wagon, I panicked, and I'm afraid Ash ended up discovering what we'd done."

"He was terrified," Wren said shortly, "and rightly so." She rejoined us, pointedly not looking at her sister. "You were still in there—captured, for all we knew—and with every chance Lord Leander would discover how you gained entry."

I shook my head. "We can relieve his mind on that, at least. Leander thinks we got in by the escape passage."

Wren's face relaxed. "Well, that is a relief, at least. In fact, I think I might go to the bakery now to let him know. He has to be up so early to bake the bread, and I daresay he's struggling to sleep with this hanging over him."

I blinked but hadn't formulated an answer before she disappeared out the door, pulling a scarf over her hair and her cloak around her shoulders.

"What in the kingdoms is Ash going to think when Wren turns up at his door in the middle of the night?" I whispered, although there was no one left in the kitchen but Audrey and me. "I thought she was trying not to encourage him."

Audrey gazed toward the doorway where her sister had just disappeared. "I don't think she quite knows what she wants." She sighed. "And in actual fact, it's not just fear that's been bothering Ash." She looked back at me and grimaced. "Telling Ash the truth meant he discovered that Wren had been using him. He was so pleased when she asked to visit, and so proud of her interest in his sample cakes. No doubt he thought she was finally coming around to his courtship. And now he's crushed. She feels terrible."

A pang shot through my heart. I had just rejected someone myself, and it was an utterly uncomfortable feeling. Poor Wren. And I couldn't dismiss my own part in the drama.

"If only there had been another way," I murmured.

Audrey sighed again. "I shouldn't have reacted so openly. He wouldn't have found out the truth and been crushed."

I shook my head. "No. We concealed it from him beforehand out of necessity, not because it was the right thing to do. How would it be better to leave him in ignorance, thinking Wren was finally ready for him to progress his courtship? He's been more than patient with her—giving her as much time as she needs for her grief—but it can't be easy for him."

I frowned. I understood something of grief myself—if not the loss of a husband—and I could understand the years Wren had chosen to spend alone. But she was different now—more peaceful than she had been when she first arrived, and less melancholy.

Juniper loved Ash, and I knew Wren wanted a father for her. And Wren herself always laughed at Ash's jokes and seemed to take his advice with utmost seriousness. And now she had jumped up and run out of here—eager to carry the good news to him so he might sleep more soundly. So why did she still push him away?

I didn't have the chance to ask her until two nights later, when Juniper was tucked soundly in bed and my voice had returned with the darkness. I had spent the day on tenterhooks, hoping for Gabe to appear with news of when the royal guards might arrive, but when he showed up at the haven, he made no mention of them.

Gregor was being particularly querulous, and Gabe had helped me keep him comfortable and entertained—his presence both welcome and trying at the same time. I had no easy way to ask him my questions—although he seemed to anticipate anything else I might need, being there with the cushion or glass I was reaching for whenever I turned around. I spent the whole day waiting for nightfall, only for him to disappear before the light left.

There was no doubt that Gabe had made caring for Gregor a great deal easier, but I couldn't shake the feeling that he was trying to court me—acting as if a threat to the kingdom wasn't lingering on our doorstep. All in all, it had been a tiring day, and I was more than ready to put my feet up and accept a cup of tea.

Audrey had left in high dudgeon at our teasing abuse of her terrible smelling beverage, so only Wren and I remained.

I watched her for a moment as she pottered around, and it was no difficulty to imagine her installed in the bakery, with its spacious apartment on the floor above.

"Did Ash appreciate your visiting him despite the late hour?" I asked, as she joined me at the table.

She nodded. "He was most relieved." She looked down into her cup. "Although I don't think he was entirely glad to see me. I'm just thankful he opened the door at my knock."

"It was dark," I said. "He probably thought something terrible had happened. And I'm sure he wouldn't turn his back if you or Juniper were truly in need—no matter how much it terrified him."

"Oh." Wren looked startled. "I didn't even think that my arrival might scare him. How thoughtless of me!"

"You aren't thoughtless, Wren." I took a deep breath. "And you seem to care for Ash. Have you considered welcoming his suit?" I hesitated. "I think Juniper would love to call him father."

"And leave the haven? Certainly not." Wren cradled her cup in both hands, sipping at her tea, and I had the distinct impression she was hiding behind it. She had said nothing of her feelings —or his.

"You would only be down the street," I said. "You could return each day to teach the children. I'm sure Cora hasn't been expecting you to spend the rest of your life here."

"Certainly not," said Cora in a weary voice. She took a seat across from us and gratefully accepted the cup of tea Wren offered to make.

"If it's not one thing, it's another," she muttered to me, as Wren poured the water. "I've been run off my feet all day. Now if only old Aunt Florinda had left me a giant sack of gold along with this old heap." She sighed. "If the roof makes it through two more winters, I'll count us lucky."

"We'll find a way to get it properly fixed," Wren said from the stove. "You always do find a way, somehow."

I nodded. "Your aunt would be proud if she could see what you've made of your inheritance."

"Old Florinda?" Cora snorted. "Clearly I haven't told you enough stories about my aunt. She would have rather seen every one of these rooms sitting empty and unused. Sometimes I think I only turned this place into a haven to spite her."

Wren and I exchanged wry smiles. Both of us knew Cora too well to believe that.

"I see you two grinning." She chuckled. "It's good to have you back here in the evenings again, Lady. And to hear your voice."

"It's good to be back," I said sincerely. I could at least be grateful for the one aspect of my situation that had changed for the better.

As soon as Wren sat back down with the fresh cup of tea, Cora fixed her with a stern look.

"You've been a great help to me, Wren, I won't try to deny it. But I ran this place long before you arrived—and I'll run it long after you're gone. I've kept my peace and let you run your affairs as you please, but I have to agree with Lady here. It's getting downright ridiculous. Not that I dislike having fresh rolls and cake hand delivered for nothing by our local baker, mind you." She winked at me, and I hid a grin.

"I don't..." Wren looked between us and sighed. "I suppose there's no point trying to deny that I like Ash very well. And he's wonderful with Juniper—she loves him."

"But—?" Cora prompted.

"But I just don't think I can," she whispered.

She looked up, and the raw pain in her eyes took my breath away. I bit the inside of my cheek, unable to think of a response.

"What if something happens to him? What if I lose him too?" Her soft voice was barely audible.

"Then you will continue on—as you've done before," Cora said.

I stared at her, thrown by her brisk response to such open emotion. Her face held sympathy, though, and kindness. She reached across and placed her hand over Wren's.

"I have lost everyone I ever loved—eventually. Only you girls are still here—and I know you'll move on soon enough. You're young, and that's the right and proper way of things. I wouldn't try to hold you back."

I sucked in a breath, but she continued without pausing.

"And just you watch, someone else will come along, needing my love, and perhaps they'll be the right one to stay." She shook her head. "I'm not saying it's easy, and I'm not saying you'll ever forget, but you can't live without love. Juniper needs a mama who's opened her heart to love again. It takes courage, but you're strong enough for it. You know you are because if you're honest with yourself, I think you'll find you already love Ash. You just need to give yourself permission to let someone else hold your heart again. You can't regain what you lost, but you can create a new future for yourself."

I nodded, my eyes focused on Wren, but my friend wouldn't look at either of us. Tears coursed down her cheeks, and she rose shakily to her feet.

"I think I need my bed," she said in a choking voice and fled from the room. I stood to follow her, but Cora gestured for me to sit back down.

"Leave her be," she said. "There are some things we have to process alone."

Reluctantly I sat, wishing there was something I could do to ease my friend's fear and grief. Perhaps when the guards arrived and we found a way to dismantle the rest of Leander's enchantments—freeing the kingdom from his mantle of fear—she would find the courage she needed to say yes to Ash.

"But never mind about Wren," said Cora suddenly. "I don't

know what you were doing sitting there nodding your head. You're worse than her. I can't think when I've ever seen such a bad case of the pot calling the kettle black." A laugh sounded in her voice, but no echoing amusement rose in me.

"What do you mean?" I asked stiffly. "I've never even been in love before."

"Ho! Have you not?" Cora actually chuckled. "Well, be that as it may, I believe the issue in question was having the courage to trust your heart to someone after loss."

I frowned. Her words echoed Leander's, pressing on the raw pain of my rejection of Gabe. Cora talked as if she thought me incapable of love, yet I loved Cora herself—as well as Wren and Audrey and Juniper. I even loved Vilma and Gregor, though they drove me to distraction sometimes. I could love—but that didn't mean I should give my heart away carelessly.

"I don't pretend to know everything," Cora continued. "But I know a little more of your history now than I did, and it only confirms what was obvious from the moment you turned up on my doorstep—you were abandoned by everyone who should have loved you. By choice or through death."

I turned my face away, fighting back tears.

"Something like that leaves scars," she said, her voice soft, "and they're leading you to hold yourself back. I daresay you love all of us here at the haven—but do you trust us? You would give everything you have to help us, I dare say. But what we really want—what a certain tall and handsome prince wants—is for you to let us in. It's hard to have an equal relationship when you're always willing to help us, but you don't trust us enough to let us help you in return."

"I…" My instinctive protest died immediately.

"Precisely," said Cora. "You're like a daughter to me, Lady, and yet you never asked me for help when you were cursed. You never even trusted me with the truth. And then when Audrey found out and reacted like the hotheaded young fool she is, you immediately concluded your fears were founded. Did you ever stop to consider what an insult it was to me to group me in with Audrey?"

I gulped, hot tears filling my eyes. Cora had cared for me when I had nowhere else to go, and she had the largest heart of anyone I had ever known. Her words burned me.

She heaved herself to her feet and placed a gentle hand on the top of my head.

"Oh relax, child. I understand. You're not so much older than Audrey yourself—you're both of you children to me. And you were motivated by love—you didn't want to see harm come to any of us, and I respect that. But it's not your role to protect me. It never has been. I feel I've done enough to earn your trust in the last five years, and I think you should ask yourself—if you can't give it to me, who *could* earn it? If the answer is no one, then you have a problem. So I would suggest, dear heart, that you are not so different from Wren. If you want any hope of love in your future, you must cast off the fear that holds you back."

She patted my head once and departed, leaving me sitting alone. I felt chastened and small, but it only took a moment's reflection to realize she was right. I loved my friends, but I had also held myself back from them. I was willing to care for them, but not to let them close enough that they could hurt me with any betrayal. And what sort of love was that—that held itself back and built up walls, safe and protected? You could argue it was no love at all.

And yet, people betrayed you. They hurt you and turned their back when you needed them most. That also was undeniable, and I didn't know how to reconcile those truths.

CHAPTER 23

I slept poorly, tossing and turning all night, and rose to the buzz of an entire town preparing for an evening of dancing and festivities. Nothing could have been less aligned with my mood.

When Gabe appeared mid-morning I dragged him aside, not willing to spend another day dancing around what I truly wanted to know.

<You haven't heard back, have you?>

Gabe could have read my words four times over in the length of time he stared at the parchment. Finally he looked up and sighed.

"No, I haven't. And I'll admit, I was expecting I would have by now."

<You predicted it, remember? This is the reason Leander has worked his enchantment on the whole kingdom. Who's going to stand up to him? You need to go yourself and rouse them into action. You know you do.>

"I don't want to leave you," he said. "Not here with Leander."

<I can't come with you. Obviously. And you have to go. So you have to leave me, there isn't any other choice. After two

years, I don't think Leander is suddenly going to send wolves after me now.>

Gabe still hesitated, and I could tell he wanted to argue further. But I gave him a stern look, and he deflated. As much as he hated to turn tail and run, he knew I was right. No one but Gabe could hope to bring the royal guards back here. Not with the current, deteriorating state of the kingdom. Those at the capital would do whatever they could, and use any excuse, to avoid such a dangerous course.

Relief filled me at his acquiescence. Gabe would be far out of reach by the time the celebrations commenced. As the night of the party had approached, my tension had increased. Alone, I could not keep Gabe safe. If the royal guards weren't going to arrive in time, then Gabe needed to be far from here. It wasn't an argument I had bothered to put forward, however, since I had known his own safety would weigh little with him. But for his kingdom, he would leave.

At least, having made up his mind, Gabe acted with decision, gathering supplies and departing without hesitation. He had his stallion, Cobalt, with him, and he would move as swiftly as any messenger. There was no chance he would be able to bring the guards back in time for the celebrations that evening, however. Would he bother to send apologies to Leander? The party was supposed to be in his honor, in name at least.

Sure enough, a disturbance swept through town some time after he left. The innkeeper had reported his departure far and wide, and everyone wondered if the festivities were to be canceled. But no such word was received from the Keep, and everyone soon resumed their preparations.

Wren needed extra assistance most of the day since the children were unsettled by all the excitement and resentful they were not to be allowed to go. Naturally, given their irritability, Audrey was nowhere to be found, and I didn't manage to escape until they were all settled in bed after the evening meal.

Juniper had been safely deposited with Cora—only the promise of being allowed to spend the night in Cora's room consoling her to the news that her mother intended to attend the party without her.

"Lord Leander may be a villain," Wren told me, "but the other attendees are all our neighbors. And I want to dance."

I had hopes that this sudden desire to attend was motivated by Ash, so I made no argument against it. It was Gabe who Leander had designs against, and he was safely out of the way. For my own part, however, I had no desire to attend.

But when I returned to my own room, I found Audrey waiting for me on my bed. She bounced to her feet at my arrival.

"There you are! I've been waiting forever."

"And why is that exactly?" I asked warily.

"Because I brought you a dress," she said, her eyes alight with restless energy.

"I'm not going to the party, Audrey."

She put her hands on her hips. "Don't be ridiculous. Of course we're going to go. There's still another godmother object somewhere in that stone heap that is keeping both your swans and your voice captive. And if we don't find and destroy it before Gabe's guards arrive, who knows how many men and animals will die? And what better opportunity could we get to make it past the gate?"

I frowned. "Leander will know we're there."

"Will he?" she asked with a troublesome grin.

"What do you mean?" I asked warily, concerned that this time I was to be stuffed in the back of a wagon in a ballgown.

She lifted something from the bed and held it out toward me.

"A mask?" I examined the complicated concoction of green feathers and ribbon. "Won't that be a little suspicious?"

"Not in the least," she said. "I've spent the last two days sowing the seeds around town, and I've convinced everyone it's a masked ball. You should see some of the costumes the townsfolk have managed to cobble together."

"Audrey!" I gasped.

"What?" She shrugged. "It's genius. No one will know who we are, least of all Lord Leander."

"I don't know..." I said.

"Just take a look at the dress I got for you, at least," she pleaded.

Reluctantly I nodded, her enthusiasm making me nervous for my willpower. It had been a long time since I had been given the opportunity to wear a beautiful dress, and if she was that certain of the gown, then it must be—

I gasped. The dress she held up was the softest of creams, feathering lace creating a bodice that flowed into soft, full layers of tulle. It was a dress for the height of summer—or a crowded ballroom—but it was still spring, and the nights were cool. I wouldn't be cold, however, since it came with an elegant, full-length wrap that completed the ensemble with feathers and the faint suggestion of...

"Wings," I gasped. "It looks like swans' wings. Wherever did you get such a thing?"

"The seamstress's daughter-in-law keeps swans." She gave me a satisfied smile. "And as soon as I saw it, I knew you had to have it. And look at this."

She held out a second mask, this one made from a cream material and covered in swans' feathers which swept elegantly up from above the right eyehole.

"You have to wear it," she assured me gravely. "You just have to."

"Fine," I said, and then tried to tell myself I had been convinced by her initial arguments and not the gown. Because she was right. If we could find and destroy the remaining object tonight, we might save a lot of bloodshed.

"I have this for you, too," she said, holding out a small cream bag. "A few essentials for the night, such as needle and thread."

I laughed. "Anyone would think we were young ladies preparing for a ball."

"Aren't we?" She grinned and slipped over to the door. "I have a dress to match that second mask that I need to put on. And I think we should arrive separately, to make us harder to recognize. There's a constant stream of carts and wagons heading that direction, so just hail the first one with space and hop on board. I'll meet you to the left of the main Keep doors."

She was gone before I could protest or ask questions, so I turned my attention to the dress. It fit beautifully, soft against my skin. Impossibly, I began to feel an echo of the townsfolk's excitement for the event. It had been a long time since I wore something so beautiful.

I pulled my hair up myself, keeping the style simple and letting the natural waves show. All too soon, I was ready, but as I moved toward the entryway, a memory returned to me. I had promised Vilma that I would visit her in my dress. And it turned out that here I was, in a beautiful gown, on my way to the dance, after all.

I changed course and headed for the far wing. The sitting room used by the elderly residents appeared deserted at first, until my eyes picked out a small woman in a large chair.

"Oh, Lady," Vilma sighed. "You look even more beautiful than I imagined."

I blushed. "It's an incredible dress."

"And an equally incredible girl," she assured me, coming over to admire me more closely. She glanced up into my eyes. "It's nice to hear your voice again."

The smile I gave her trembled. She had asked no questions when I stopped speaking, and she asked no questions now. All of the residents of the haven had treated me with remarkable forbearance, and I had repaid them by withholding my trust.

"You've been married for so many years," I blurted out. "And Gregor has cared for you all that time—and you for him. How did you know at the beginning that you could trust each other?"

Vilma blinked. "That's a big question." She glanced around her. "Here, come, sit down." She led me over to an armchair, and I perched on it carefully. "Have a drink." She held out a glass of water, and I accepted it, although I wasn't thirsty.

Once she was sitting as well, she took a moment to ponder my question.

"I suppose we knew because we grew up together," she said. "We had seen enough of each other to know how we acted in all different situations. Neither of us has ever left this town, you know. Gregor was born only four houses down from mine." She smiled fondly at the memory before looking over at me again, her brow creased.

"But it's an uncertain world, and we are none of us perfect. So what choice do we have but to love and trust regardless? It would be a lonely life if we did not."

"But you chose well," I said, softly. "Gregor never betrayed you."

I had not chosen my brother, but I had grown up beside him, and I had believed earnestly in his love. Sometimes I wondered if it was my own blindness that scared me more than his betrayal.

"Actually, he did," Vilma said.

"What?" I stared at her. "But the two of you…"

"Oh, this is many years ago now," she said. "I had almost forgotten it. The children needed new shoes, and so I had taken in some laundry work—something I didn't usually do." She shook her head. "I worked so hard for those coins, and I entrusted them to Gregor to purchase the shoes from the cobbler. But he ran into an old friend, just passing through town, who invited him to the tavern for a drink. One thing led to another, and they ended up in a game of chance. Gregor came home without the coins or the shoes."

She shook her head. "For weeks afterward, when I saw our poor children with their cold feet, I thought I would never forgive him."

"But you did," I said. "How?"

"By remembering my own mistakes," she said. "And the times he forgave me for them. As I said, we are none of us perfect."

"But even if you chose to forgive, how could you trust him after that?" I asked.

"Oh I didn't, at first. Not with the coin, anyway," she said, perfectly cheerfully. "But he was so repentant. He was determined to win my trust back, and for years he refused to set foot in the tavern at all, although before he used to enjoy an occasional drink there with friends. And he insisted that I take charge of any spare coin we had—although it wasn't often we had spare coin in those days. How could I hold onto his mistake in the face of all that?"

She sighed, looking around at the empty room. "There's reason enough in a place like this to think only of those not worthy of our trust—and they exist, of course. If Gregor had not been repentant, if he had made no effort to win back my trust, I don't know what I would have done. But if you choose someone who is able to admit when they're wrong, and change when change is needed, then you can weather any obstacles together."

She reached forward and patted my knee. "We all have a choice, Lady, when it comes to those we love. We can be forever holding onto the bad—because there will always be bad—or we can choose to see the good. First, choose yourself a man with a good heart, and then choose every day to see the good in him."

Was it that easy? Could you just choose to trust someone, even though it might hurt one day?

"But I don't know why you're here nattering to me," Vilma said with sudden briskness. "You're wearing a beautiful dress, and a dance awaits. And also, I'm guessing, a certain handsome prince." She winked at me. "If I were just ten years younger, I'd be

217

hobbling up that forest road by your side. I always loved a dance."
A dreamy look filled her eyes.

I chuckled. "I bet you would, too. And fight a dragon, as well,
if it came to it." Vilma had always had more fire than the other
residents.

"Of course I would, dearie, if I needed to," said Vilma, as
calmly as if I'd suggested that she might water some daisies.

I remembered the water in my hands and put it down carefully on a small table.

"I'll dance an extra dance for you, Vilma," I promised.

"Make sure that you do, my dear," she replied.

CHAPTER 24

*V*ilma's words circled in my head as I hitched a ride on a hay-filled wagon beside merry townsfolk who didn't seem to recognize me, just as Audrey had predicted. But I forgot my troubled thoughts for a moment when we arrived at our destination.

The courtyard had been transformed since the last time I saw it, turned into a vast ballroom, open to the sky. Spring flowers twined everywhere, and a small orchestra played on a raised stage. Long tables laden with food—Ash's cakes displayed proudly—stood to one side, surrounded by a crowd.

Many of the inhabitants of Brylee had been less strict than Cora, and children darted everywhere while couples danced in the center of the space, dresses twirling as masked faces flew past me. It combined the best of both a ball and a village dance, and my feet twitched, wanting to dance to the lively music.

The group around me dispersed, and I moved deeper into the throng, not wanting to draw attention to myself. I immediately began to look around for Audrey's green mask, but with so many people—most of them moving—it was hard to see far. Eventually I gave up, heading straight for the Keep's doors instead as she had instructed. Thank goodness for her foresight in setting a meeting place.

I passed the food table on the way and stopped briefly for a slice of cake. Out of loyalty to Ash, naturally. Or that was the excuse I was preparing for Audrey if she saw me with it. But when I reached the door, she wasn't there.

I waited for some time, watching the dancers swing past and listening to the music mixed with the laughter of the children. But I recognized a flash of hair—less distinctive than Audrey's flaming locks, but still recognizable to me as Wren. I dove into the crowd, chasing after her, in case she knew what had become of Audrey.

When I caught up with her, however, I hesitated. She had already abandoned her mask, which now dangled over one wrist, and she was wrapped in someone's arms as he guided her through the dance. They spun in my direction, and I recognized Ash.

I was just debating interrupting them, when he leaned in to whisper something in her ear. She blushed, the color faintly visible from the many lanterns and torches that lit the courtyard, and allowed him to lead her out of the dance to a slightly more secluded spot where a bench waited, twined round with vines.

He settled her gently onto it and then sat beside her, both of them murmuring, heads close together. I had just decided it wasn't a moment I could interrupt when he took her into his arms and pressed a gentle kiss against her lips.

I swung around, my own cheeks flushing at having been watching them. But the color quickly faded, the warmth moving to my heart. She had done it then. She had overcome her fear—or taken the first step in doing so.

For the first time since I had arrived, I wished desperately that someone would take my hand and sweep me into the dance. And if I was honest with myself, there was only one person I wanted to perform such a service. Which was foolishness on my part—he was probably most of the way to the capital by now.

The masks were distracting, though, hiding identities and causing my heart to jump every time I caught a glimpse of a tall man with brown hair. Cora had laughed at me when I claimed never to have been in love, and I admitted to myself that she was right. I even admitted to myself that I had always admired Prince Gabriel of Talinos—even as a young girl. I had simply been too proud to admit it—not when all the other young princesses were in love with him too.

I stopped abruptly, the thought catching at me. What foolishness it had been, to lie even to myself. Our father had been the one to teach us to be proud, and he had directed far more of his energy on my brother than on me. If I could forgive such pride in myself, perhaps I could forgive the twisted pride that had wrought such destruction on Dominic after our land was cursed. Gabe said that he had changed...perhaps I needed to give him a chance like Vilma said.

I nodded to myself. If this curse was ever broken, I would agree to travel to Palinar once more to see my brother and meet his bride. And, as for myself, it was time to change. No more turning my back on the truth. I was in love with Gabe, and I wished desperately that he was here to ask me to dance.

"Will you dance, Addie?" a familiar, deep voice asked, a tall figure appearing in front of me.

My heart stopped and then took off, not stopping to ask how he could possibly be here. And for once, I let myself follow it.

"Yes." I placed my hand into his waiting one. "I was just wishing you would ask me."

His broad smile was reward enough as his fingers closed over mine. He pulled me in among the dancers. A moment later he had one arm firmly around my waist, grasping me close as he navigated our way across the makeshift dance floor.

"You look beautiful, my swan," he murmured in my ear. "More beautiful than I could have imagined."

"The costume is incredible, isn't it?" I could feel my cheeks warming at his compliment.

"I knew it must be you as soon as I spied it," he said. "But I wasn't talking about the gown or the mask."

"The wrap, then?" I asked cheekily, and he laughed, the warm sound enveloping me.

"Yes," he said gravely. "I was most certainly talking about the wrap." But the sparkle in his eyes told me otherwise.

"But what are you doing here?" I asked, my mind finally reasserting control. "Don't tell me you met the guards already on their way here?"

His arm tightened slightly around me. "No, I'm afraid not. But I was chased down by a messenger who said I had to come back, that you were in danger."

"Me?" I stumbled, missing one of the steps. "Who would send such a message? I'm not in any particular danger. You're the one in danger! And now you've ridden right into the heart of it to save me—when I didn't need saving."

I could feel my voice rising, and I pulled away from him, moving to the edge of the dance floor to stand partially obscured behind an enormous potted tree. Gabe followed me.

"I won't apologize for coming back," he said. "I couldn't ride away and leave you in danger."

I turned to him, ready to explain that I didn't need saving, but the words died on my lips. He had come back for me. Knowing the danger to himself, he had turned around without second thought for me.

All this time I had accused him in my mind of being daring and foolhardy, and I had closed my eyes to his bravery and self-lessness. My mind whirled back over every interaction, remembering how I had spun everything in a negative light, just as Vilma had said. And even when he had not met my expectations

—pausing when I had expected him to rush in—I had refused to see anything but the danger I had already decided was there.

It was true that he could be reckless. But, like all qualities, his daring nature had positive sides as well as negatives. And he had matured since we were children—calling for help or sending scouts when such things were needed. I remembered a time when he would never have thought of such a thing. And I remembered my recent revelation about myself. Did I want him to remember only that I had once been proud? Or did I want him to see me as I was now—as he already did?

"I'm sorry, Gabe," I said. "I haven't been fair to you."

He frowned, taking one of my hands. "What do you mean?"

"And worst of all," I added, "I haven't been honest with myself. I said you could never free me from this new curse because I didn't love you, but…"

I swallowed. The words were hard to say.

"It's not true," I said at last, looking up at him. "I do love you."

And just like that, a lightness filled me. Already I couldn't remember why the words had been so hard to say.

"I love you, Gabe. I love you."

He laughed, picking me up and twirling me around and around.

"It seems I should ride away more often," he said when he at last set me on my feet again. "I love you, too, Adelaide."

And then his lips were on mine with the fire his last kiss had lacked. I threw aside all thought of propriety and twined my arms around his neck, kissing him back. My fingers caught on the soft curls of his hair as he deepened the kiss before pulling back with a sigh.

"As soon as this set of dances ends, I'll take the stage from the orchestra," he promised. "I'll pledge my love and our betrothal and free you from this new curse. Then I'm getting you safely out of here. When the royal guards dismantle this place stone by stone, we'll find the object that will give you back your voice."

I blushed and agreed. It was an easy thing to do since his desire to get me away would see him safely removed from the celebration as well. And for the rest of the song we engaged in the delicious process of reliving various moments of our time together and explaining our true feelings on each occasion. Gabe, in his good nature, merely laughed at all the times I had denied my feelings for him and thought only the worst.

"Oh, but I must find Audrey," I said when the music paused between songs. "She's probably been waiting for me all this time."

I had completely forgotten both my friend and my true purpose in coming, and guilt flooded me. I would find her, and then we would make our case to Gabe. Before I left, Audrey and I had a task to accomplish, so he would need to leave the party alone. We couldn't afford to wait for his guards to find that object —too many of them would die in the process.

"She said to wait for her here," I said, pulling away from him and heading toward the Keep's doors.

I had to push through a particularly dense knot of people, leaving Gabe to trail behind me. As I pressed past them, I heard snatches of conversation.

"What a party," I heard a young man say, and a young girl answered, "I'm so glad Lord Leander decided to make it a masked ball."

I shook my head as I kept going through the revelers—Audrey had done a good job of fooling everyone, apparently. Had she claimed the directive came from Leander himself? She was bold enough for it.

But when I finally slipped free, right by the Keep's wall, there was still no Audrey to be seen. I scanned the crowd. Where could she be? Worry began to tug at me, and I turned to ask Gabe if he could see her with his extra height, but he had disappeared in the crowd.

I stood on tiptoes, straining to see over heads in my efforts to find either of them. No more than a few seconds had passed, however, when someone gripped me from behind around the waist.

"Oh, there you are!" I twisted to look up at Gabe.

I blinked once in confusion and screamed, but the sound was muffled by a hand. The arms encircling me belonged to Leander, not Gabe, and they dragged me backward into the Keep.

CHAPTER 25

I struggled, kicking backward against his legs and attempting to prize his arm off me. I had nearly wrenched myself free when he suddenly let go. I staggered and hadn't regained my balance when new arms restrained me, this time pinning my arms against my side and lifting my feet from the ground altogether. I renewed my struggles, even stretching down to try to bite his arm.

"Tut tut," Leander said. "You shouldn't be so rude. I believe you've met Brock here before—out by one of my lakes."

I stilled instantly.

"That's better," Leander said in an oily voice that slithered across my skin.

We stood inside a large entranceway I hadn't seen before, and my darting eyes could pick up no sign of whatever killer animal Brock controlled. I didn't resume my struggles, though. There seemed little hope of breaking free of his grip, and I preferred to save my energy for a more hopeful endeavor.

Brock said nothing, carrying me up the stairs as if I weighed no more than the feathers that adorned me. What would Gabe think when he realized I had disappeared? Would he come charging into the Keep? Was that Leander's plan?

My stomach churned, and I had to fight to keep it in its place. I was bait to lure the man I loved to his death.

We climbed upward. The main, carpeted staircase of the Keep had a much more gentle curve than the servant's stairs or the escape passage. It still seemed as if we climbed forever, though, and I marveled at Brock's ability to carry me such a distance.

We hadn't quite reached the top when Leander turned onto a generous landing and opened a door. He ushered Brock inside, and the man dumped me on the ground near a window.

As soon as he stepped back, I leaped forward, launching myself at Leander. Brock blocked me with an arm, knocking me to the ground.

"Now, now." Leander frowned at me. "None of that, please. You can't really think you'll be able to hurt me with my good friend around, do you?"

I put all my hatred into my glare, but he merely chuckled. When he gestured, Brock stepped back and took up a post next to the now closed door, but I could feel his eyes boring into me.

Slowly, I rose to my feet, taking stock of my surroundings. I stood inside a smaller version of the guest suite we had stumbled into on the top level—this one a single room. The canopy on the bed looked faded and worn, and the air of the room suggested no one had been here for a while. The curtains confirmed the impression—hanging askew from multiple places where the material had slipped free from the large bronze curtain rings.

"I chose it for the view," Leander said idly, as if we had been discussing the room.

I fought with myself for a moment but couldn't resist stepping over to pull the curtains aside, revealing a full-length window. It opened onto a small stone balcony which blocked the view some-what, but to one side, a sliver of the lake could be seen as a dim patch of darkness, and on the other side I could still see most of the Keep's courtyard.

In ordinary circumstances, I would have enjoyed the sight of the celebrations spread below me—the lanterns globes of light, and the greenery and flowers softening the tables and chairs and lending everything a magical feel. Dancers swirled in an unfamiliar local dance, oblivious to my abduction.

"What do you want, Leander?" I snapped, pretending I didn't already know.

"What I have always wanted," he replied. "To prove that we make our own destiny. To prove that I was meant for more than the minor title I was born into." He shook his head. "My father was disgusted with my research and experiments, you know. But then he was also content to be an insignificant lord in a forgotten stretch of the kingdom—wasting what resources we had on undeserving rabble. I am a patient man, and I planted the seeds for this moment many years ago, knowing that eventually my efforts would be rewarded. And how right I have been. Soon I will have the throne, and when I hold all of Talinos in my hands, he will see how wrong he was."

"Isn't he dead?" I asked, cutting off his diatribe. "I mean, he must be if you inherited the Keep and the title."

"Of course he's dead," Leander snapped, looking thrown off for the first time. "I had to make sure of that when he would have thrown away everything I was working toward."

A chill ran through me.

"When your family got themselves cursed, the fool thought we should go rushing off and confront whatever evil had taken hold in Palinar. He would have gotten himself killed soon enough, if I hadn't done the task for him. My seeds needed time to grow—and sure enough they blossomed soon after, providing just the solution that was needed. It's taken me five years to effectively propagate caution throughout the whole kingdom, but you could say I was doing everyone a favor. No one will be heedlessly rushing to throw themselves into harm's way now."

The sickening smile that accompanied his words made it clear that protecting the people had nothing to do with his real motivations.

"Brock over there doesn't look meek and mild to me," I muttered. "I suppose you don't care if he comes into harm's way."

Leander laughed, and if I'd hoped to discomfort Brock, those hopes were thoroughly dashed. He gave no sign he had even heard me.

"I assure you, Brock can look after himself," Leander said. "As can all of my mercenaries. And if they can't, well, they have some furry friends to help them."

His smile showed all his teeth, and I had to suppress a shiver. But he was giving me information, whether he had intended to or not, and I needed to use it to my advantage. As I strained to think of a way to subtly ask him how he had enchanted the entire kingdom, he frowned.

"But really, there is no need for all this talk," he said, and my heart sank. Apparently Leander had come to the same realization. "I have gone to a great deal of trouble to orchestrate this fine moment, and I would hate for you to miss it." He gestured again to the window, but I refused to look.

"What are you talking about?" I asked coldly.

"Why, your young princely friend, of course," he said. "Playing right into my hands."

"Gabe won't come running in here after me, if that's what you're expecting," I said. "He's too smart for that." It took every shred of trust I had to hold onto the hope that was true.

"Oh, I should hope not," he said. "But I'm sure he'll do just what he's supposed to."

"What do you mean?" I asked, my stomach swirling as a sick feeling rose up my throat.

Leander chuckled. "You must judge me a fool, Princess. Did you really think I would tell you the truth of your enchantment—especially with a young prince hanging around?" He regarded me with amusement. "Oh, don't look surprised. Surely you didn't think I would fail to notice the way the two of you have been sneaking around the forest—even into my own inner sanctum."

Anger crossed his face before it was smoothed away with a smile. "I told you exactly what I wanted the two of you to hear—and yes, I did know you were both there."

So he had known Gabe was hiding in the forest while he told me of the new curse. What else did he know?

"You mean the curse can't be broken by a declaration of love?" I was proud of how steady my voice sounded when inside, everything shook.

"That part is true enough," he said. "These sorts of enchantments are delicate matters, and it isn't always safe to tell outright falsehoods where they are concerned. However, an omission, on the other hand..."

He let his voice trail off, clearly wanting me to exclaim and inquire as to his meaning. I refused to give him the satisfaction, and after a moment he continued anyway.

"If your true love stood before everyone and proclaimed his love and his promise of fidelity, you would be freed. But I left out a rather important point. If that same true love declares his love for another, you will die."

I pulled in a long breath, my churning insides slowly calming. I had come too far to give way at such an early test. I could trust Gabe with my life as I had already trusted him with my heart.

"I don't know what you think is going to happen, but Gabe would never do such a thing," I said.

"Ah, but did I not promise you a show?" Leander pointed once more to the window.

This time I didn't even try to resist, looking down quickly at the party. It took me a moment of searching, but I managed to locate Gabe, standing not far from the base of the Keep, half way between the tree where we had kissed and the door. The crowd that had blocked my way earlier had dispersed, somewhat, and he was looking all around, clearly searching for me.

I frowned across at Leander, but his eyes were trained on the scene below with a self-satisfied smirk, so I looked reluctantly back down. My eyes picked out Gabe again, just in time for a change to come over his demeanor. He reached out both arms, and someone hurried toward him, placing two hands into his.

I blinked and then blinked again, pressing myself up against the glass with both hands flat as I tried to understand what I was seeing. I was up here—watching the party from above—that much was unassailable. But somehow I was also down there. The same cream dress, the same winged wrap and swan mask. I could just make out the soft brown waves of hair, pulled loosely back in a simple arrangement.

"I...I don't understand," I stammered.

"Do you not?" Leander kept his own gaze locked on the scene below. "Personally, I have always found my servants to be perfectly amenable to my requests. You know, I wouldn't have been able to arrange any of this if you hadn't so helpfully sent your good friend into my Keep. But she has been so very helpful. She sent a message to recall the young prince when he nearly escaped. She convinced you to come. And she passed on the dress I provided—the one I had instructed to be made in duplicate. Gabe is not fool enough that he would think she was you if he had not already held you, and talked to you, and kissed you while wearing that ensemble."

Leander continued to watch the people below while Gabe led the now-brunette Audrey through the crowd.

"It's hard to tell up here, but it's noisy down there. Noisy and crowded and dark. And one of the interesting things about having a distinctive physical feature—like your friend's red hair —is that you become surprisingly hard to recognize without it."

"Audrey would never agree to help you," I said, clinging to the hope that this was all part of some plan of hers.

"No," he said. "I don't think she would have...which is very interesting. None of my other servants are so defiant. I think I will have to study her, when this is all over. But everyone can be persuaded one way or another."

"What did you do to her?" I asked, horror in my voice.

"Why, nothing." He sounded surprised. "Your friend is unharmed—as you can see for yourself."

I frowned back down, but it was too far to notice any specifics of her features.

"You know, you're a gift to me, Princess," he said. "When your kingdom was first cursed, I was a little...distracted."

I fisted my hands into my skirts, fighting down my repulsion over his casual mention of what he had done to his father.

"I didn't recognize who you were immediately," he said. "I didn't notice you at all, in fact. And then my seeds bore fruit, and I was rather occupied ensuring the entire kingdom got to taste my fearsome harvest."

He smiled, clearly pleased with his word choice, and my stomach turned.

"By the time I had leisure to look around, it seemed fairly clear you weren't a threat. And then I received word about the unexpected new arrivals from the Old Kingdoms." His face twitched.

"You knew of the Old Kingdoms?" I asked. "I thought few even remembered them before the way was reopened. Surely you do not follow the ways of the High King and his godmothers?" The persistent question of my godmother's intentions wormed its way back into my mind.

"Ha! I should have known you would be one to believe in such fairy stories." Disgust twisted his features. "You mark my words, there is no High King—just a bunch of women with too much power, using it to shape our world as they see fit. But if we're careful and cunning, we can take that power and turn it back against them. And then we may shape the world as *we* see fit."

"I don't wish to live in any world of your shaping," I said.

"How fortunate," he said calmly, "since in a few hours you will be dead."

I followed his gaze to where Gabe had nearly made it through the crowd to the stage, Audrey trailing behind him, holding onto one of his hands.

"But don't worry," Leander continued. "I won't leave you alone to die. I've become quite fond of you in the two years you've been in my keeping." He shook his head. "It is strange the whims of affection."

"I was never in your keeping," I spat, glaring at him. How dare he suggest he had any affection for me?

"Oh, but certainly you were," he said. "Not at first, of course. The disappearance of Palinar removed our kingdom's most valuable ally, and I was busy exploiting that weakness. It took time to properly set my plan into motion. But then news came of unexpected happenings at your brother's Tourney. I have studied broadly, you know—much to my father's disgust at what he called a waste of my time. I knew that the return of the Old Kingdoms would herald a return of the godmothers as well. And from there it was likely only a matter of time until Palinar returned to full power. Suddenly, I realized how fortuitous it was that I should have you on my doorstep. As long as I could keep you here, I would have a tool at my disposal if ever I should need to... dissuade your brother from involving himself in Talinosian concerns."

I was only half listening to him talk of his apparent brilliance, my eyes glued to Gabe, waiting for the moment when he realized it wasn't me holding his hand.

"Of course, the initial enchantment I used to bind you to the lake didn't work quite as thoroughly as I had hoped," Leander continued. "Which you no doubt noticed. But I am a meticulous man, and my plans are carefully laid. I had a backup enchantment with me, and I daresay you were still stumbling through the forest when I released it. I had to be sure you were fully ensnared."

He shook his head. "That one didn't work exactly as I intended, either, but my brilliance soon saw the broader applications. Turning you into a swan would have trapped you at the lake, certainly, but connecting a person with a group of wild animals? Now that is truly useful. Once again, you had assisted me with your mere presence. It has taken me two years, but I have nearly built my army to the necessary size. And then you attacked my study."

His eyes narrowed. "No doubt you thought you had struck a blow against me, and I confess to being angry for a moment. But you had not invested the years upon years into studying these objects that I have done, and your efforts were in vain. I will admit, I had hoped not to have to release this second part of the enchantment that now binds you. But really, it's all for the best. I could have killed the prince at this party, as I originally intended, but I can kill him later just as easily. No, my brilliant mind has found a far more useful role for him."

"And what is that?" I asked, the words falling reluctantly from my lips.

He turned to beam at me. "Why, for him to betray—and, thereby, kill—you. I hear King Dominic is tearing Palinar apart looking for you. Do you think he will rush to Prince Gabriel's rescue after he discovers what the prince has done to you?"

Leander adopted a false expression of grief. "What kind of heartless man would woo a young girl without family or friends, make her love him, and then promise himself to another in front of everyone—leaving the girl to die alone?"

"My brother would never..." My words trailed off.

But would he? What did I know of him now?

"Oh, I think he would," Leander said. "He may even join me in overthrowing Gabriel's family after this. And will the other kingdoms blame him when they see the disaster that Talinos has become?"

CHAPTER 26

*L*eander had claimed he intended to remain by my side, but a servant came looking for him, knocking tentatively at the door and ignoring my cries for help as he relayed a message to Brock.

"I'm afraid I shall have to leave you, after all," Leander said when he heard it. "It seems my people call for me."

"Good riddance," I snapped, not turning to look at him.

Leander merely chuckled, leaving me at the window. The door opened and closed, and I waited a moment before turning to check that Brock had departed as well. As soon as I saw I was alone, I raced to the door and tried to pull it open. It wouldn't budge.

The solid timber stood up to every assault I tried, and I quickly gave up and returned—drawn irresistibly—to watch the scene unfolding below. The dancing had stopped, and Gabe was speaking to one of the musicians. Audrey hung behind him, her face slightly averted.

I sank to my knees and covered my face. I couldn't watch. Even if I could break the door down, I would never get down all those stairs and out there in time to stop what was about to happen.

And yet, I couldn't sit here and do nothing, either. My mind flew from one hopeless thought to another, desperately grasping for something that might save me. But it would need the impossible.

I froze. The impossible. That was the province of the godmothers. And I had one of those—she was the one who had precipitated me into this predicament by placing me in Brylee to start with.

"Godmother!" I cried. "Godmother, where are you? I need you!"

I had never tried to call on her before, and I didn't have much hope of it working now—so I almost toppled over in shock when a voice spoke behind me.

"These abandoned rooms always have a smell, don't they? No matter how regularly they're cleaned."

A short woman with steely gray hair and bright eyes surveyed the room from her perch on the bed. She might have been a guest at the Keep—someone's grandmother, even—if not for the wings.

"Excuse me?"

For a moment shock drove every coherent thought from my head. She had actually come.

And then my desperate need reasserted itself, and I glanced frantically back out the window. Gabe was on the stage now, coaxing Audrey up to join him.

"I need help—"

"Again?" The godmother regarded me with a mildly surprised air. "I put you right where you needed to be, you know."

I fought down a surge of bitterness. "I trusted you five years ago. And yet you placed me in the middle of danger. I've been cursed for two years…and now I'm going to die."

I glanced out the window. It was too late. Gabe was already speaking to the crowd.

"Oh, my dear." The godmother rose and crossed to place a gentle hand on my head.

Her scent enveloped me, a smell I couldn't quite place but that filled me with a peace I hadn't expected. My pulse slowed, and my breathing calmed. Even my aching heart throbbed a little less. I would die calmly, at least.

I looked up at her.

"I can promise you that we are always working for good," she said. "I placed you in the haven because I knew it was a place where a friendless thirteen-year-old would be safe and sheltered. But there were other such places. I chose that one because the plans I serve are bigger than you can see, and you are not the only person in the kingdoms."

The weight of her hand disappeared, and I looked up, intending to question her further, only to find myself alone. I looked back down as the whole crowd burst into applause. Their clapping hands looked like an undulating wave from this distance.

I had called on my godmother, and she had come. But it had changed nothing. I was alone, and I would die.

But the calm that she had brought with her had wormed its way down, taking root inside me as it changed into something else—determination. She had been cryptic, in the way godmothers were said to be, but I had understood her.

She had placed me in the haven because five years ago Leander had already killed his own father and was on his way to introducing a great evil to this kingdom. She had placed me here so that I might grow old enough to do something about it. And, so far, I had done nothing but free myself from the lake.

But it was not too late. I was not dead yet, and I was here, in the heart of Leander's Keep. Earlier, at the lake, he had said the curse would make me sicken and die. And that meant I had time. Even as I weakened, I would keep searching. Audrey had used our search for the remaining object to lure me here, but she had not been wrong. If I could find and destroy it, it would change everything.

As I pushed myself to my feet, I felt the change. I swayed slightly, my knees nearly buckling beneath me. There was no pain, just a bone-deep weariness that begged me to crawl onto the waiting bed and close my eyes for a moment. But I turned my face away. If I lay down, I would not get back up.

Grief tugged at my mind—for my own future, now gone, but also for Gabe and the horror he would feel when he realized the truth. It made my heart break to have to leave him like this. And Audrey. The thought of my friend almost made me double over. Leander had no doubt hoped her betrayal would be a double blow, a death to my spirit as his curse was death to my body.

But now, when the moment came, I knew Cora had been right. Enough years had passed for my friends to earn my trust, and for all Audrey's impetuosity, only the direst circumstances would have forced her to act in such a manner. I would not allow her mistakes to cloud my eyes to her loyalty and love. Just as none of them had rejected me for the mistake that had sent Audrey straight into Leander's arms.

And the more I considered it, the clearer it became that she was working with him unwillingly. She had done as Leander commanded in the areas he had named—influencing Gabe and me to be here and now taking my place. But she had not betrayed our various plans to him. He might have worked out our presence at the lake and in his study—but he had not been waiting for us in either place, nor had he prevented our freeing me from the first enchantment.

A fresh wave of grief filled me. How she must have hoped that we would find a way to defeat him before today came. And how much it must have hurt her to be forced into such a position. I hoped I would have the chance to see her before I died, to tell her that I understood and didn't hold it against her.

I made no move toward the door, already knowing I would

239

have little success with it, and instead examined the rest of the room. No other doors lurked anywhere, and I could see no possible exits. Next I examined the window itself, looking at it instead of through it this time. It opened easily which gave me a moment of hope, but when I stepped out onto the balcony, I could immediately see that there was no way either up or down from this vantage. I had no desire to hasten my death by falling to the ground below.

I refused to give up hope, but I was rapidly running out of ideas. I tried waving and screaming to the distant figures below, but it did nothing except release some of my pent up emotion. And soon I ran out of energy for it, my arms impossibly heavy to lift. I stopped and rested my cheek against the cool, smooth surface of the glass.

A flash of white caught my eye, followed by another and another. I straightened, peering out into the night. A wedge of swans flew into view. My swans.

I resumed waving and calling, and they wheeled toward me, honking and bugling as they came. One by one they glided in to land on the balcony, surrounding me. I sank to my knees and pressed my face against their feathers, tears running unheeded down my cheeks. They had sensed I was in trouble, and they had come. If only they were big enough that I could climb onto one of their backs and soar away.

A wild thought caught me. I ran back into the room, rushing to the bed and stripping off the top sheet. Bundling it in my arms, I rushed back to the window, nearly tripping twice, my weak arms struggling with my burden.

For all I knew I was courting disaster, but my swans had proven themselves so much more capable than they had any natural right to be, and I chose to believe that they could manage this too. I had to try something.

With a single yank, I brought the curtain down, rod and all, almost collapsing in the process. Removing four of the large rings proved simple, and I quickly tied a corner of the sheet to each one.

Dragging my creation behind me, I returned to the balcony where my swans waited. Sammy was the steadiest and most reliable of my friends, so I approached her first, wishing for daylight and the ability to speak in their language.

But when I held out the ring, she seemed to understand anyway, allowing me to slip it over her head and down to the strong base of her neck. The others all pressed in around me, and I had to shepherd them back, keeping only Snowy, Sunny, and Shadow herself beside me. Soon they were all attached to a corner of the sheet.

The remaining three hopped up to the edge of the balcony, dropping out of sight before soaring back up above us. My chosen four also hopped up, ready for their own departure. But they paused before throwing themselves off, looking at me. I couldn't hesitate, that would only give my body time to deteriorate further—and my mind time to think better of the dangerous plan.

Climbing up among the swans, I perched on the edge of the balustrade, cupping myself in the sheet. Despite my determination not to hesitate, I closed my eyes and took a deep breath. But a sudden force at my back sent me plummeting off the balcony, the material tangled around me.

I screamed as I fell, honks and flapping wings surrounding me, before I slowed, jerking and finally beginning to rise. Somehow, impossibly, it was working. My four swans spread out in a square formation, carrying me between them in the sling created by my sheet. I loosened the death grip on the fabric bunched in my hands and twisted myself so I could peek over the edge.

Big mistake. I pulled back, my head spinning. We were high. I had expected them to lower me gently down, but instead they lifted me higher, angling around the curve of the Keep.

"Where are you going?" I asked, but only received a bugle in reply.

Peering out again, I saw that Stormy seemed to be in the lead, something held in her beak. Sweetie flew behind her, Eagle coming last.

"Wait!" I shrieked as Stormy flew directly at a window.

She didn't hesitate, however, the stone in her beak ramming into it at full speed. I gasped as she fell, dazed, the stone plummeting beside her. But her wings flicked out and caught her just in time, bringing her in for a soft landing on the lake.

Sweetie followed her lead, aiming for the exact same spot, where a spiderweb of cracks now branched out across the glass. I watched anxiously as she too caught herself before hitting the water.

Eagle flew in last, moving faster than the others to my eye.

"Not too fast," I called, just as she smashed into the window. It shattered around her.

She disappeared from sight as her momentum took her into the room. The birds carrying me flapped hard, lifting me level with the windowsill, and I grasped hold of it, scrambling into the room in a flurry of waving arms and legs. I landed on a number of objects, all showered in glass, and winced as the shards sliced at my beautiful wrap. But at least I had avoided any larger pieces that would have pierced through to my skin.

It only took a second's glance around to recognize where I was. Everything became clear. Stormy had led us all to the window where she had seen Leander on her scouting expeditions. My swans had known what I needed without my having to say it.

My eyes fell on the dazed Eagle, a trickle of red splashed against the surrounding glass beside her. Slipping and sliding, I stumbled over to kneel beside her.

"Come on, girl," I whispered. "Come on."

She stirred, opened one beady eye, and honked at me. I helped lift her to her feet where she regarded the chaos around us with a disapproving air. I laughed—a weak chuckle, but still a laugh—and managed to rise to my own feet, although I now swayed dangerously, my head spinning.

"Lady?" whispered a small voice, and my blood froze.

Peering further into the room, I could just see a pair of bright eyes and tangled hair peeking out from behind the overfull desk.

"Juniper?" A surge of energy replaced a portion of the strength I had lost and allowed me to scramble over the mess toward her.

"Lady, where are we?" Juniper bolted from her hiding spot, careening into me and nearly sending both of us over.

She began to cry, noisy tears that tracked down her smudged cheeks. I no longer had to wonder how Leander had ensured Audrey's cooperation. I could only imagine the threats he had made.

"I didn't know the men," she wailed. "But Cora said to be quiet and behave."

"What men?" I asked, but I suspected I already knew the answer.

"I don't know," she said. "The men who brought us here."

Us. She had said us.

"Where's Cora?" I looked around.

"She won't wake up," Juniper cried, and I almost collapsed beside her.

No. No, no, no, no, no. Not Cora.

"Where is she?" I managed to rasp out.

Juniper grasped my hand and tugged me back around the desk. Eagle followed, picking her careful way across the scattered debris.

I had little feeling left in my body, aside from the alternating hot and cold flushes that swept through me, and I no longer

243

knew if it was a physical symptom of my impending death or a result of the shocks of the night.

We rounded the desk to find Cora sprawled out flat on the ground, one of her arms across her stomach, and the other flopped above her head. Juniper immediately let go of me and fell on her, shaking her wildly.

"Wake up, Cora," she shouted. "Wake up."

"Quietly, Juniper," I said. "Quietly." The only thing that could make this moment worse would be Brock bursting in on us.

Juniper's hand, resting against Cora's ribs, rose and fell. I gasped. Leaning in close, I checked again. There, another breath. Juniper was right, Cora was asleep.

I gasped in a grateful breath, steadying myself, and then joined Juniper in shaking Cora. She made a soft sleepy groan but otherwise didn't stir.

"See," Juniper said. "I can't wake her up."

"Yes, I see," I said. "What happened to her?"

If she had been hit on the head, her non-responsiveness seemed like a bad sign.

"They came to the haven, right into Cora's bedroom," Juniper said. "They kept saying I had to go with them, and Cora said not without her, so then they made us both come."

I could imagine the scene, reading between the lines of the four-year-old's narration. My heart was in my throat, a lump that made me feel as if I might be sick.

"I looked for Mama or you or Auntie Audrey," Juniper said, her lip wobbling and tears leaking out again, "but they made Cora walk too fast. And once we got up here, they gave her something to drink. She got all slow and strange, and she seemed..." Juniper hiccuped, as if this were the most terrifying part of all. "She seemed scared. But Cora isn't scared of anything."

"Scared?" I stared at the little girl.

It was a familiar word, and I had lived with the effects of it all around me. But this was something else—something stronger.

Whatever had overtaken Cora was far more potent than mere timidity—almost as if the fear had made her give up on consciousness altogether.

Juniper had said Cora wasn't afraid of anything, and it might seem that way to her, but Cora was normally only slightly less fearful than everyone else—she just hid it better. Well, except for Audrey—she could do with a little more fear in her life. Perhaps she had rubbed off on the haven's proprietress. Either that or she had learned from Vilma—ready to take on a dragon, despite her age.

I frowned. Audrey. And Vilma and Gregor. Now that I thought about it, it made no sense. How had I never wondered about it before? How had Gabe never questioned it? Surrounded by meek and timid Talinosians, Audrey stood out, stark against the rest. Even Leander had commented on it.

How had Audrey—out of the whole kingdom—retained her dauntless courage? And Vilma and Gregor too.

I stared down at the sleeping Cora. They had given her something to drink…

My mind worked slowly, grasping at the pieces, until suddenly everything clicked into place in a rush. We had so many lakes in these forests because we were near the mountains—the source of the two rivers that fed Talinos. If Leander's enchantment was something you drank, and if he put it in the water up here, it would slowly flow down to the rest of the kingdom—strongest here, perhaps, but working its enchantment everywhere.

Small pockets might escape, maybe, but not enough to make a difference. Especially not when fear was so catching.

Pockets like Vilma and Gregor who insisted on drinking the odd-tasting water from their private well. Water Vilma had shared with me today and had no doubt shared with Cora and Wren on many an occasion—both of them far too kind to refuse. And Cora and Wren had always seemed less susceptible than most. As for me, I drank largely from my enchanted lake.

Leander no doubt dosed his servants directly to ensure they remained extra compliant, but I had seen with my own eyes his mercenaries carting in large jugs to their forest hideout—no doubt full of clear water.

Palinar had its own rivers that originated in the mountains across the border, and one of those rivers fed Marin. There couldn't be a tidier way to reach all of Talinos without touching the other kingdoms.

Clearly whatever Leander had used to dose the rivers was low in concentration, taking years to build up in the body and take effect—Gabe had been spared by spending so little time in his own kingdom. But what of Audrey?

I could think of nothing to explain her immunity. She had always refused Vilma's offers of water, wrinkling up her nose and claiming it tasted odd. Which was ironic coming from—

I jerked upright, my racing thoughts snagging and slowing. Audrey largely drank her disgusting tea, the one only she liked, that she claimed had all sorts of healing properties. None of us had ever taken her seriously, but what if she was right? What if she had somehow found a natural substance resistant to whatever had caused this enchantment?

I ripped off my wrap, fumbling through its folds for the bag she had given me. Audrey had made me an emergency pack for the ball, and if I knew her...Yes! I pulled out a packet of the tea, the odor hitting me as soon as it broke free.

Cora stirred, muttering something inaudible in her sleep. I threw the rest of the bag aside and thrust the tea packet directly under her nose, fumbling it open and letting the leaves spill out directly onto my friend.

"What are you doing?" Juniper asked, but I ignored her, my sole focus on Cora.

Her hand moved first, fluttering to her head, and then she moaned.

"Where am I?" she asked groggily, and then memory must have returned because she sat up so sharply she fell back down again, my hands reaching out to cushion her fall.

"Junie?" she cried. "Where are you?"

"She's right here," I said. "Just rest a moment. She's fine."

"Lady?" Cora's eyes fluttered back open and fixed on me. "What are you doing here? And where is here?"

She sat up more slowly this time, looking around as she distractedly brushed at the tea leaves that clung to her.

"What is that awful smell?" she asked. "Is Audrey here? It smells like that tea of hers—but much worse."

"It is that tea of hers," I said, with a sniffle. "And I think it just saved you."

Quickly I sketched a rough outline of everything that had happened, skipping the part about my death because Juniper was watching me with wide, fascinated eyes. Cora's wits returned quickly, her sharp gaze saying she knew I was holding something back.

When I swayed, she reached out to support me, our roles reversed.

"Lady…" she said softly.

"It's not good," I said in a grim whisper. "Don't ask."

She hesitated then nodded, switching topics.

"If Leander has been poisoning the whole kingdom's water for years, then he must have a supply of it somewhere. And a way to make more. We need to find it and destroy it."

I nodded. "And we need to find the enchanted object that he's using to control me and all those other animals."

Eagle honked loudly, in agreement or to remind us of her presence, I wasn't sure.

"This place is a mess." Cora surveyed the room with disgust. She would never countenance the haven falling into such a state.

"Yes, he doesn't allow any servants inside, so I think it has been accumulating for years," I said. "But we looked through a lot of it the other day, and I'm sure we didn't miss anything as substantial as what he must need for the rivers. Leander mentioned experiments, and I think..." I paused and gulped. Inevitably, the search had brought me back here to the one place I didn't want to go. "I think there's another room."

CHAPTER 27

J pointed at the door beside the tapestry. It no longer leaked smoke, but somehow it looked just as ominous. The same fear that had filled me the first time I saw it still lodged behind my ribs, but my certainty had only grown that whatever substance Leander used to put fear in the rivers of Talinos was brewed behind that door.

Wait. Fear. Of course I was so afraid of it! What better indication could there be that what we needed to find was behind that door? I leaned over and inhaled deeply over some of the discarded tea leaves. My desire to avoid the door was replaced with determination.

Cora gave me an odd look but said nothing. Scooping Juniper onto her hip, she strode over to pull the door open.

Instead of revealing a room, as I had expected, it opened onto a single flight of stairs. I gaped at them, looking sideways at the tapestry. It made sense, I supposed—the door going up and the door going down beside each other. And it explained why the Keep seemed taller than its top floor—there was an extra secret story.

Cora had already started up the stairs, so I tried to hurry

behind her, the weakness in my legs making it hard to move with any speed. Eagle brought up the rear, waddling even more slowly than me. We made an odd procession, Juniper staring back over Cora's shoulder at us, her eyes straying constantly to Eagle and seeming to get rounder every time.

"Her name is Eagle," I told her.

She frowned. "But she's a swan."

I smiled, Juniper's innocent confusion somehow breaking through the horror of the evening.

"Yes, she's a swan, but her name is Eagle. She has the heart of an eagle."

The swan honked her agreement, and Juniper giggled.

"Huh." Cora sounded surprised, so I forced my legs up the final stairs, coming to a stop beside her.

The vast, open room before us could not have been more different from the one below. Pristine and tidy, nothing littered the floor here or crowded on the many long benches that lined the walls and ran down the middle of the room. Leander might give no effort to the room below, but this must be where he conducted his experiments and studied the godmother objects. I could only imagine how bemusing this aspect of his son must have been to the old lord—by all accounts a genial man but not a scholar.

How many of the items on the benches were enchanted in some way? My eyes latched onto several terracotta pots holding a variety of plants. The most impressive was a small tree, large enough to bear odd-looking fruit almost like dates in appearance, although they couldn't possibly be dates.

Nearby, a large open hearth contained a banked fire, a sizable iron pot hanging above it. Cora put Juniper down with a stern instruction not to touch anything and strode over to the pot. She peered inside and then looked back at me.

"There's liquid in here," she said. "And I don't see anything else that could hold liquid."

I scanned the room before joining her and looking into the pot myself. Several shapes floated in the watery substance in different stages of disintegration. I glanced back at the potted tree. It looked like whatever strange fruit it bore was feeding this unknown concoction.

"Seeds," I said, making Cora look at me in confusion. "Leander kept talking about seeds and fruit—I thought he was talking metaphorically, but now I think he was being literal."

I stared at the tree. I had heard of types of fruit that were godmother objects, but I had never considered that if someone planted the seeds from one, a tree might grow. But what had tainted it so badly that it would grow such fruit as this? *Can you not guess?* whispered a voice in the back of my mind. I had seen first-hand an entire kingdom poisoned by the kind of evil that led someone to kill their own family. I shivered.

"I intend to destroy what's in this pot and that tree along with it," Cora said.

"Personally, I'd feel more comfortable if we destroyed everything in this room. Just to be sure." I met her eyes, and we shared a grim nod. "And I suggest we work quickly."

She probably thought I meant that we might be interrupted, and it was a legitimate concern. For all I knew, Leander might already be aware of my escape and searching the Keep for me. But the real reason for my rush was my own state.

The weakness had invaded every one of my bones, turning them heavy and cumbersome, so that each movement cost more energy than I had to spare. But I was determined to live long enough to complete this task. Leander had done me a favor by bringing Cora here—I could never have lifted the pot on my own.

She took it down from its hooks without hesitation, setting it on the floor away from the fire.

"I would recommend not breathing in anything that's coming off that," she said, and I nodded fervent agreement.

Kneeling, she prodded the fire in the hearth to life, feeding it kindling from a small box beside the fireplace. As soon as it had taken, the flames leaping higher and higher, she sat back on her heels with a satisfied sigh.

"Let's get it in," she said. "All of it."

"Can I help?" Juniper asked.

"No!" Cora and I exclaimed at the same time.

"Don't touch anything," Cora added, with a stern look for the girl.

"You shouldn't either," I said to Cora. "Who knows what enchantments might be on these things?"

Cora frowned at me, but I shook my head at her.

"There's nothing that can hurt me now," I whispered.

"What do you mean?" Junie asked, staring at me.

"Hush now, young one," Cora wrapped her in her arms, her eyes full of sadness. "We'll talk about it later."

"But I want to talk about it now," Juniper said, but I had already turned my focus to the rest of the room.

Scooping my skirts into a makeshift basket, I moved along the benches, slowly sweeping anything I could find into them. Papers, plants, wooden sculptures, clothes—all of it went in. As I worked, I wondered why the bottle binding me to the lake had been downstairs when it would have been more at home up here. Had he needed it in view? Had it somehow changed when I was away from the lake at night? It might explain how he had always managed to appear, and why he had kept it in view. But I would likely never know the full truth of it.

When my weak arms could no longer take the strain, I hobbled back to the fire and let everything I carried tumble in. The flames roared, consuming the items far faster than seemed natural.

"Here, I'll help." Cora formed her own skirt into a similar receptacle.

I hesitated, but we would go much faster that way, and she

wouldn't actually have to touch anything. Moving more quickly, we threaded our way up and down the benches, me sweeping anything and everything into Cora's skirts.

When Cora took a second load to the fire, I remained behind where we had left off, taking a moment to catch my breath. She returned, and we continued. My legs shook under me, but I willed them to keep going.

We had done everything except the far wall, Cora having just deposited a load in the fire, when Juniper—forgotten for a moment in our absorption—spoke.

"*What* is *that?*"

I looked across the room, but I couldn't see what had caught her interest. Both of us converged on her, only to stand and frown at what held her attention.

It looked like a knitting project that someone had abandoned part way, the shoulders and arms of a shirt formed but the rest still missing. Except it had been made from the strangest looking thread I had ever seen.

Cora leaned in close.

"Don't touch it!" Juniper said, her nose wrinkled. "It looks like stinging nettles. My mama says not to touch those."

"People don't knit clothes out of stinging nettles," I said but then stopped. Could I really say anything with authority about this strange room?

"Stinging nettles?" Cora turned to look at me. "I remember an old tale about stinging nettles."

"Oh!" Juniper tugged at my hand. "I know that one, too. About the princess who had to knit shirts out of nettles to turn her brothers back from swans into people. She couldn't talk the whole time, either." She wrinkled her nose. "It's not a very good story. I want to be a princess one day, but I don't want to knit with stinging nettles."

Cora and I gaped at each other. I vaguely remembered the story from my own childhood. I remembered thinking that I would have done it for Dominic if he were enchanted. Of course, I had never stopped to ask myself if he would do it for me.

"It looks like he's unraveled it," Cora said. "Taken some of the thread away to use for something else."

"Like that?" Juniper asked, pointing at something slightly obscured to one side of the shirt.

Gingerly I reached forward and tugged the item into view. My mouth dropped open.

"What does it say?" Juniper asked, standing up on tiptoes to try to see better.

"Princess Adelaide," whispered Cora, staring from the embroidered letters to me. "It says Princess Adelaide."

The plain cotton was still stretched across a wooden embroidery hoop, and there was no question what material had been used to sew the rough letters or to secure the swan feather that had been attached below my name. I glanced back at the shirt and its missing threads.

"What are those?" Cora pointed at what looked like a neat pile of hoops behind the one I had pulled forward.

I took down the top one and stared at an unfamiliar male name and a crudely sewn image that looked a bit like a...

"Is that a bear?" Cora asked, looking over my shoulder. "And are those hairs sewn in among the nettles?"

"Fur, I think," I said tersely. "Get them in the fire. All of them."

Cora grimaced. "Don't touch any of the nettle with your hands, though."

"STOP!" A bellow from the doorway made us freeze.

But only for a second. The moment of shock passed, and we were all moving at once.

"In the fire! Quick!" Cora cried, already running across the open floor on a collision course with Leander who rushed toward us.

"Get under a bench," I called to Juniper as I abandoned caution and picked up the strange shirt in my bare hand.

Ripping off my wrap, I bundled the shirt and all the hoops into it. My fingers and palm had already begun to sting, however, an itchy sensation crawling across my skin. It was a sensation I had felt once before, just after I met Leander at the lake for the first time. I ignored it, trying to run, but my legs no longer properly obeyed my commands. I tripped and fell, landing hard.

Leander swerved at the last moment, avoiding Cora and running toward me. I tried to push myself back up, moving agonizingly slowly. Eagle honked, announcing her presence, and grabbed at the corners of my wrap with her beak.

Juniper giggled and cheered her on—oblivious to the danger we were all in—as the swan waddled toward the fire dragging the wrapped bundle behind her. Leander gave chase, quickly closing the distance between them, and I screamed as his hands stretched out to grab her.

He fell short, however, brought crashing to the ground by Cora in a flying leap. She promptly put her full weight on him, pinning him to the ground. I finally managed to scramble to my feet and stumbled toward the sprawl of human limbs and feathers. I reached the fire in time to wrest the bundled shirt and hoops from Eagle and throw them all deep into the flames, my wrap with them.

"Nooo!" screamed Leander as the flames caught the material, burning it all to ash in mere seconds. "I'll kill you!"

I hobbled slowly up to him. "You already have, remember? You've destroyed my life, and now I've destroyed yours. It only seemed fair."

"Why, you—"

His words were cut off as Eagle sat on his head, prompting more squealing laughs from Juniper. I met Cora's eyes.

"I can't do the pot, Cora," I murmured, "or the tree."

My words must have reached Leander through all the feathers because he began to thrash, trying to break free of the combined hold of Cora and Eagle.

Juniper screamed as a flash of movement darted out from Leander's writhing shape. Cora gasped, and red appeared, leaking down to soak into Leander's clothing.

I threw myself forward and wrestled the knife from his grip.

"Eagle," I said grimly, and the bird instantly stood, exposing the lord's head.

Twisting the blade in my hand, I brought the hilt down hard on Leander's skull. It made a shocking thump and then he went still.

"Cora? Are you all right? Where are you hurt?"

I tried to pull her up off Leander's now still form and only succeeded in nearly collapsing on top of her.

"The blade only cut my thigh," she said. "I'll live."

She tore a long piece of fabric from her skirt and wrapped it around the wound, tying it off tightly.

"But I would like to recover somewhere far from here," she said. "So let's get this over with."

She braced herself on me, using mostly her own strength to heave herself to her feet, and together we hobbled back toward the pot and the tree. Stopping to take several breaths, she took the tree's trunk in both hands and wrenched it from the soil. Carrying the entire thing over to the fire, she laid it across the burning wood, pausing until the flames licked at the branches, consuming the fruit.

"What are we going to do with the pot?" I asked.

"Use it to put out the fire," Cora suggested, eyeing the way the flames had already raced along the trunk, escaping the confines of the hearth.

"Good idea."

I wasn't sure how much help I could be, but I took one handle while Cora took the other. Together we upended it, my grip wobbling and making the pot tilt toward her. The liquid inside gushed out, nearly missing the fire, but at the last moment, I threw myself sideways, righting it enough that the second half of the contents splashed over the flames. They hissed and fizzled, great billows of steam rising up.

We both dropped the pot, hastily backing away from the steam. Ushering Juniper ahead of us toward the stairs, we followed Eagle's lead. The rolling steam engulfed Leander's unconscious form, blocking him from view. If the steam worked as the pure liquid did, I didn't think he would be waking up anytime soon. But I had no problem with that.

Somehow the four of us made it back down the stairs and into the chaos below. I didn't have much time left, I could feel it, but I hoped that with the destruction of the shirt, Eagle, at least, was now free from my coming death. But she needed to rejoin her wedge.

"I need to rest," Cora puffed, lowering herself to the ground.

"I'm just going to help Eagle out of the window," I told her.

First I had to knock all the remaining glass shards from the window, a task that took far longer than it should. And when I was finally finished, I realized I had long since lost the strength to lift her. Instead, I crouched down, and she somehow clambered up and over me, using me to launch out of the empty hole with a triumphant bugle.

Answering bugles greeted her, and I leaned against the frame, hoping to catch a final glimpse of them all. But I had misjudged my center of balance, my weakness making me clumsy, and I toppled slowly out, unable to catch myself.

"Lady!" Juniper screamed somewhere behind me, but I couldn't see her, my reaching fingers scrabbling for something to hold.

Then feathers surrounded me, easing my fall, and I slid down into a sling made of cotton. Just like before, we all dropped, two heartbeats passing before the swans' powerful wings caught us, lifting us back into the sky.

I slumped down, curled into a ball, and gave myself over to exhaustion. I had hoped to see Audrey again, and Gabe, one last time, but I had no energy left to try to direct the birds. They would take me where they willed.

Long moments passed in which I slipped in and out of consciousness, somehow still clinging to life. Eventually I roused enough to notice that we were flying slowly, our pace decreasing and our altitude dropping. I peered around, trying to get my bearings through the dizziness and nausea.

Everything looked different from up here, seen from a swan's view, but at last I recognized it. The swans were taking me home to my lake. I nodded and let myself slip back down again. It seemed a fitting place to die, among friends.

They must have been tiring of their burden because by the time the lake appeared beneath us, we were perilously low. I tried to find the voice to warn them that I could not land on the water as they could, but I remembered that I had no swan words in the darkness.

And then we jerked and dipped, Snowy faltering and crashing to the lake below. Her corner dropped, and the sling catapulted me out and into the dark, cold embrace of the water.

CHAPTER 28

The shock of the impact, followed by the cold water, revived me somewhat. I thrashed around, struggling for the surface. Finally I broke free into the cool moonlight, gasping for air, but the brief burst of energy was already subsiding.

My legs kicked weakly, but my arms and shoulders slipped beneath the surface, the water swallowing me slowly. I looked around for something to grasp hold of, thinking perhaps I could cling to one of the swans, but it took me a moment to find them.

The seven shapes on the water barely moved, their necks drooping and their small movements feeble. My heart contracted. It had not been exhaustion, then. They shared my fate, just as Leander had threatened. My hands fluttered and my feet scissored, but my skirts weighed me down, and I sank.

"Adelaide!" A strong voice shouted my name, followed by energetic splashes.

The water moved around me, new life injected into the lake as Gabe appeared, swimming fast in my direction.

"Adelaide," he cried again, coming to a stop beside me, and slipping his arm under me.

I breathed a sigh of relief and stopped my efforts, letting myself hang there, while he kept us both afloat.

"What are you doing here?" I managed to whisper.

"I saw you fly overhead," he said. "And I guessed where the swans would take you. I ran all the way."

I could hear his labored breathing now, and new fear clutched at my heart. It was far too late for me, but Gabe shouldn't be out here in the middle of the lake, exhausted and trying to support my weight. I thrashed weakly, trying to push him away.

"Addie, stop! What are you doing?"

"Go," I said, my voice as weak as my body. "It's too late for me. You need to go."

"No." He sounded stubborn and strong. "I won't leave you. I don't know what trick Leander has been playing tonight, but no matter what, I won't leave you."

Fear for him proved as effective as cold water at giving me a burst of energy. I grasped at him. "Then we will both die. You have to swim back."

I could feel it even more, the way we kept dipping down. He had to exert more and more energy to keep us both afloat. I tried to disentangle myself, but he was the one clinging on now, and I couldn't get myself loose. I would be the dead weight that dragged him to the bottom, his energy drained in his attempt to hold back the inevitable.

"Gabe, no," I managed to say, and then we both sank, water rushing around my nose and mouth and eyes and cutting off my words.

For a horrible moment, I panicked, pushing and clawing in my attempts to get my head back above water. And then I remember who I pushed against and stopped, everything going limp once more. But Gabe's arm came alive beneath me, propelling me up toward the surface.

I broke free, gasping and spluttering as I sucked in precious gulps of air. But Gabe hadn't emerged, and I let myself sink again, feeling around for him. Instead of Gabe, my reaching fingers grasped fistfuls of fabric, and I realized what had happened.

Somehow the swans had freed themselves of my sheet sling, and Gabe had become entangled in it. Gabe's head emerged, but he managed only a single breath before sinking down again. I went with him, both of us fumbling around, our movements slowed by the resistance of the water as we struggled to unwrap the material.

But neither of us could kick now, and my feeble arms did little to help. The dark water stretched in every direction and in a moment of utter panic, I could no longer be sure which way was up. Perhaps I thrashed and struggled merely to drive us deeper into the depths.

Gabe went still beside me, and I grasped onto him and screamed into the silent lake. This wasn't how it was supposed to end.

And then arms broke the surface, thrashing and bubbles and shouting surrounding us. Someone gripped me, tearing me from Gabe, and I struggled, but too feebly to be of any use. Someone dragged me through the water, and I felt the moment their feet found solid ground, arms cradling around me and carrying me the rest of the way.

The arms placed me gently on the ground, and for a moment everything spun around me. Then my vision steadied, latching onto my rescuer's face.

"Dominic?!"

I tried to sit up, but my brother held me down. I struggled and fought, desperate to see what had happened to Gabe.

"Gently, gently," he said, but I strained against him still.

"Gabe," I managed to gasp out. "Gabe."

Dominic finally understood, lifting me so I could see where Gabe lay, a short way along the shore line. Two men appeared to have just finished dragging him out of the lake, and he wasn't breathing.

"No," I cried, my voice ragged. "No."

I tried to crawl to him, but Dominic restrained me, his gently cradling arms helping me to my feet. One of the men who had pulled Gabe from the water looked at his pale, still face and dropped to his knees beside him.

"What is he doing?" I cried as he pressed hard against Gabe's chest.

Dominic didn't reply, continuing to hold me back, and a second later a fountain of water erupted from Gabe's mouth. He began to cough violently.

The men rolled him onto his side, and from there he rolled himself onto his hands and knees, his head drooping as he struggled to regain his breath. As soon as it evened, his head shot up, his eyes searching until they latched onto mine.

"Addie," he breathed.

I hurried toward him, sinking down at his side and letting him wrap me in a dripping embrace.

"You reckless fool," I said, my tears joining the lake water that already soaked him. "You nearly died for nothing. It's too late for me, I'm already dying."

"Are you?" asked a new voice in calm inquiry.

I froze before turning slowly to lock eyes with my godmother. She stood at the back of the scene, calmly observing, although she hadn't been there before. Taking stock of my body, I noticed that I no longer felt so weak, and my head had stopped spinning.

"Well...I was." I said.

"Fortunately for you," she said briskly, "there is something more powerful than any curse, more powerful than even true love's kiss. True love's sacrifice. Your prince was willing to die for you—and, in fact, did so, if only briefly. Leander explained that the curse was tied to you, and to your love, but he failed to mention it was also tied to him. If your love betrayed you, you would die, but if your love sacrificed himself for you, Leander would be the one to die. Why do you think he was so reluctant to activate this particular binding? And with his death, the curse is dissolved."

"I'm free?" I asked, struggling to comprehend the words. "Truly free?"

"Yes, indeed," she replied.

"And my swans?" I turned quickly toward the lake.

Already I could see the strength returning to them as well, their heads lifting again, their necks curving gracefully. I let out a relieved sigh, that turned slowly to sadness. And now I would lose them, the one bitter pill in what should have been unalleviated happiness.

"We are no longer bound together," I murmured. "I'll lose them now, after they saved me. Saved us all, really."

"Well, that is to be seen," the godmother said. "Animals are tricky creatures, and these ladies have been enchanted for a long time now. It's hard to say exactly what changes have been wrought."

"Addie." Gabe pulled my attention back to him. Despite the news from my godmother, horror filled his eyes. "Were you dying because of me? After my announcement, I took you— Audrey, I mean—aside somewhere quieter, and that's when I realized..." He swallowed, seeming to find it difficult to breathe. "She broke down and told me what Leander made her do, but I couldn't understand the point of it all. All I knew was that you were gone, and something terrible was happening. I was searching for you when I saw you fly overhead."

He stood to his feet, swaying once but then steadying, and pulling me up along with him. He grasped both my arms, his eyes burning into mine.

"You know I would never betray you, don't you? All my promises were made to you regardless of who stood beside me."

I nodded. "I know." A deep certainty, a peace, settled inside me. I believed him—I trusted Gabe completely. And a life with him was worth any risk that one day he might cause me pain.

He slipped his arms around me, and I leaned into him.

"Ahem." The disruptive throat clearing made me draw back, my searching eyes finding my brother.

"Dominic. You're here. How is it possible?"

"I sent for him at the same time as I sent for help from my parents," Gabe said, one arm still around me. "I thought in the circumstances I might find better help from Palinar than from my own capital." He grinned. "And I knew one mention of your name would bring Dominic running, no convincing needed." He turned to my brother. "I'm not sure how you got here so fast, or how you found this lake in the nick of time, but I'm certainly glad you did."

Gabe dropped his arm from around me and held his hand out toward Dominic. The two clasped arms, whacking each other on the back.

"We rode without ceasing is how we got here in time," one of the men with Dominic muttered. "Frequent changes of mounts, and we took turns sleeping tied to our saddles."

"Plus, a little help from me," the godmother added. "I thought they might have a little trouble finding their way to just the right spot."

When I looked over at her, she gave me a prim smile. "You did ask me for help, did you not? And I think there's one last bit of assistance you might need."

She waved a hand, and Gabe and I instantly dried, a pleasant warmth rising from our clothes. A delighted smile broke over my face, and it must have been thanks enough for her because a heartbeat later, she had disappeared.

"I hate it when they do that," Dominic muttered, and our eyes met, my mood instantly falling.

I knew my brother and I were in the same place in our minds —the last time we had stood together in the presence of our godmother. On that occasion, both of our parents' broken bodies had lain below us at the bottom of a long flight of stairs thanks to my father's rage. A sob from deep within my belly broke free.

"Dominic," I gasped, as he whispered, "Adelaide."

And then we were embracing, the years of separation and pain falling away.

"I'm so sorry," he murmured, his voice low and broken. "I'm so sorry."

"I forgive you," I said, and I knew I meant it, no shade of anger or betrayal remaining behind to poison my future. "It was so long ago, and we are different people now." I paused. "I hear you've changed."

He pulled away and smiled, the expression reaching deep into his eyes in a way I never remembered seeing before.

"I have," he said. "And I swear to show it to you. And I'll also show you the girl who helped me do it."

"I've heard about her," I said. "Sophie."

He nodded, a new glow lighting up his face at her name. "She was desperate to come along to meet you, but she couldn't have managed the ride."

"Ah yes," Gabe interjected, "congratulations. Double congratulations, I'm told."

"Thank you?" Dominic said.

"Ha!" Gabe clapped him on the shoulder. "That's not supposed to sound like a question, you know. You might want to work on that before Sophie hears you."

"Double congratulations?" I asked, looking between them.

"I might have forgotten to mention that." Gabe looked guilty. "I've had a few other things on my mind."

My head whirled as I struggled to absorb the new information, my capacity for the day long since reached.

"I'm going to be an aunt?"

"Twice," Dominic said with a smile, but Gabe laughed again.

"You might want to work on that hint of fear, as well. It's not kingly." He winked at me. "He's just afraid he'll get two small versions of himself. It would be enough to terrify the mightiest of men."

"Very humorous," Dominic said, eyeing Gabe.

How strange it was. Like old times—and yet different in so many ways. Dominic turned to me.

"I know Sophie will love you, and you will love her. And the babies will love to have their aunt around. I can't wait to finally bring you home."

"Ah. About that." Gabe stepped sideways and wrapped an arm around my waist. "I'm afraid Adelaide has already agreed to make a new home here—with me."

"So you've found her just to steal her away?" Dominic didn't sound impressed.

Gabe, however, was undaunted. "You didn't think it would happen any other way, did you? She's altogether too lovable."

He dropped a quick kiss against my hair, and the glare I was giving him softened.

"No one is stealing me," I said sternly to them both. "I choose my own home." I gave Dominic an exasperated look. "And don't even pretend you're going to withhold your blessing. We both know the crown prince of Talinos is a worthy alliance—even for the king of Palinar."

"I don't care about alliances," Dominic said. "I only care about you."

I blinked and then smiled. He had changed indeed.

"How fortunate," Gabe said. "I feel precisely the same way." He turned to me, shutting Dominic from the conversation. "So, tell me, my love. Where exactly do you choose to make your home?"

I drew close, letting him pull me into his arms. "With you, of course. My home is with you."

And then his lips were on mine, while the swans bugled from the lake behind us, and my brother awkwardly cleared his throat. I wasn't sure whether I wanted to laugh or cry from happiness, so I settled for kissing my prince instead.

EPILOGUE

*O*nce again the courtyard of the Keep had been covered with greenery, soft fabric, and lights and filled with all the inhabitants of Brylee. But this time the children from the haven ran merrily between the adults' legs, laughing and calling to each other.

"It's perfect," sighed Audrey, beside me. "I just wish it was a double wedding." She grinned cheekily at me.

"So does Gabe," I said with a chuckle. "But just remember, this way you get to be an attendant twice—and you get a trip to the capital as well."

She brightened immediately before shrieking and rushing off to stop Juniper from throwing herself into a patch of mud, white dress and all. Part of me wished it was my wedding day, as well, but I couldn't get married without my brother by my side. And the price of being a princess was that I couldn't get married in a remote location in the middle of the forest, either.

Dominic and Gabe's parents had fought over which capital would host our wedding, and King Clarence and Queen Sapphira had only won because of Gabe's status as crown prince. But my new sister-in-law, Sophie, had sworn that she would find a way to get herself there—regardless of how enormous she had become by that point. When I left Palinar to return to Talinos for Wren and Ash's wedding, she and Dominic had still been debating whether a boat or a well-sprung carriage would provide a softer journey.

A month in their company had been more than enough to convince me that my brother had truly changed. And it hadn't taken more than a day to know that I would love my new sister just as well as Dominic had claimed.

But neither would I forget the sisters of my heart. Wren had already promised that she would join Audrey as one of my attendants. Ash's assistant was going to be taking charge of the bakery during their short wedding trip, so Wren had convinced Ash to leave his store for a little longer and take the whole family to the capital to join me.

"The Keep has shined up nicely for the occasion, I think," Cora said proudly from beside me.

I turned to smile at her. "It looks completely magical. Wren is going to be delighted."

"Well, it was the only way," Cora said with a snort. "It was hard enough moving all the oldsters out here in the first place, I wasn't carting them all back into Brylee for a wedding."

"Who are you calling old?" Vilma asked, a sparkle in her eyes.

"Vilma!" I gave her a hug, and she squeezed me back.

"I heard you'd arrived," she told me. "But I had to see for myself."

"I missed you," I said. "And I promise I'll be back to visit as often as I can."

"Which won't be often enough, I'm sure, what with all your royal duties." She shook her head and laughed. "Royal duties! Just imagine! A princess living among us. Gregor is still in shock, you know."

"I wish you could both come to the capital for the wedding," I said.

"Oh, goodness no." She clasped my arm. "We would be out of place in a palace. But we'll be thinking of you on the day." She drew herself up and winked at me. "Cora's asked us to keep an eye on the place in her absence, and it's a big responsibility."

Cora rolled her eyes. "I don't know what came over me."

I grinned at her, still pleased I had convinced her to come to my wedding despite its distance from Brylee. It helped that there were various official tasks she needed to complete in the capital, now that she was Lady Cora.

Even after all these weeks, the inhabitants of Talinos were only slowly coming out of Leander's enchantment. King Clarence and Queen Sapphira had been overcome with gratitude when they learned how the kingdom had been saved, and it had only taken a suggestion from Gabe for them to agree to grant Leander's now empty titles and lands to Cora in thanks for her role in freeing them.

I knew it hadn't been just gratitude that motivated Gabe's request, however. He had seen first-hand that no one deserved the title and role more. Cora had already dedicated her life to helping the people of this area—the official position would just mean she had the resources she needed to keep doing it, and the recognition she deserved as well.

With a new, larger building, and all the wealth attached to the title, Cora would never have to worry about how to keep the haven running again. And the inhabitants of Brylee already knew to direct anyone who turned up at the old haven's doors out of town to the Keep.

Audrey delighted in coming up with outrageous suggestions for how the old building could be used, and even Cora and I had spent an enjoyable hour the night before discussing the topic while we wove flower garlands for the wedding and tried to avoid the smell of Audrey's awful tea. No one liked to tell her not to drink it now we knew how important it had been. Audrey herself was convinced her noxious fumes had helped protect us all and was terribly smug about the whole thing.

A flash of white drew my eye upward. A wedge of swans flew overhead, bugling loudly as they glided down below the level of the Keep's walls to splash down into the lake beside it.

"So they really did follow you to Palinar and back." Cora shook her head. "You have a way of inspiring devotion, Lady. A quality that will stand you in good stead when you're queen one day."

"I'm glad I didn't lose them," I said. "After everything we've been through together, they deserve a life of ease as royal birds."

I couldn't talk to them as I once had, and they no longer seemed quite as attuned to my wishes, but neither did they behave like wild swans either. Snowy and Sweetie had attached themselves to Sophie, seeming to instantly sense her physical discomfort, and I had almost been afraid they might stay behind when the rest of us left. Eagle, on the other hand, had tried to bite Dominic on three separate occasions. Apparently my godmother had been right, and you couldn't enchant an animal in such a way without making permanent changes.

Gabe had been pleased for me but also concerned initially, wondering if his forests were now to be filled with aggressive wolves and bears with heightened intelligence. But his anxiety had proved unfounded. No reports of animal attacks had come in, and the bears hadn't been sighted at all, apparently choosing to head deep into the uninhabited parts of the forest once they were freed. Most of the wolf packs had dispersed as well, although we had begun to hear tales about a woodsman who had somehow acquired a pack of wolves to hunt beside him.

The hounds had been the only ones to make their way into town, and many of the townsfolk now had new members of their households, while the Keep itself had gained a whole family of hounds. Already the stories of their feats were spreading beyond

Brylee, and I imagined the creatures would soon become legendary.

"Lady! Cora!" Audrey called to us from the doors of the Keep. "I mean, Lady Cora *and* Princess Lady." She began to giggle. "You two are so confusing."

"Did you save Junie's dress from the mud?" I asked.

"Yes, she's inside now. And we need both of you. It's nearly time to start the processional."

Cora and I hurried in, ready to take our places beside Wren who had insisted we both be attendants. When I saw the bride, dressed in softest pink accented with pearls, and with flowers through her hair, I stopped.

"You look beautiful." Tears filled my eyes.

"As do both of you," she said, reaching to clasp hands with both of us.

"Just wait until you see the courtyard," crowed Audrey, almost bouncing in place. "I think I outdid myself."

We all laughed, but from what Cora said, it was true. Audrey had thrown herself into the wedding, devoting herself to giving her sister the perfect day. We had all assured her over and over again that none of us blamed her for what had happened, but she seemed to need a physical outlet to demonstrate her remorse.

Leander's threats against Juniper had been enough to keep her from telling us the truth, but I had been right that she had been hoping she could help us secretly defeat Leander before the date of her betrayal arrived. We hadn't succeeded, but it had all worked out in the end, and no one was going to hold any of it against her.

The rest of us were already dressed in the deep rose-pink gowns I had brought from Palinar for the attendants. I had insisted that since I couldn't be around to help with the other preparations, I would bring all the dresses back with me. Wren had already taken me aside this morning and told me that it was too much. The pearls on her dress were worth more than the rest of the wedding put together. But I had laughed and told her it was royal privilege and that I would soon be her crown princess, so she couldn't refuse my gift.

"Just make sure you sell them afterward and use the money for Junie—and any future babies who might soon be on their way," I had said with a wink.

She looked down, blushing rosily, and I laughed and nudged her with my shoulder.

"Junie would love a younger brother or sister, I know. Or two or three."

She had chuckled at that and pushed me away, refraining from commenting further on the dress. And seeing her now, I was pleased at my choice.

The look on Ash's face as we joined him in front of the gathered townsfolk only reinforced my pleasure. And when I glanced sideways at the appreciative look on Gabe's face as he gazed at me, I blushed as well. Before I knew it, it would be my turn to stand in front of my family and friends and promise to spend my life with the man I loved. And the moment couldn't come too soon.

NOTE FROM THE AUTHOR

Read what happened while Adelaide was missing starting in *A Dance of Silver and Shadow*, or see where it all began in the first book in the Four Kingdoms series, *The Princess Companion: A Retelling of The Princess and the Pea.*

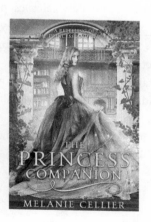

Or for more romance, adventure, and intrigue in a new world, try my Spoken Mage series. In Elena's world words have power over life and death—but none more so than hers. As a commonborn, Elena has always been forbidden to read and write, until a startling new ability thrusts her into the Royal Academy where she finds herself among the mageborn including the enigmatic Prince Lucas. You can turn the page for a sneak peek.

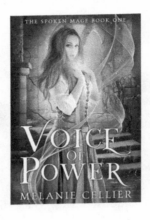

To be kept informed of my new releases, please sign up to my mailing list at www.melaniecellier.com. At my website, you'll also find an array of free extra content, including a bonus chapter from Gabe's perspective as he sets out to look for Adelaide.

Thank you for taking the time to read my book. I hope you enjoyed it. If you did, please spread the word! You could start by leaving a review on Amazon (or Goodreads or Facebook or any other social media site). Your review would be very much appreciated and would make a big difference!

CHAPTER 1

J was hurrying home along the dirt road, already late, when I heard the cry. It clearly came from a young child and was too loud to miss and too pained to ignore. With a sigh, I slowed and tried to pinpoint the source. I had spent longer in the woods than I usually did on my herb-gathering expeditions, and the sun was already drawing low. But I was well outside the village now, so no one else was likely to hear or intervene.

An angry voice followed by another cry sent me around some bushes and onto the flat patch of ground bordering the small river that flowed past our town of Kingslee. A small child who I vaguely recognized—not more than three years old—cowered in the dirt away from a boy and girl my own age. I leaped in, placing myself between the child and his attackers, before my brain caught up. I shot a pained look at the girl in front of me.

"Really, Alice?"

She winced. "We had to step in, Elena. He was endangering us all. You would have done the same."

I turned to glance at the boy who now clung to my leg. He didn't look dangerous. Tears ran down his cheeks, one of which bore the distinct red mark of a hand. I turned back to glower at the other two.

"I really don't think I would have."

Alice winced again. "Well, maybe not that. Samuel got a bit carried away, perhaps…"

"No, I did not." Samuel narrowed his eyes at me. "That boy needs to be taught a lesson, and even you should know that, Elena. Isn't your family's house just down the road?"

I rubbed my head. I was too tired today for riddles.

"What are you talking about, Samuel?"

Samuel just pointed at the scuffed dirt beside where we all stood. I looked helplessly across at Alice.

She leaned over slightly, pointing more closely. Reluctantly I bent down as well, frowning at what appeared to be a single short, curving line drawn in the dust, deeper than the other muddled depressions.

"It's a…line?" I picked up the crying child, who was now attempting to climb my leg, and settled him on my hip. "So he's been drawing in the dirt. What of it?"

"Yes, just a line. Thanks to us." Samuel stepped forward, his posture belligerent, and I fell back a step. But only because of the boy. I didn't want Samuel taking another swipe at him.

But Samuel ignored the child, pointing instead at something on the other side of us. It appeared to have been pushed aside and partially concealed by a bush during whatever scuffle had occurred before my arrival. But half a page was still enough to see what it was—a single sheet of printed parchment.

I gasped and jumped back instinctively, nearly dropping the boy.

"What—? Where did that come from?"

Samuel crossed his arms in front of his chest and regarded me again with narrowed eyes. "And now you see. We've saved us all. And that child needs to be taught a lesson."

"He's only a baby," I protested, my arms tightening around him. "He doesn't know any better."

But I could feel the shake in my limbs as residual fear burned through me. How close had we all come to death? I scrubbed at the dirt with my foot, removing even the faint traces of whatever had been marked there.

"Why haven't you burned it?" I asked. "Before someone else sees it. Like a guard. You know the penalty for possessing writing, let alone the danger…"

Samuel shook his head. "We'll burn it once that boy has learned his lesson."

I stepped back again as he leaned forward threateningly. But Alice put her hand on his arm, restraining him.

"I think you've scared him enough, Samuel. Look, he's still crying. Elena is right. We should burn it."

For a moment Samuel and I stood frozen, our gazes locked. But then Alice pulled at his arm again, and he sighed, shaking her off.

"Very well."

As he pulled out tinder and flint, I tried not to look at the parchment. But the firm black marks called to me, and I couldn't resist stealing several glances. I couldn't read what they said, of course. None of us could. But I knew enough to recognize words when I saw them. Their loops and curves and straight edges fascinated me. What mysteries would they unlock, if only I could decipher them? If only I hadn't been born Elena, of Kingslee, daughter of two shopkeepers.

But as the first bright lick of flame ignited the paper, the forbidden letters burning away, I shook myself. I wouldn't trade my family for anything. Not even the wonders of the written word and the magical power it could unleash for those from the right bloodlines.

"Well, that's done then," said Alice when the parchment had

turned completely to ash. "We should be going." She looked over her shoulder at the road, clearly eager to be gone.

But uneasiness stirred in me.

"But surely the real question is where did he get it." I looked down at the boy who had snuggled into my shoulder, his tears finally fading at the mesmerizing sight of flames. "Where did it come from? Kingslee doesn't need that kind of trouble." Not when we stood so close to the capital, in all too easy reach of any number of the king's guards.

Samuel grunted. "Didn't you see earlier? A couple of fancy carriages came rolling through on their way to Corrin." He gestured up the road past my house where the capital lay, far out of sight. "They deigned to stop, and the mages inside even went into your parents' store. I've no doubt one of them dropped the thing, and this idiot found it."

At his angry tone the boy began to tremble, attempting to burrow into me. I hoisted him a little higher on my hip and glared at Samuel again.

"It's not his fault. He's too young to know better. Things like this aren't supposed to be lying around."

"He's obviously a smart one." Alice watched him with sadness lurking in her eyes. "To try to copy what he saw."

"Smart? Ha!" Samuel barked a laugh without humor. "Idiot fool, more like. He could have exploded us all with a single word, you know that."

"Well, he didn't!" I snapped, my nerves having eaten the last of my patience. "And it's getting late. I'm taking him home." I narrowed my eyes, daring Samuel to try to stop me, but he merely glared back.

"Do you know where he belongs?" asked Alice tentatively.

I nodded. "I recognize him. I'll have him home soon enough."

Neither of them moved, so I took off, winding around them. I would have preferred to walk behind them, but I didn't have time to wait around. Not now that I would have to return to town before heading home.

I walked quickly, the boy's weight growing heavier by the minute. I considered putting him down and letting him walk, but the slow pace would have killed me. Instead I pushed on, stopping only once to switch hips.

So someone from the mage families had passed through today. It made sense since no one else would have written words with them. If I hadn't been out gathering, I would have seen them for myself. Spoken to them even, perhaps, if they had come into the store as Samuel said.

What would they have been like? It was one thing to learn the facts of them in school. How they alone could control the power that written words always unleashed, and therefore they alone could be trusted to read and write. About the way they built the kingdom with the power of their written compositions. Even about the different color robes they wore to signify their various disciplines. But that wasn't the same as knowing what they were like as people.

Proud, haughty, and disagreeable? That was how I always imagined them, and how the ones who occasionally rode through Kingslee usually looked.

But what if they had instead looked normal? Friendly even. A person just like me, only wearing fancier clothes. Would that be worse? To know that no more than an accident of birth separated us.

I pushed open the door of a small cottage, set a short way back from the main road, without knocking. A young woman, her eyes red, looked up and gave a small shriek.

"Joseph! There you are!" She rushed forward and snatched him from my arms, wrapping him in her own. I had thought he looked like Isadora's boy, although I had forgotten his name.

She regarded me with wide eyes. "Where did you find him, Elena?"

I shifted from one foot to the other. "Down by the river."

She shrieked again and squeezed him so tightly that he protested and tried to wriggle free. I only just refrained from rolling my eyes. This was a lot of dramatics for someone who hadn't even been out searching for her child.

I wanted to hurry away, but something kept me locked in place. I cleared my throat.

"He wasn't in any danger from the *river*," I said and instantly received Isadora's full attention.

"What do you mean?"

"He didn't show any inclination to go swimming. Perhaps because he'd found something." I glanced around but could see no one else in the small two-room house. I lowered my voice anyway. "A piece of parchment. With words. Samuel thinks someone in those carriages from earlier must have dropped it. Joseph had found it and..." I paused. "He was trying to copy some of it. In the dirt."

I had been sure my revelation would earn another shriek, but Isadora had apparently been shocked into silence instead. She looked round-eyed between me and her young son.

"And..." Her voice wobbled. "Samuel knows of this? He was never one to know when to keep his mouth shut."

"Don't worry," I said quickly. "Joseph is practically a baby still. And we burned it. I'm sure Samuel won't stir up any trouble, no matter what he says." I hesitated. "But you need to make sure he understands—" I bit my lip. "He must be very smart. Has he...has he ever tried anything like that before?"

"Of course not!" She looked offended this time. "He's never even seen words before. Where would he? But he loves to draw. He's always trying to copy the shapes from the pictures at the market, and from the signs..." Her words trailed off, and she dashed her hand across her eyes. "He's smart like you say." She shot me a look. "Like your brother, Jasper."

I smiled, but it felt false, tension still radiating through me.

"That would be fortunate indeed for him. For you all." I refrained from letting my eyes run over the poorly kept interior of the cottage. "But first he has to live long enough."

Isadora shuddered. "It's been burned, you said?"

I nodded.

"Well..." She sighed. "Hopefully that will be the end of it." But I could see the fear lurking in her eyes as she watched Joseph who had managed to work himself free and had run off to play on the other side of the room.

"Yes." I inched toward the door. "I'd better be going..."

"Of course, you'll be wanting to get to your dinner. Thank you, Elena."

Joseph looked up, as if on cue, and repeated, "Thank you, Elena," his high voice mangling the words slightly. His mother's face melted, and even I couldn't resist a smile.

But it fell away as I jogged back out of town. Isadora should have been more careful. Should have been watching her son more closely. He was old enough now to understand. I shivered. Or perhaps he wasn't. I could hardly remember Clementine at that age, let alone what it had been like to be that age myself. Still. A whole village had been lost only last year. One big bang and the whole thing had disappeared. No one knew exactly what had happened, of course. Not after the fact when there was nothing left.

Just that the explosion had been untrained, out of control. Deadly. Someone had been writing. A commonborn without the control to shape the power that flowed out of them as soon as they began to form written words. A commonborn like me and every single other person in the kingdom not born to a mage parent.

And that could have been Kingslee. Nearly had been, perhaps. I swallowed and veered off the path to collect my leather satchel which I had abandoned in the bushes when I rushed to defend Joseph. Not that I remembered doing so. Jasper would scold me as he always did if he ever heard of it, telling me I was far too protective.

"And you're not even the oldest, Elena," he would say, pulling affectionately on my hair. "Aren't I supposed to be the protective one?"

I always smiled and played along, but we both knew the truth. Jasper was our shining light. The one who was going to lift us all out of poverty. The genius with perfect recall who could compete even against the mages when it came to academics.

One day he would secure a lucrative position and take us to the capital. Which meant it was left to me to do the protecting, of both him and our younger sister Clementine. Although he was far away at the Royal University, these days. Too far for either teasing or protecting.

It had always been clear that Jasper would not be accepting our family's conscription responsibility. Any more than there was any question of weak, sickly Clementine being left to go to war.

So if I was to bear the ultimate burden of protecting my siblings, then why not start early? Even if my eighteenth birthday was still more than a year and a half away.

When I pushed open the door to our home, my sister greeted me with a glad cry as she always did. Unlike the house I had just left, everything here was neat and in good order, the furniture sturdy and every surface scrubbed clean. Even the curtains looked newly washed. It was larger, too, with two more rooms tucked away, as well as a loft where Clementine and I slept. The reward of my parents' careful running of their small store. That and their willingness to live out of town where there was room for a bigger house.

I tried to smile, but Clementine knew me too well. Her face fell, and she hurried over to take my hand.

"What is it, Elena? Is something wrong?"

I shook myself. "No, indeed. Don't mind me, Clemmy. I'm just tired." And it was true. Nothing was wrong, now. But still I couldn't dislodge the feeling of unease that had settled over me beside the river.

"Oh, poor thing. Of course, you're exhausted, traipsing through the woods all day." She hurried to take my bag from my shoulder, gesturing for me to sit down while she emptied it, laying the herbs inside out neatly on the table.

"We had some special visitors while you were gone." She giggled. "Well, not visitors exactly. Customers."

I ran a hand over my eyes. "I heard. Mages, were they?"

She nodded, looking a little crestfallen that someone had beaten her to the news. "One of the ladies caught sight of some of our fresh fruit and had a 'hankering that couldn't be denied' apparently."

I rolled my eyes, but Clementine was obviously fascinated by her brush with the upper class. Our oppressors. I pressed a hand to my head. I must be more tired than I realized. Now I was the one getting dramatic.

The mages might wield all of the power and much of the wealth in the kingdom, but they were the only ones able to control the power. And we did all see at least some benefits from it. If only because their growers and wind workers ensured the crops grew, and their creators built roads. Even their healers were available to those who could afford them.

"I hope they paid well," I said.

"That they did," said Mother, bustling into the room. "And extra. As if counting out the correct amount wasn't worth their time." She shook her head in wonder.

"That'll be us one day," said Clementine, pride in her voice. "Once Jasper graduates, and we all join him in Corrin."

"Aye, that it will," said Father, coming in from outside. He picked Clementine up and swung her around, although at eleven she was really too old for such things. None of us protested, however.

When he put her down again, his eye fell on the neat rows of gathered herbs on the table. He raised his eyebrows.

"You did well today, Elena."

I sat up straight and smiled back at him. I had managed a good haul, although the subsequent events of the afternoon had driven it from my mind. I had always been the best at finding the hidden spots in the woods where the rarer herbs grew. The ones that would fetch a good price in the store—either fresh or dried.

My family would miss me when I turned eighteen and signed up to go away to war. I knew they would. But better me than Jasper or Clementine. No one said it, but we all agreed on it. And the law was clear. One child from every family must sign up to join the army when they turned eighteen. And if no one stepped forward to volunteer, then the youngest would be forcibly conscripted on their eighteenth birthday.

I had heard it debated from time to time, but no one seemed able to agree which position was less enviable—to be an older one, forced to choose, or the youngest, without a choice at all. I saw the sadness and the fear in my mother's eyes sometimes, when she watched me. Most families sent their brawniest son and hoped he could survive the three years until he had served his term and was free to return home.

I sometimes wondered if that was why Mother had fallen pregnant again, a full five years after my birth. It had been clear by then that Jasper was special, and that he could not be wasted on the front line of a never-ending war. My parents had already begun to save their coin, in fact, knowing how much tutoring he would need once he finished in the Kingslee school at age ten.

Perhaps my mother had hoped to bear more sons, who might have been better suited than me to surviving in battle. But she got Clementine, the sweetest—and weakest—of us all.

I had never actually had the courage to ask, though, so perhaps that had not been it at all.

"Did any of them drop anything?" The words were out of my mouth before I realized they were hovering on my tongue.

"Who?" Father looked confused.

"The mages, you mean?" Clementine tipped her head to one side, regarding me quizzically. "Why?"

"Oh, them." Father returned to packing up the herbs.

"Not that I saw," said Mother. "Although from the careless way of them, it wouldn't surprise me one bit. Why do you ask? Did you stop by the store and find something?"

I shook my head. "Not me. But young Joseph—Isadora's little boy—found something it seems." I hadn't meant to tell them what happened, but I couldn't keep it to myself—not with the way it weighed on me. The story wanted to escape.

Plus Samuel had been there. I didn't trust him to keep his mouth shut, and once he started talking, it was hard to know how others would react. I just hoped he hadn't recognized Joseph or seen which house I went into to return him. Thankfully he wasn't the sort to pay attention to details.

"Something valuable?" asked Clementine. "Do you think they'll miss it? The mages, I mean."

"I certainly hope not." I sat up, drawing in a breath. I hadn't even thought of that. "It was words. Some sort of printed dispatch or something."

All movement in the room stilled.

"And young Joseph found it, you say," said Father, after a breath.

I nodded. "Samuel and Alice found him down by the river. We burned it. But..." I took a deep breath and finished in a rush. "He was trying to copy it. In the dirt before I arrived, apparently. They only just stopped him in time."

"Trying to copy the...the letters?" Clementine stumbled over the words, her face white.

"If he'd managed a whole word..." Even my father looked afraid.

I swallowed and nodded. "But he didn't. That's what I keep reminding myself. He didn't. And he's only a child, too. Perhaps... perhaps the power wouldn't have grown strong enough in him to do much damage."

No one responded to my hopeful suggestion. Because we all knew the power of words. Words had the power of life—and the power of death. Written words shaped the power, released it from inside us out into the world. But only the mage families could control that power.

Certainly not people like us. Or young Joseph. If any of the commonborn wrote so much as a word, the power would come rushing out in an uncontrolled explosion of destruction. Just like in that poor village up north. In one instant gone forever, wiped off the map. How many letters had it taken? And who had written them? We would never know.

I might hate the system that trampled us into the dirt, but I understood it. There was a reason none of us could ever be permitted the wonders of reading and writing. Without the bloodline that would enable us to control the power once we accessed it, it was just too dangerous. One slip up, and...

The door banged open, and we all jumped.

Thomas, the young boy who sometimes helped in the store now that Jasper had left, leaned against the doorframe, panting.

"What is it, Tom?" asked Father.

"Trouble," he panted out. "Trouble at the store. Something about those mages."

Palinar

Eldon

Eliam

Marin

Talinos

Trione

MAP

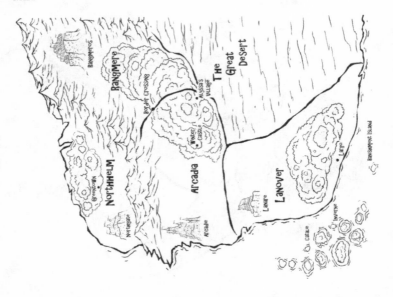

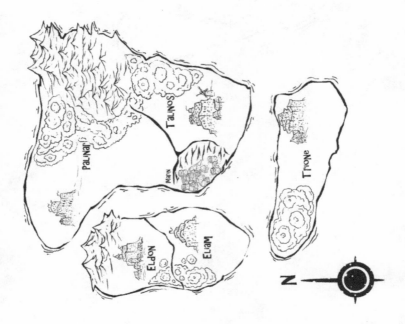

ACKNOWLEDGMENTS

I've had a break from fairy tales with my recent fantasy series, and coming back to them only reminds me of what I enjoy about the genre. It has once again been a delight to weave an old tale into something new, even if the writing process itself was sometimes a challenge. This book didn't immediately want to fall into line, and I'm so grateful to all of those who stuck with me as I fought through to find the characters and story. (First Gabe wanted to be the point-of-view character, and then Adelaide kept reminding me she was no longer the sweet thirteen-year-old girl all the other characters had been remembering for the last four books. But working out her journey back to wholeness brought the whole book together.)

As always, the first thank you belongs to my husband, Marc. My books are a team project even if he never writes or edits a single sentence because without him my life would fall over—I wouldn't write a word while I had to deal with more pressing issues like feeding myself and remembering what day of the week it is.

My beautiful children keep me sane and grounded, and I'm so grateful for them, as well as the rest of my family—both by blood and law. Having a support network is so important, and I truly enjoy the company of all my family.

But of course my support network isn't only made up of family, and I'm so thankful for my amazing friends and beta readers, Rachel, Greg, Priya, and Ber. It is a joy to be able to discuss my books with each of you, and to feel your ongoing support at my back.

And for a virtual shoulder to cry on and laugh to be shared (insert laughing gif of choice here), I can't imagine better friends than my fellow authors. Kitty, Kenley, Shari, Aya, Brittany, and Diana—thanks for everything!

And, of course, my professional team are equally valuable—thanks to Mary, Dad, and Deborah for looking at everything from story and character to my constant incorrect grammar and bizarre typos.

A thank you to my cover designer, Karri. I've already had comments from some people that this might be their favorite of my covers.

And of course all of this is done for you—the reader—so I'm incredibly grateful to you too. As I am to God, who is far more patient with me than I deserve.

ABOUT THE AUTHOR

Melanie Cellier grew up on a staple diet of books, books and more books. And although she got older, she never stopped loving children's and young adult novels.

She always wanted to write one herself, but it took three careers and three different continents before she actually managed it.

She now feels incredibly fortunate to spend her time writing from her home in Adelaide, Australia where she keeps an eye out for koalas in her backyard. Her staple diet hasn't changed much, although she's added choc mint Rooibos tea and Chicken Crimpies to the list.

She writes young adult fantasy including her *Spoken Mage* series, and her *Four Kingdoms* and *Beyond the Four Kingdoms* series which are made up of linked stand-alone stories that retell classic fairy tales.

CPSIA information can be obtained
at www.ICGtesting.com
Printed in the USA
LVHW041034280422
717455LV00001B/106

9 781925 898149